Conception

ÖZGÜR UYANIK

FAIRLIGHT BOOKS

First published by Fairlight Books 2020

Fairlight Books
Summertown Pavilion, 18–24 Middle Way, Oxford, OX2 7LG

A CIP catalogue record for this book is available from the British
Library

1 2 3 4 5 6 7 8 9 10

ISBN 978-1-912054-87-9

www.fairlightbooks.com

Printed and bound in Great Britain

Designed by Marina Drukman

This is a work of fiction. With the exception of any public figures,
names, characters, business, events and incidents are the products of
the author's imagination. Any resemblance to actual persons, living or
dead, or actual events is purely coincidental.

In loving memory of Dad.

Dedicated to Granny, Mum and Sis.

A nation devoid of art and artists cannot have a full existence.

Mustafa Kemal Atatürk

I

Don't make fun of my accent, that's all I'm asking. It's transatlantic and bringing attention to it makes me self-conscious. The fluidity of my inflection is because I was taught English in Turkey where I was born and the American enunciation predominates there. Later, after many years in London, the Queen's English seduced me and I am thus left stranded somewhere in between.

Anyway, I'm full of Darjeeling First Flush from high tea with Mother at The Lanesborough on Hyde Park Corner. Her maiden name, aptly, is *Dağkıran* – 'Breaker of Mountains'. Nibbling a finger sandwich from a silver tray – the only time I'll deviate from my gluten-free diet – I make mention of an agent called Joseph and try to explain his function to her.

'The job of getting you a job?' She frowns, biting into one of those ubiquitous cupcakes that I intend never to understand the appeal of. I tell her that this Joseph is going to act as my intermediary for getting me directing jobs in the realm of advertising in order to provide a much-needed cash injection in my life. Mother's micro-expressions of disdain for the words

7

'job' and 'advertising' are concealed momentarily behind the lip of her bone china teacup as she sips pensively.

'My boy, you are an artist,' she says, narrowing her eyes in a way that makes me feel I am six years old again. 'TS Eliot had to be rescued from being a bank clerk before he wrote his best work. I don't recall Dali or Picasso having to work in job-type-jobs either.'

'So you want me to starve. To suffer for my art, Mother.'

'Suffering is emotional pain telling us to solve our problems, darling. You know this. And artists solve their problems by vomiting them up on to canvas and whatnot.'

'You're right of course but... I'm sick of having no money of my own.'

'I'm warning you, darling,' she says with a finality that chills my heart. 'A job will be the end of you.' Seeing me blanche, she adds:

'I'm teasing of course,' and pours out more tea for herself. She then remembers to pour some out for me as well. 'And if you need money...'

'No Mother, please. We've been through that.' I give her a level look that denotes my unwillingness to accept her patronage any longer.

She shrugs. It is worth noting that she is a very proud woman, my mother, to the extent that I am an extension of her and thus a potential mar on her otherwise unblemished reputation as a person of leisure, high culture and immaculate taste. A staunch secularist and a woman of the Turkish Republic, she resolutely faces west and has internalised a quest for progress, success and the pursuit of happiness alongside her more fatalistic and spiritual Turkic cultural heritage.

'But my boy, why *advertising*?' she asks, whispering the last word. 'What makes you think you want to do that sort of thing?'

'Don't forget, Mother, that I studied film-making before I went to art college.'

'And you gave up your dreams of Hollywood far too readily.'

'I never wanted "Hollywood", Mother. I never wanted to win an Oscar or anything… a Palm d'Or, perhaps. Anyway, I was in love with the end result and not the process. To be a film-maker you have to be passionate about the whole kit-and-caboodle – the writing of the script, raising the money, working with actors, dealing with crew, the editing! I wanted to be an auteur, Mother, in charge of the whole barely controllable chaos and to do everything myself, which is impossible – in film you cannot be a one-man band. It doesn't work that way. I'm just too egotistical for anything else and here I am almost on the wrong side of forty—'

She cuts me off, 'I hardly think Fellini had a small ego.'

'Well, I suppose not but—'

'No, what you mean is that you are a perfectionist. But you don't want to end up a dilettante jumping from branch to branch, do you? Stick to the art. It has to be your everything. Everything.'

'Well, it's advertising or—'

'No. Not that. Never.'

With that proclamation Mother vetoes the other option, which was floated earlier before the tea arrived: to abandon my artistic career due to my current and persistent financial woes and return to İstanbul where Father, surely, would allow me to lodge in one of his many rental investment properties.

My father takes a much dimmer view of my artistic exploits and he'd be more than satisfied to see me live out my days as an almost-was. I could, conceivably, teach. At least, in his eyes, that is an honourable profession. I could teach film-making, perhaps. As if reading my mind, Mother says:

'No my boy – don't listen to your father – you are not going back. He never took enough risks in his life so now he can't bear to watch you do things he can only dream about.'

Mother had divorced him a few years after we had all moved to London in the 1980s when Father's Turkish engineering firm opened a branch here. Away from the social glue of their respective families, they had drifted apart like oil and water.

'Go ahead and make a television commercial once or twice a year if you must,' she continues thoughtfully, 'but make sure you do not get drawn into that evil world of marketing claptrap.'

'I won't, Mother, I won't—'

'You must live and breathe art,' she says and delicately bolts the remainder of her cupcake.

'You're right. I was being silly... what would I do in İstanbul, anyway?'

'I've never been wrong about people, least of all my own flesh and blood. You've come this far, don't let the naysayers get to you, for goodness' sake.'

She believes in me, my mother, more than I believe in myself sometimes, and I feel that she needs me to flourish in every endeavour or else a part of her will, presumably, perish.

*

To shake off this debilitating attack of self-doubt I decide to take an invigorating walk once the bowler-hatted doorman has summoned a cab and Mother is away. In the overcast and fragrant late-summer London air, laced with pungent toxins redolent of childhood, I head through Mayfair to Sloane Street via the sedentary stucco of embassy-strewn Belgravia. I go past Gucci, Prada, Armani and co to end up in Knightsbridge. Still somewhat on edge and in danger of being late for my meeting with Joseph, I continue through Hyde Park and veer into Green Park's whispering canopies. Eschewing Trafalgar Square's vulgarities, I branch away via Pall Mall and up to Regent Street and the raucous hubbub of Piccadilly Circus where, standing in the glare of the backlit video hoardings five storeys high, the back of my brain – quite unexpectedly – is tickled by a new idea. It tantalises me and then retreats mischievously back into the folds of my grey matter for the time being and, thwarted, I am sucked back into the present. My least favourite place.

Distressed by the commotion of traffic and tourists, I swiftly duck in behind Shaftsbury Avenue and weave through the stinking streets of Soho to reach the beacon of my private members club, called Home, nestled aristocratically above a rat-infested eatery that I used to frequent as an art student – dreaming of fame and glory. I was in love with London then and her promise that she was a magical place where one could nuzzle in her rolling bosom, sure of the success that is granted to those few who can thrive in her ancient thoroughfares. Having entered through the discreet front door with its quaint unused brass knocker, I mount the tight but soothing olive-green staircase to reach the smiling sentinels – an immaculately groomed girl and an exquisitely coiffed boy – at the heavy oak reception desk. I leave my mark in the leather-bound registration book. It is not my actual signature, of course; an artist's signature is their sacred sigil. I see that Joseph has already arrived. He is being held, as if he were an asylum-seeking refugee, by the magazine racks in the reception area, unable to venture any further into the clubhouse. A man-child, he sports a cherubic face with curly blond hair uneasily fused to an expansive beer gut above stilt-like legs. His deplorably mundane clothes radiate absolute mediocrity. I demand higher standards of comportment in my associates, having been brought up to understand that image matters. I will have to have a serious chat with him about it at some point.

'Hello, Joseph,' I say and he looks up with a startled expression, his mouth in the shape of a little pink 'o'.

'Hello – sorry – didn't see you there,' he says and stands for a handshake. I affect limpness in my wrist to convey my indifference for such social conventions but I doubt he gets the message.

'You're early,' I say pointedly. An early arrival suggests that he is not that busy, which gives me a poor impression of him as my representative in business. I doubt that that message gets through either. 'You should've given my name and gone up,' I add.

'There was someone up there I'm trying to avoid,' he mumbles as he shuffles towards the stairs. A socially anxious agent.

I wonder to myself why I trust Joseph to succeed at his job at all. I plan to dabble in promotional videos for the ever-expanding black hole of the Internet or occasionally a pop promo. The income will supplement my meagre earnings from my true métier – art. Making art is my calling in life but it doesn't pay the rent to on my Rotherhithe loft apartment or a weekend of cocktails in dimly lit basement bars off Tottenham Court Road. I met Joseph at a private view somewhere in Swiss Cottage where some up-and-comer of the BritArt stable was holding court at the height of his fame and I distinctly recall the stabbing emptiness in my stomach as I yearned for the same recognition for my talents. However, money is not an end in itself but merely a facilitating factor for my on-going quest to become a fully formed creative being passing through the cold emptiness of space and time. I suppose I have to admit that it is a similar instinct that motivates individuals to inundate the Information Superhighway with their inane self-portraits on digital feeds that are throttling our collective consciousness with the pernicious tentacles of the banal. The illustrious architects of the World Wide Web most likely did not envisage their colossal creation becoming a mazelike sewer for human angst but there it is. We are all motivated by simple emotions, inherited from ocean-dwelling ancient fish no less, but the more interesting outcomes that can be derived from our utterly meaningless existence seem to be exercised through the practice of art – a mysterious and deeply arousing process that has gripped my imagination since as far back as I can remember. That is as close to a *raison d'être* as you'll get out of me, thank you very much.

'You shouldn't hide from people, Joseph. It's not a very attractive trait for someone in your line of work.' I regard the remarkable flatness of his buttocks behind the drape of his dismal, grey corduroy slacks as he mounts the steps.

'Seriously, sometimes you have to,' he insists on replying and my confidence in his abilities to secure work for me in advertising plummets to a new low.

On the other hand, I am not easy to work with and Joseph has very thick skin and no matter what I throw at him, he keeps coming back for more. The fine art domain doesn't offer a regular revenue stream, unless you are 'a name' such as Emin, Gormley or Koons. Andy Warhol actually came from advertising (he made a living illustrating women's shoes) and brought that keen sense of consumerism to his artwork – he knew how to make the viewer yearn. The act of selling myself is an odious one to me, so my gallerist – Maximillio Zvwark in Manhattan – is an essential component in the eco-system within which I dwell. Maximillio promotes my art to the best buyers and in between sales Joseph is engaged to supply me with work-type-work. Mr Zvwark is akin to the pitiless men in abattoirs who are essential to my enjoyment of a Chateaubriand whilst Joseph, I suppose, resembles a bin man; pure utility. Suffice to say, I try to stay well clear of the blood and guts of the marketplace in order to preserve a modicum of self-respect.

That brings to mind one of my earliest memories. A sacrificial sheep hanging upside down from a hook on the back of a flatbed truck. The neighbourhood butcher on the Asian shores of İstanbul skinned its fleece, pulling and tugging it down to reveal its pink body. When I demanded of my father why the man was taking off the creature's coat as it would surely need it during the coming winter, he looked down at me with a look of mild and detached amusement. This childhood experience may be the reason why I eventually became a vegetarian when I left home for university. I am extremely squeamish round raw meat and if I so much as glimpse a drop of my own blood I will faint.

I am a pragmatist by nature, constructing my career step by scrupulous step, and I expect men like Joseph to pull their weight to keep me in funds for the real work of making the art that will, one day, make me famous and I can prove to my father once and for all that I am not a wastrel, as he contends. It's Joseph's job to sell me, like I said. That sounds awful and base but there it is. I must build up my standing in the art world by producing singular work for a jaded market inundated with product for an ever-dwindling yet ever-richer class of safe-asset-seeking, independently wealthy people. My strategy is to build awareness round my name so that I have the chance to have my work placed in a prestigious collection that will lead to increased demand and higher prices. Provenance is key to a sustained and successful career as an artist. Placing work with the right collector and constructing a desirable provenance falls to the gallerist (heaven forfend you should call them an art 'dealer'!).

The right labels are crucial. Maximillio has access to the top art fairs round the globe from Maastricht to Miami Beach. He has skilfully increased demand for my work by pricing it at an affordable level for serious new collectors and then refusing to sell it to them. He puts them on a waiting list and the buzz from that simple gesture itself helps the work build a reputation. Some might view these manoeuvres as decidedly uncivilised and I would agree. That's why I make sure to keep my distance from the vagaries of the souk, unlike some others I could mention who, it has been widely reported, buy back their own work when it fails to reach a good price at auction just to keep their values stable.

'Joseph, I know you think art is frivolous and that artists are insufferably pretentious—' I begin to say as we take our seats at a corner table in the drawing room on the third floor.

'I don't think you're pretentious,' he butts in.

'I was speaking in generalities, Joseph.'

'Right, of course.'

'As I was saying, art is not everyone's cup of tea but surely you can use my up-and-coming reputation to seduce these ad executives – I was long-listed by Arts Regalia for their Emerging Artists scheme last year and I have under my belt several prestigious nominations including the inaugural Kremala Award not to mention wins such as the Girtin Prize, don't forget. These things are all in my biography, Joseph.'

'I know,' he responds with open palms.

'Hello guys.'

It is a waitress. She drops to her haunches and regards us with alacrity at just below eye level. The waiting staff here at the club are consummate professionals. They have been trained to exude the sense that they feel they are our equals and that attitude takes away the awkwardness of servitude quite nicely.

'Hi.' I smile at her warmly and order a black Americano.

'And I'll have a flat white, please,' says Joseph with what he must imagine is a winning smile. After she rises and leaves I am compelled to advise Joseph, with a quick calculated glance at his midriff, to hereafter avoid indulging in too many dairy products.

'Milk and coffee go together like bread and butter,' he grins and I roll my eyes at him.

'Don't get me started on milk, Joseph,' I say with a false jollity that I undercut straightaway with a serious expression. Then I resume, 'Set up some more meetings Joseph. Let me lay out my vision, a vision that is sorely lacking in today's advertising arena.'

'Sure, but—'

'The world is so debased that clients can't be sure any more if the public is even responding to the tripe that's being churned out – assailing our eyeballs from every conceivable outlet,' I say and sigh languidly. 'You were saying?'

'How can I put this… they don't really connect with that scene. Art makes them sort of queasy, I guess. Art and commerce—'

'Joseph, I am sensing a passive-aggressive tone,' I interject with a bitter smile. He at once relaxes with the relief that comes from having his hand forced so that he can let the mask of his toadyism fall at last.

'Okay. I have to say this because as my client you deserve to know the truth,' he declares and purses his lips in readiness.

'Go ahead.' I sit back comfortably then realise, with some anxiety, that I have crossed my arms defensively. After a sufficient pause, I unwrap them ever so slowly, ready to receive his clearly designed-to-be-upsetting message.

'These ad agency guys are tough to sell to and we need a more, how can I put it, a more – not diffident – no, not at all… it's good to be confident, don't get me wrong. They need to see that you are in control but—'

'Oh for God's sake Joseph, just spit it out.'

'You have to soften your tone. After the last meeting I arranged for you, the feedback from the executives was that, well, you came across as somewhat, erm, stand-offish, I suppose.'

'You want me to bend over for them.'

'No, I wouldn't put it quite in those words,' he splutters.

'They want to feel that they're not being spoken down to by a – you know – "highfalutin artistic type",' he chuckles with a pair of abominable air quotes to bracket the insult with insincere irony. 'They're very proud of what they do.'

'It wasn't a question. You literally want me to bend over for them so that they can feel like the big swinging dicks in the room.'

'Okay...' He hesitates. Then, 'Will you be able to do that?'

'I'll tell you what, since it's my fifteen per cent you're taking, I should think that the onus for bending over is on you, no?'

His milky English veins run hot; I can see the glint of irritation in his glassy pupils. I have awakened the basic Saxon in him. I wait for the boy-man to explode.

'It makes my job very difficult if the ad agencies don't, well, you know – like you,' he blurts out finally. I can see the catharsis fairly rack his torso as he looks up at the ceiling and lets out a controlled karmic breath.

'Good. This kind of candid and clear communication is essential for a successful professional collaboration,' I say and wait for him to calm down, building a wall between us with my silence. I do not support his view that advertising agency executives are put off by my in-your-face attitude. Whether it be a twenty-eight-second TV spot for a property development project or my latest art piece for La Biennale di Venezia, I am all about one thing. Passion.

Joseph lacks a true set of balls behind his haughty British rhetoric. As I, quite involuntarily, picture Joseph's genitals – an albino mouse-tail dangling over a shiny pair of pink cherries – I am only vaguely aware that he is speaking. Still gazing contemplatively into the blurry middle distance betwixt his undulating ribcage and his pallid face, I imagine, in quite brilliant detail, the delicious act of sodomising him with a – culturally appropriate – cricket bat.

Emerging moments later from my violent reverie fully refreshed, I don't bother to ask him to repeat what he just said but instead wind up the meeting by suggesting that if he does his job then everything will work itself out. He must have had too much sugar and caffeine by then because his jaw is clenched like a fist. He mutters a goodbye and leaves. Regardless of his sour exit, I do feel that I have made a positive impact on his psyche and that our working relationship will benefit from my open and honest approach.

I notice that Joseph hasn't had the wherewithal to leave any money on the table. Having made an indelible mental note of this faux pas, I elect to linger a while longer to observe my surroundings. Let me be clear; I don't do 'people watching' and I find the comparison to that vacuous time-killer abhorrent; for mine is not an opportunistic act of cheap voyeurism but a deeply analytical meditation. Unhappily, there is nobody here, so I settle the bill, with a healthy tip for my attentive waitress, and leave the club, hungry for a distraction after my sordid encounter.

*

My human safari takes me along familiar trails, which tourists roam, in the sleazy spectacle that is London's West End. In a sybaritic mood, I saunter into the nearest coffee shop franchise and settle down on a high stool with a double espresso. I scan the savannah of the teak-and-taupe corporate-branded interior landscape and I listen to the low-level cacophony of humans at rest. I have the rare ability to follow two or three separate conversations simultaneously. It amazes people at social gatherings.

Once, a few years ago, I was practising this ability in Turkey, diving at will into several conversations happening around me. It was at the opening of a new art gallery in İstanbul's Pera district, on the European side. A irate Turkish man told me, sporting the customary frown and wrinkled forehead of the alpha male coiled tight with testosterone, to stick my nose out of his business. In fact, I had been answering a question that the woman standing next to him had asked me. In her heels, she towered over the pot-bellied gentleman in whom I had aroused such vitriol. He was quite ready to put me in my place in front of his, as it turns out, wife. She was far too self-possessed, young and beautiful for him but she had evidently acquiesced to the match for reasons that shall remain mysterious to me. I was not a little attracted to her flavour of intersexual allure: short cropped hair, a strong nose and bony, hard demeanour swathed in the most feminine of outer skins, glistening blood-red lips and coal-black sensuous eyes. I was frankly besotted with her and, I'll admit, leaning in too close. She either found me endearing or it was her act in front of her increasingly agitated husband to treat my presence as though a naughty but amusing puppy had invaded her space. I had a cocaine-fuelled flash-fantasy of taking her roughly from behind in one of the toilet stalls and my arm went round her waist for a split second. Her husband caught a glimpse of the move and almost burst into flames with fury. The host and gallery owner, alerted to the build-up of tension, quickly interceded to explicate with loud jollity that I was one of many 'super-talented' artists to have passed through his galleries, what an interesting fellow I was and did anyone need any more champagne... Then, having defused the hectic atmosphere, he introduced me to the tetchy little husband and, just as swiftly and gallantly, he carried me away from the married couple on a raft of effusive reminiscences.

I imbibed many a glass of champagne that night interspersed with excursions to the facilities in order to keep cocaine levels in balance with my alcohol intake. I was enjoying my evening thoroughly up to the moment I ran into the angry Turk outside, on the steps of the newly refurbished nineteenth-century apartment building that housed the gallery on its raised ground floor. He was trying to ignore me, dragging on a cigarette, when I began.

'All the most elegant structures in this neighbourhood were built by foreigners, weren't they?' I teased. 'Italians, the French, Greeks and so on.' I let that sink in before lighting a cigarette of my own. 'Are we just passing through, like our nomadic ancestors did through the steppes? Sort of looking after it because we have to – to keep UNESCO and the troublesome Europeans off our backs? What line of work are you in, sir?' I asked, then jested smoothly, 'Hope it's not construction!'

He continued to ignore me when all I wanted to do was break down the partition of reticence separating us as human beings. In a way I wanted to prove that we can take a joke, us Turks, because we are stronger when we can laugh at ourselves without fear of being seen as weak. True weakness is revealed when our sense of humour fails us. By his mannered posture, age and dress I could tell that he was a serious man who believed that Turks had every right to exploit our fertile lands and build up our choking cities just as the westerners had done over a hundred years ago with their own. It would have made a good point in the argument, had he proffered it. I swiftly took a different tack.

'She looks very Eastern European, your wife – is she a hundred per cent Turkish?' I said and waited for a response that never came. Then I said, 'There's definitely some foreign blood in her somewhere. Of course, the genetic evidence points to the fact that almost all Turks are a mixed bag in any event. After all, the Turks are a dominant culture and have left their indelible mark across swathes of Central Asia, the Balkans and beyond, no?'

He looked at me with a blank expression and I felt like a disembodied voice on the night breeze. 'Oh, let's forget about your wife – that's a sore subject, obviously,' I said and looked round at the architecture.

Some men are so easily provoked. I could take offence about a thousand times a day at what I see or hear around me yet I choose not to express myself with unproductive rage but to channel those energies into my work. Perhaps in this way, we artists have the greatest psychological advantage over the masses. We can find peace in the act of creation, able to dump the toxic from our minds that ordinary people have no outlet for. The lack of a creative vent poisons men over time, seeping in and scouring their brains and they explode with impotent and self-righteous wrath. Which is what happened.

They call it an Ottoman slap and it comes at you, invariably, from a good distance as the perpetrator winds up his arm like a trebuchet and whips it forward, palm open, to deliver a devastating impact to the side of the head. The jolt from such a blow can be quite terrific. The Turkish male, when he wants to surprise and humiliate an adversary, will use the slap rather than the punch. A punch implies a pugilistic code of masculine honour and sense of fairness. In contrast, the dismissiveness of the smack proclaims that you are an inferior specimen with the status of a prepubescent boy, too feminine to thump properly in public. I was drunk enough that I didn't feel anything when I hit my head on the stone steps and rolled – as it was later reported to me – down to the gutter of the backstreets of old İstanbul, in ancient times simply The City, where once painters, Orthodox patriarchs and prostitutes strode the cobbles and rode in polished phaetons to tantalising appointments lost to time with the haunting echo of the *boza* vendor prowling the night.

'Bo-o-o-za... bo-o-o-zaaaa...'

Mother, when she had returned to İstanbul for a spell after the divorce, had advised me to file a charge of grievous bodily harm following the incident. However, I chose not to do so as the police and courts of the land are weighted dramatically in favour of the well-connected thug. The usual defence of the violator is that they were provoked; provocation need not be proved but simply pointed out. I attempted then to walk Mother through my reasoning but all she could see was the shiny bruised face of her one remaining progeny.

'I've lost one child already and I refuse to lose the other because of some common gangster,' she had said, her countenance solidifying like cooling lava into a basalt statue of rectitude and maternal rage. What had happened to my twin brother (congenital end-stage renal failure) in our seventh year on the planet had sown the seeds of my parents' eventual divorce and had cleaved me to her more than ever. I was suddenly her only child and she stayed in a state of shocked grief for many years while Father became an increasingly distant figure of perpetual sadness. I felt secretly that they were unable to look at me without being haunted by my dead brother; I was the strange living ghost of the one they had lost. In their dealings with me, up until puberty kicked in when I was mercifully no longer the mirror image of my unageing twin, I sensed or imagined an anguish. I was a cruel reminder that perpetuated their guilt for going on without him. I did not suffer bereavement in the same way as them, however; perhaps locking away the hurt of separation for another day or, being so young, I simply hadn't grown as attached to him as they had. He was simply there one minute – competing for attention and toys – and then he was gone. It was as if a defective product had been recalled to the celestial factory where humans are assembled, my childish brain had mused. His abrupt exit amounted to a summons from a disinterested cosmos fixing a clerical error.

After listening awhile to my mother lingering fondly over the punishments she would ascribe to the perpetrator, I had interjected, 'Mother, it's only a black eye.'

'You could have been killed falling down those steps,' she had said, holding back her tears as she spoke in clipped tones designed to pre-empt any emotional outpouring on her part. 'He cannot be allowed to get away with it.'

'I don't want to waste time and energy on it. I've got bigger fish to fry,' I had said with manly insouciance. I always try to have as little to do with the police as possible. Their arbitrary power and sense of entitlement terrifies me and they can smell the fear. My nightmares invariably involve a pack of hounds, usually the massive Anatolian shepherd dog breed called *Kangal*, sniffing the air as I walk past nervously. My dreams are terribly obvious and require little or no deciphering.

'Darling, your father once looked at me as if he was about to raise his hand and do you know what I did?' she had asked, unblinking.

'What did you do?' I had asked automatically, this particular parable having been served up many times before.

'I divorced him.'

'This isn't the same thing...'

'It's exactly the same thing; we do not tolerate violence of any kind, threatened or actual in this family. You're not a violent man. I know because you take after my side of the family, thank God. This man... this *animal* should be made to stand up in court and be seen for the criminal ape that he is. And pay some sort of compensation for the emotional and physical trauma he has caused us. I'll talk to Metin *bey*.'

Metin *bey* was our in-house counsel at the time and a distant relative who pursued and administered Mother's various court-related acts of justice. I believe that, bar the Americans, Turks are the most litigious people on earth. Everybody is always taking somebody to court over something. I get tired just thinking about lodging a complaint at a police station whilst others do it as if it's a trip to the local post office. I have that British need, semi-assimilated as I am into their culture, to avoid confrontation, I suppose. That only applies when the Brits are stone cold sober of course. We all know what they can get up to when they're drunk on booze, or power for that matter. I've seen how vile they can be, terrorising the delightful pavements of Amsterdam, stoned and tanked-up, or rampaging like a medieval plague along the peaceful promenades of Bodrum in south-eastern Turkey. At the height of summer and callously inebriated, they infiltrate idyllic towns and cities in Cyprus revealing themselves as brutes. The British slaughtered thousands when they ruled India; they sent convicts to Australia – their ingenuity is undoubtedly remarkable – and nearly wiped out the Australian aborigines. Not to mention their doctrine of divide and conquer, shamelessly pitting Arab against Turk so that they could carve up Mesopotamia between themselves and their European allies. One hundred years later the Middle East is still mopping up the blood. They started a war with China to force them to buy their opium. Inspired! They conceived the Golden Triangle of the original slave trade and taught everyone to quake at the shrine of the Industrial Revolution, sacrificing the lives of millions of their own poverty-stricken citizens, women and children, in order to serve the machines and work the mines that would cripple many millions more, all for the profit of the few. They invented the cancerous capitalism that continues to strip-mine the planet's resources without mercy to this day. These facts were fastidiously side-stepped during my schooling in England, of course. I was educated to respect and wonder in awe at the achievements of the kings and queens of the land through the centuries, as if they were cut from the cloth of legend and myth, myths and legends stolen from Celtic heritage and passed off as their own – there is no end to their voracity – instead of seeing them as they truly were: megalomaniac islanders and empire builders.

On the other hand, I do love them for their aplomb in spreading Britishness across the seven seas. Who wouldn't want mastery of the oceans and their mother tongue to be the lingua franca of the globe? It would be quite disingenuous of me – being so Anglicised – to argue that their unbridled ambition does not have its appeal.

'This hateful little man hospitalised you and over what? What did you do to him?' Mother had demanded to know.

'Nothing,' I had murmured, picking up the thread. 'I made a joke and it went over his head.' There had been a dash of shame in my voice for now I felt as if I had stood down from a fight, my honour in tatters, accepting premature defeat due to deplorable weakness of will. It probably won't surprise you to discover that Mother's favourite author is Ayn Rand.

'We don't take things lying down in this family and we won't let ruffians walk roughshod over us. What joke?'

'I don't remember.'

'Are you concussed?' she cradled my chin with her hand in alarm.

'No, Mother, I'm fine now.'

'Good. I'll talk to Metin *bey* and we'll file a complaint first thing at the Beyoğlu police station.'

The whole sorry episode with the fat man and his wife taught me that public intercourse with people can have bothersome consequences if one becomes too exuberant in the moment and abuses one's talents. Over the years I have therefore learned to appreciate the art of sitting back from it all and observing rather than diving in with the naïve assumption that other people are operating at the same level as I am. You may think that's arrogant but there's nothing I can do about that. Anyway, as I was saying before the bittersweet segue down memory lane, I am sitting with my espresso and trying to concentrate on the sights and sounds of my surroundings:

A moribund tableau of consumerist excess renders in front of me in this faux-continental patisserie franchise. I can see *Homo sapiens*, the only surviving hominid species with their evolved small teeth and big brains, plugged into various devices. They are cyborg ungulates chewing cud, vacuously consuming stimulants and pausing their overtaxed brains before their next shopping foray or entertainment venue. Amongst these forlorn beings, the kicking of the embryonic idea I glimpsed earlier is losing its placental integrity in the womb of my skull. It is in danger of being flushed out like menses before I can get to grips with it, so I abandon my observations and decide that I must move on to greener pastures at once.

There is a particular tribe that is more profitable to observe. The New Mothers. They are to be found this time of day in the pleasant ghettos that exist in the hinterlands of the King's Road, in the Royal Borough of Kensington and Chelsea, or on the implausibly well-manicured high street of Primrose Hill, as phoney as a Wild West main street film set. The hankering to view these women in their natural habitat intensifies as I hurriedly exit the morass of the West End, pushing through the aroma of cabbage and roast duck in Chinatown, and insert myself gratefully into the Tube system at Leicester Square with its own special musty odours evocative of my first travels as a child in an outlandish subterranean realm.

Once I am breathing exhaust fumes above ground again on the bustling shopping precinct of Sloane Square, I know that my quarry is near. I dip into a serene mews, where millionaires reside in converted stables and old servants' quarters backed on to redbrick Victorian buildings, in search of the swollen-breasted nursing brigade. In the hallowed weave of thoroughfares that stretch longingly towards the royal palaces, I walk past shops called Billionaire, and alongside Lamborghinis parked at the side of the street, shipped over from their desert homes before the start of Ramadan. Those fun-loving Gulfsters. The vehicles are in sickeningly bright hues of lime and tangerine, lined up like a packet of what used to be called Opal Fruits. As I turn the corner of a pink sandstone depot converted into offices and a gym, it reveals itself to me. The proprietary coffee and cake shop in what was once a pub – a horrifically poignant transmogrification. I push through the saloon-style doors to be hit by a dense aroma of cinnamon and the shrieking of steam eviscerating milk. Incongruously, the pub decor is intact but caked with a fresh colour scheme of burnt orange and chocolate-brown lacquer. The heady perfume of baking has replaced the smell of damp wood and yeasty urine of bygone days. Once frequented by working-class men from proximate allocations of council housing in the heart of upper-crust Chelsea, the space has been appropriated for a new clientele. There they are, corralled into a zone of oestrogen nearest the toilets, where they must spend half their cafe time changing nappies and relieving their chai tea latte-distended bladders. I detest the latte. It's a scandalous adulteration of the noble coffee bean. Raw milk and coffee should never be mixed. Milk ought to be banned altogether, in fact. A disgusting mammalian ooze of runny fat that no human being should consume unprocessed. The mothers are delicately bolting sugary goods – at reassuringly extravagant prices – with their little charges strapped into hi-tech prams apparently designed by racing engineers at McLaren, Ferrari and Porsche. They prattle together, high on motherhood. I could listen to them for hours, their chatter as soothing as white noise.

I find a low seat at a discreet distance, as like the seasoned hunter I do not wish to startle them. The only other male aside from me in this doughy playground for the affluent white female is slicing carrot cake with a frilly paper hat on his emasculated crown. Perhaps this is man's destiny, to be the faithful drone to the queen bee, worshipping the Mother Goddess once again after a disastrous hiatus when God the Father took on parenting duties. It happened several thousand years ago when the put-upon males realised that they had something to do with the 'miracle' of birth and assigned woman's divine authority to rule over to themselves with a novel invention; the one true God. A bearded male deity who was on their side and scolded the womenfolk for shedding blood without dying, admonished them for attempting to take His place as the head of creation and, to add insult to injury, took their life-giving breast milk and diluted His coffee with it. After many hours of what I call 'distance contemplation', I reach the inescapable truth of the matter: these women are consuming parts of themselves. Sure, the mothers all love their offspring but that's simple brain chemistry. In the public sphere – this particular sphere of the privileged – their precious fruits of procreation are on full display like extracorporeal rogue organs, their erstwhile incubi, the parasitic embryos that were mercilessly fused to their bodies then became detached from the docking bay of their wombs and were expelled to a fanfare of shrieks.

Expelled.

I look at my notebook, its leaves open invitingly on my lap.

I jot the word down. Then I find myself penning the words
'organ', 'fused' and 'fruit'. Something clicks deep within my
corrugated lobes and the cortical activity has a powerful
adrenal effect; for a moment my sight is clear and my city-
sullied ears pop. It is the moment of conception for my next
artwork. Will it be the one that will catapult me to stardom
at long last?

II

It is within a week of my biggest solo show to date in İstanbul, bankrolled by Maximillio and organised by my illustrious mother who is also my de facto personal manager. I am cooking in an effort to distract myself. My current portfolio of work is already dead to me – almost from a past life – and I am still excited by the concept that has been teasing me lately but refusing to reveal itself fully. The current pieces that will be exhibited should sell and that would help pay the rent as Joseph has singularly failed thus far to procure the advertising work I was hoping to get. It is a matter of cash flow and I am loath to ask Father for another hand-out or puncture Mother's delusion any further that I am a successful artist since revealing my moribund pecuniary status to her recently. I hanker to produce something fresh and new – I almost have it in sight yet it remains a chimera of incongruent composite parts too vague to pin down.

Anyhow, I am presently basting lamb shanks in a clay *palayok* I bought in Manila. Dead animal parts have not entered my kitchen in decades yet I was compelled to visit a local butcher's today where I almost retched at the sweet fetid aroma of raw meat hanging in the air. As I go about my cheerless task I listen to my guests seated in the open-plan kitchen and dining-room space in my Rotherhithe residence on the supine spine of the cloudy brown Thames. They are talking about, of all things, art. Do they not have an ounce of empathy? I place the lid on the cooking pot and tear myself a sheet of aluminium foil as I realise that I desperately need to take my mind off all that and yet there they are discussing the state of contemporary art as if I'm not here. I parcel up some vegetables in the foil to oven steam and observe my assistant S sitting quietly with them, gripping her wine glass as though it's a gyroscope keeping her vertical. She looks exhausted. S has been working extremely hard, coordinating the opening of the show in İstanbul. My current beau, Brett, is regarding a young man called Seb with the intensity of a person who is ready to take over the conversation – but he is too timid to change the subject. I wish he would.

'That man calling himself Moomoo has discovered the secret to flogging art,' says Seb, once intern and now assistant to low-level art dealer (yes, 'dealer' for he is not of the same ilk as Maximillio) Cranston Michaels of the Portobello Road, also present. I know Cranston and Seb from the bad old days – fresh out of art college – peddling paintings in exchange for dirty martinis at the Empire Club. Seb and his girlfriend Chifre were invited to my intimate soirée in some convoluted manner that evades me right now and they are both having the time of their lives, drinking red wine and mixing with the art crowd round my bespoke one-piece dinner table hewn from maple. I commissioned it after seeing a similar piece on a trip to Sri Lanka. I place the vegetables in the top shelf of the oven and the blast of hot air exacerbates my already frayed temper.

'In the past, any of that clandestine street-art stuff would've caused no more than a raised eyebrow. There's no wit there,' Seb continues as I remember to slot the lamb shanks, beautifully simmering in their own juices, back into the oven and let the door slam shut. This produces a satisfying thunderclap that puts Seb off his stride. Now Cranston weighs in, even though he is too drunk to think coherently, the hoary soak.

'What's fascinating is that he's marketing himself to the marketers – or *marketeers* – is that a word?' he says with amused incredulity.

'Yes, by commoditising the mystery that is essential to possessing the, er...' Seb cuts in then stumbles. 'The glow that surrounds—'

'The key ingredient that attracts buyers like flies to compost – the word you're looking for, dear Seb – is aura,' says Cranston.

'I just said that,' whines Seb, the captious bastard.

'Without that you're dead in the water.' Cranston nods, ignoring Seb, and stoppers his mouth with a wine glass, drinking deeply.

'Moomoo's aura is so obviously and crassly manufactured,' rejoins Seb. 'And in the most abysmally obvious way – withholding information! The death knell of any market comes when someone gets too clever and stupidly reveals the magicians' tricks in a last-ditch attempt to milk the scene dry before the bubble bursts.'

I stroll over to them in my handmade Caucasian moccasins, which Chifre has been eyeing covetously all evening, whilst twisting the meshed polyethylene sleeve from a wine bottle between my fingers. I am staring daggers at, in turn, both S and Brett; how much more of this diatribe must I take? As the gracious host with a Turkish heritage that holds guests in the same category as the divine, I am loath to interrupt them when they are having such a great time hearing the sound of their own voices. However, since I have other visitors equally discomfited as me by the pretentiousness of Seb's conversation, I am compelled to intervene.

'There,' I say and theatrically pitch the crumpled-up plastic lattice on to the table. There is a moment of deliciously confused hush and then I say, 'Art.' I had conceived the gesture as a moment of jest, an approximation of what art was to my mind at that precise moment of exasperation – a satirical swipe if you like – but as soon as the words escaped my lips it felt like the truth.

'Bravo.' Cranston applauds and adds with a devious wink, 'Very well said indeed.'

'I'm not sure I get it,' babbles Chifre who had been mercifully quiet thus far.

'It's art because he says it is, my dear,' explains Cranston with a delighted tremolo, confirming the transmogrification of chemical compounds into desideratum.

'Well, he's in danger of ruining everything with his... his stencilled shit,' Seb says with a vanquished tone, his eyes stuck on the crushed netting unbending jerkily like a deceased spider. I exchange a micro-expression of triumph with Cranston at our mutual trouncing of Seb's pet theory that he must have saved up and rehearsed for the occasion, the affected pretender that he is.

'Stencil is the oldest trick in the book,' pipes in Brett, possibly trying to change the subject at long last. 'Australian aborigines did it thousands of years ago.'

'Whatever. I mean, his method isn't the actual point here,' blurts Seb and blares on. 'Art is there for us to experience life through the eyes and minds of others, surely. We want the art to be expressive of some line of thought,' he says, and I find myself beginning to agree with him, the little twerp.

'I wouldn't be surprised if he's some infantile post-Dadaist committee.' I pout and drink some of the passable Rioja that someone brought along, seating myself at the head of the table.

'Exactly,' Seb splutters and I immediately regret adding fuel to his fire as he booms on noxiously, 'It's terrifying that people like this Moomoo are peddling their crap to the willing so bamboozled by illusionist methods that they cannot see they are undermining the value of the assets they have already acquired—'

'Must we talk about art?' I cut in, revealing my true feelings at last. I hate doing it but sometimes you have to nail your colours to the mast and simply demand that people respect your mood. After a short but rather awkward silence hangs in the roasted-lamb-scented air, Chifre pipes up again:

'What's that creature who eats its own tail from Greek mythology?' She enquires of the group, apropos nothing – possibly trying to save Seb's blushes.

'It's on the tip of my tongue,' lies Cranston. Another silence.

'The Ouroboros,' says S. Well, she did study art history and philosophy. The kitchen timer starts to ping and blessedly draws a line under the topic. I call upon Brett to help me serve the meat. He springs to his feet, grateful of the escape route

I have provided for him, and trails me to the kitchen. He's a beautiful boy, Brett, but not too bright.

*

Wine is being drunk, the slow-cooked lamb, derived from a dimly remembered recipe I saw my grandmother make once, is going down very well and I feel the stress of the evening melting away. I describe my amusing get-together with Joseph (it hardly qualifies, in retrospect, as an actual 'meeting') and have barely moved on to my observations in the coffee and cake emporium when Chifre, who was happily chortling along with everyone else, bursts into tears and flees the room.

'Why did you have to do that?' Seb asks, fairly brimming with menace.

'Do what?' I say, nonplussed. Seb stares at me.

'What's going on?' bleats Brett.

I glance from the simmering visage of Seb to Brett, who shrugs at me quizzically. Then I gaze at S and she seems to know something that I do not, judging by her pursed lips. Cranston is a blur at the edge of my peripheral vision, swaying gently in a wine-drenched stillness. Perhaps it's the Rioja, but everyone appears to be reflected in a concave mirror, distant and receding with each pulsing second.

'You know what.' Seb spits out. He stands up rigidly in a pastiche of wronged indignation and goes after Chifre. Then I remember, dimly, that she had a miscarriage some time ago. Or was it a stillbirth? I don't recall exactly.

'It totally slipped my mind,' I say. 'But to be honest I rather think she's had too much wine. I wasn't talking about her.'

'I don't get it,' says Brett to me. Then, receiving no response, he turns to S. I am suddenly too addled to speak. I must recover my senses.

'Chifre had a miscarriage,' explains S and Brett makes an 'ouch' face then an 'oops' face followed by a 'what now?' face as he looks at me.

'Poor thing!' Cranston chimes in.

'She's overreacting,' I say.

'The thing is, old chap, if she took it the wrong way then perhaps there's a way to put it right with a well-placed apology,' says Cranston.

'Apologise? For holding a conversation at my own dinner table about my day?' I reply. Soreness is developing in my gut. Moments ago I was coasting along on a river of alcohol and free-flowing chat. That idiot Chifre is probably weeping into my sink and pulling fistfuls of toilet paper in an agonised rictus of self-pity in my bathroom.

'Fuck.' I seethe and stare at the table, trying to marshal my anger. Brett reaches out to put a mollifying hand on my forearm but I spot it creeping up lizard-like and jolt out of the way. I glance at S; she still appears to be horrified and quite useless. Perhaps old man Cranston is right and, as the host, it's best to defuse the situation by being the better person, acting with the refined manners I was brought up with. I breathe in and out slowly thrice to centre myself and give a reassuring nod to the table that I will take the best course of action to smooth all ruffled feathers and close the evening on a happier note.

Presently, Seb returns from the bathroom with Chifre sniffling under his arm like a wet child.

'I wasn't making any references,' I say kindly, 'and I am sorry for the misunderstanding.'

'Yeah, he didn't mean anything by it,' says Brett.

Seb, his lithe Englishman's body taut – a bow about to snap – says, 'He knew perfectly well what he meant, Brett.'

'Look here,' says Cranston in his best tenor, 'he said he was sorry, now the thing to do is to accept the ap—'

'Fine,' cuts in Seb without a note of graciousness. Chifre remains cocooned in her maudlin muteness.

I glance at Brett and he knows to go to the hallway to fetch their coats. As we wait for him to return, the room is thick with a ghastly atmosphere of unfinished business. I apologised and they refused to accept it. In my own home after I cooked them dinner. What kind of people are they? I am close to losing my temper when Brett appears with the coats and perfunctorily hands them over to the undeservedly outraged couple. I can hear Seb breathing through flared nostrils and clamped teeth. He is obviously drunk enough to find it acceptable to insult his host who had so magnanimously brought him into his inner circle and fed him the best meal he had had in years (those were his words about an hour ago, before hostilities began). Flabbergasted, I am nevertheless going to act the adult in this distasteful predicament and offer the olive branch of an explanation, so I say:

'I think that this will all look very different to you in the morning.'

Seb bristles. Chifre places a hand on his chest to indicate that she is too tired to restart an argument. He ignores her and says:

'You looked directly at her when you said the words "fruit

of their loins" so don't give me any of that... crap.' He froths and tiny saliva bubbles appear at the downturned corners of his measly mouth; the same mouth that gorged on the organic and extremely rare English-sourced milk-fed lamb I had bought without any thought for my own deeply held vegetarian ethos. What a waste!

'You've been turning your nose up at us ever since we arrived,' adds Chifre with an enervated sigh, acting the wronged party, the simpering emotional wreck that she is. I open my mouth to let loose my feelings on this preposterous and paranoid onslaught when I am cheerfully and tactfully interrupted:

'That really was a first-rate meal,' Cranston says, grabbing his coat from Brett. 'And I do hope all goes well in İstanbul, dear boy.'

He slaps me warmly on the back, leading me to the front door with him. Seb and Chifre follow, their bodies clamped together in mutual hatred of me. I swallow my retaliatory words and retain enough sobriety in this taxing situation to remain diplomatic to the last but then I recall how Seb and Chifre ended up in my home in the first place. I was keen to have Cranston round for dinner to discuss the state of the art market as the recent Frieze Art Fair had been marred by poor sales and general buyer reticence. He mentioned that his assistant Seb was an ex-banker and had a lot to say about buyer psychology. Cranston added that Seb was going through a rough patch as he and his fiancée were having trouble conceiving. Apparently, Seb's seed suffered from 'low motility'. When they had finally managed to conceive, Chifre had suffered a miscarriage. That's when I asked him to bring

Özgür Uyanık

them both along so as to cast my eye over a couple who were suffering – as a mating pair – the sort of blockage a self-propagating artist endures alone; the devastating realisation that one's whole *raison d'être* is doomed to fail. It cannot be easy for a man to entertain the notion that his sperm is too weak to puncture the ovum's no doubt considerable defences. I may have said a few of those things out loud as Seb and Chifre were getting into the lift. I don't remember it but apparently Seb took a swing and managed to clip me on the chin before anyone could stop him.

*

I wake up in the morning and my face is stuck to the pillow with dried blood. It's seeped through the gauze dressing Brett had thoughtfully applied to my broken skin. The dim recollection of a profound dream fades rapidly as my eyes adjust to the light in the room. My body has the vague memory of having been in some sort of a tumble and the distasteful details of the night return in painful bursts throughout the morning as Brett fusses over me and implores me to see a doctor.

'Brett, if you keep looking at me like that I will scream. Except I can't scream because my head is about to explode,' I murmur, with a mug of coffee steaming in front of my face.

'Looking at you like what?' he asks, all hurt.

'Like a fucking lost puppy.' I smile wanly.

'I'm worried about you.'

'Well don't, I'm a big boy. The bastard sucker punched me.'

Once I have woven together the ill-mannered tapestry of the evening from my own fractured recollections augmented by testimony from Brett and S, I can only conclude that Seb and Chifre are members of the Sabotaging Class. When they are in the presence of creative minds, they are simply not ready to engage their own intellects and compensate poorly by overreaching their capacities. These people ought always to be properly acclimatised before they get thrown into a milieu they cannot handle. Sometimes they simply listen listlessly, overtaken by events, or flit away at an opportune moment to gather their flocculent thoughts. Other times they cannot stand to be there but nonetheless are trapped by morbid curiosity and, thanks to their own crippling sense of inadequacy, prefer to sink the whole ship instead of jumping overboard. An appetite for revenge, as a reaction to being made to feel gut-twisting envy, is an essential component of the most vicious cultural saboteur.

Not too long ago, another such vicious creature destined for obscurity entered my life in order to manifest his own, ultimately disastrous, foray into the domain of art. He had studied at the Slade School of Fine Art in London and found himself on a scheme that would match him up with a more experienced artist to act as his mentor for a period of a year. A non-profit UK arts funding institute – Arts Regalia – approached me because the young man, Selim Mehmet, had proposed me as one of his choices. He never divulged who his other two choices were or where on the list I came. However, from his adoring devotion to my every word (in the earlier stages of our affiliation, in any case), I inferred that I was his first choice. A protégé choosing his own mentor seemed an odd sort of way to go about the process of matching people together but I was to be financially compensated for my time and it felt churlish to refuse, even though I had doubts about how effective my tutoring of Selim would be after our first meeting when he came across as far too meek and middle-of-the-road.

Nevertheless, I resolved to mould his unimpressive raw materials into something with potential and he would soon become my pleasingly pliable human subject. He could have been my muse as well; however, in keeping with my contractual obligations to mentor Selim responsibly, I held fast to the unspoken rule that I was not to interfere with him, romantically speaking. After several weeks of face-to-face encounters, late-night telephone conversations and panicked emails, Selim and I parted ways. He complained to Arts Regalia that I was 'overbearing' and 'drowning his creativity with my own ego'. The archive of electronic correspondence towards the final moments of our collaboration attests to the mental and emotional breakdown of a frustrated wannabe. Selim, despite my continued and repeated efforts to inculcate him in the art of being an artist, wilfully ignored my advice on many occasions. For example, he was enamoured by the medium of video and insisted that he was a video installation artist. When quizzed as to what that was exactly, over single-malt whiskies at a central London hotel bar one night, he replied loosely and with distinct lack of confidence that he did not care to know but only to do.

'You are being evasive, Selim,' I said, boring into his watery blue eyes. I had hoped to provoke him into individualising. At the time, he was at sea in a wishy-washy miasma of relativism.

'I'm not being evasive, I mean, I don't mean to be,' he replied with a half-cocked grin he probably picked up from some movie character he admired. The conversation continued as I sought clarity in the fogginess of his inarticulacy.

'You videotape emotionally damaged people in the hope of displaying the resulting footage in a gallery.'

'Yes.'

'Then why don't you just edit the footage and construct a documentary? Would that not be far more interesting from an ethnographical point of view?' Selim, nervous then, sipped his whisky and looked away. He was staring at the marble surface of the bar where we were perched on adjacent stools when he said:

'I don't want to tell stories.'

'Then you shouldn't use a narrative device.'

'It's anti-narrative.'

'How?'

'Because I am presenting the footage unedited, in its entirety – that's the point of it.'

'Seems to me that you have a poor grasp of documentary film-making techniques and you are hiding that weakness behind a methodology that has clearly fooled your tutors but won't get much credulity from someone like me,' I said, downing my whisky.

'W-what?' he stammered.

'I think you're a fake, Selim. I think you need to hear it before you stumble out there into the real world and hoodwink a bunch of well-meaning art lovers with your BS.'

Misplaced indignation choked him and then he said with childlike rage, 'You're my mentor, you're supposed to help me...'

'Grow up, Selim. Don't waste your life pursuing something you're no good at.' I really meant it too. He was a catastrophe waiting to happen. The last I saw of Selim Mehmet was him striding away from the bar, his legs scissoring self-righteously, buttocks clenched and head held high as he walked blindly towards a future of bitter disappointment.

'Brett,' I say, staring at my oak flooring from a prone position on the sofa. 'I want you to leave.' I hear him emit a low-level whimper.

'Okay.'

And that's the last I see of Brett. It may seem like a cold-hearted way to break up with someone but I find that making abrupt decisions when it comes to relationships is a good way to remind oneself that you can't rely on anyone except yourself. People are here today, gone tomorrow. Besides, I need to divert all of my powers into the art right now and becoming celibate for a spell is exactly what is required to get that pesky semi-formed idea out into the world.

*

The moment I step into her flat in Holland Park and she sees my bruised cheek and facial cut, Mother is already reaching for a silk handkerchief to staunch her tears. I am not sure if they are tears of sorrow or exasperation. Probably both. Her displeasure flares into anger when I tell her that a dealer's assistant called Seb did this to me.

'What dealer?' she demands and I clarify that it was an art dealer. I had a longish dalliance with hard drugs (cocaine and the occasional MDMA) once and she has never fully trusted me not to fall off the proverbial wagon.

'It was a simple act of vagrancy. I had a tramp at my table and I didn't know it until it was too late. It was like a scene from *Viridiana*—'

'Stop trying to be poetic. Tell me what happened.'

'Poetry is the last thing on my mind after the insufferable atrocity that has befallen me, Mother,' I say, in order to satisfy her appetite for the histrionic.

'Who is this Seb character, darling? Speak to me.'

'Seb is a man brought up from the gutter – do you remember that fleapit gallery on Green Lanes next to the halal butchers?'

'Oh darling, do not refer to that windowless basement as a gallery.'

'Anyway, he was interning there when I met him and pointed him in the right direction. Well, the worthless little tea boy that he was, he never respected me – probably due to his innate islander sense of superiority. I made the mistake of inviting him and his partner to dinner.'

Mother walks thoughtfully to her escritoire and snatches a slimline cigarette from her packet, slots it into a filter and lights it with a vintage Ronson Art Deco Bakelite table lighter. I wonder if she is considering launching an immediate case against Seb for grievous bodily harm when she turns her spot-light glare on to me.

'My boy, why do you insist on getting yourself into these situations?'

'Mother, I was attacked – out of nowhere, might I add.' I twist in my seat so as to be able to face her.

'What happens to me when one of these days somebody whacks you and you end up in a… coma?' Her eyes close, willing the image away.

I feel that dire sensation of my intestines coiling tight in my belly, suffocating me. I feel guilty. I have caused her pain through my own negligence; allowing a snot rag like Seb to physically violate me was a disgrace. What if I indeed suffered brain damage, where would Mother be then? I have to choose my words very carefully.

'It was stupid of me, Mother. I'm sorry.'

'Learn to take care of yourself!' she explodes, taking me by complete surprise. Her normally tightly coiffed and sprayed-solid shell of a hairdo flings out a tendril as she yells, her eyes watering up and the edges of her mouth curved down. It is heartbreaking I see Mother as she would hate me to see her – vulnerable, afraid and slightly out of control. I nod and take a deep breath. The automatic body language of the chastised. Then she gathers herself as if tightening an invisible corset and strides to the French windows, trailing blue smoke. Normally I adore the way the afternoon light slants in through the plane trees on the avenue outside, but today everything has taken a maudlin tone.

'You cannot let these people drag you down. The English are the most dangerous breed,' she says and I am relieved that the subject has been changed. 'They'll put you up on a pedestal and then pull you back down again once they have used you up. They love to watch people fail.'

'Mother, if I thought that way about everybody I meet then I would be quite unable to organise a dinner party. Besides, this time it wasn't exactly planned – Cranston gave me a call and I thought I'd have him over and then he mentioned Seb and I thought the more the merrier – I wanted to take my mind off the opening and of course that backfired in spectacular fashion—'

'Disassociate yourself from the pair of them,' she cuts in and goes to her telephone. 'Cranston Michaels is an alcoholic *and* completely uninteresting – he has nothing to offer. Whatever are you doing with him?'

'He's an old friend,' I wheeze as a puff of acrid smoke hits my face as she glides past.

Mother makes a few phone calls and I fancy that I can hear the sound of doors slamming in Seb's face all across town. I feel bad about Cranston, though. Sometimes he is rather amusing – in that self-deprecating English way. Once that is over I lay out my plan for the conceptual work I will develop for the upcoming, painfully prestigious, contemporary art exhibition that occurs quinquennially in Kassel, Germany, that is authoritatively entitled 'documenta', complete with its self-regarding lack of capitalisation. Not an art fair in the upper echelons with Art Basel or Frieze but a well-respected contender where prices are 'solid' rather than 'aggressive'. In other words, not overpriced to the point where only international money launderers would be interested. Mother tells me to explain my idea.

'It's to do with...' I begin. 'Actually it's too soon to say.'

'Fine. Now, have you been to the doctor, darling?'

'No it's nothing—'

'Headache?'

'No. A bit of a hangover but that's passed now.' I smile grimly. She sighs and stabs out her cigarette in an Art Nouveau bronze ashtray.

'So, it's too soon to say...' She trails off.

My idea. Aside from a few words jotted in my notebook I had no clue. Too much contemporary conceptual art is sloshing round and even the curators are beginning to see the collapse of the market through oversupply and the deadly shadow of doubt creeping in (what was all this 'conceptual shit' about, anyway?). If enough people begin distrusting the inherent value of the works being produced by living artists then the money will crowd to safe havens like the old masters, twentieth-century titans such as Picasso and the Impressionists, for example, as well as to the affordable and thus less risky up-and-comers. Whilst the mid-career artists looking to break into the big time – including myself – will be left high and dry. Therefore I have to come up with something truly great.

'Something fresh and unique,' I say finally.

Mother catches that word 'unique' as it flails through the air, having escaped my lips like a fugitive. I should have kept that word under lock and key, in solitary confinement, until it lost all sense of its meaning and rubbed itself out, never to be heard of or seen again. But it is too late.

'Yes, it must be unique. Of course,' Mother says as she rolls her eyes to the ceiling and I know she will dedicate her every waking moment to the achievement of that purpose.

'Mother, I kind of regret saying "unique" to be honest with you. It's a truism, I know, but everything under the sun has been done before and we both know that chasing uniqueness isn't always the best plan. Perhaps inspiration will strike if I let it simmer a bit more...'

'Stop yammering and get to work. Don't believe for a second that you have failed before you've even begun. What kind of an attitude is that?'

'It's too much pressure. I need to walk in the woods and breath in the—'

'Nonsense! How can you fall back on the routine of self-indulgence and navel-gazing that has been the end of so many others?' she says briskly and adds, 'Inspiration is for amateurs.'

She is, of course, right.

III

It is a crisp autumnal İstanbul evening and I am standing in a gallery gouged out from the guts of a Republican era warehouse in the port district of Karaköy. It lies near the point on the Golden Horn where Sultan Mehmet the Conqueror of Constantinople thwarted the giant Byzantine chain barring the waterway to the city's defensive walls by carrying his battleships overland to vanquish their dying civilisation. I am stood here amongst my latest paintings with peers and assorted persons of importance about to arrive and judge my artistic output. I am knee-deep in disappointment; the accumulated tangle of these creations has haunted me daily leading up to this private view. They are the most recent manifestations of my internal turmoil and levitate about me like headstones defying gravity. Upstaged by the walls themselves, I fancy – painted in a seductive hue of white called Japanese Bone. The pieces – good pieces with solid sales potential, I keep telling myself after Maximillio's assurances – are starting to lose their Platonic essence, their form and integrity in front of my bespectacled eyes. The guests arrive. I know this feeling of doom all too well and I must quash it before the panic spreads through my veins and queers my physiology. It is paramount that I, the artist, remain anchored. Yet my work refuses to coalesce into an impression of success and thereby give me much-needed comfort. Instead, the pieces remain aquiver suggesting delicate denizens of a deep-sea crevasse, frightened that they'll fall from their pins, shatter and forthwith be swept up by a zealous cleaner. I will then have to watch helplessly, my feet frozen to the polished concrete, as my art is dumped into a bin and the invitees look on with the suspicion that they are witnessing an elaborate performance piece.

Ah, the inscrutable nature of conceptual art. No one knows what it is unless it is studiously labelled and hung in the hallowed halls of a designated place of contemplative worship, enshrined with the appropriate moniker – The White Cube, İstanbul Modern or (whisper it) Gagosian. I, too, am designated a label and must parade about in carefully chosen garments, fastidiously combed hair and a pair of overpriced Prada glasses with the brand name prominently displayed across the temples. Will anything sell? They must sell or I'll be finished – I am too early in my career to lose momentum. Maximillio would lose faith that I have a market and he would abandon me; my work would then slowly fade from the art-collecting collective memory, not even warranting a footnote, and then what? I would be without purpose. What else could I possibly do with my life that didn't involve producing art? I wasn't trained for anything else. If Joseph failed to procure me advertising work then I would have to, I suppose, if push came to shove, teach. No! This depressive daydreaming causes everything to wilt round me as I plummet into a void, the cocaine fading ahead of schedule. I must resist the urge to run away. I should have had some beta-blockers to smooth out the ride but now it's too late and I feel the rollercoaster has gone off its rails. Coming here high was a deadly mistake but I was too tense and worried about the small but very visible healing cut on my face and the lies I'm going to have to tell in order to insouciantly cover up its provenance, should I be quizzed on the topic.

The process of people unknown to me entering and exiting my orbit, asking art-related questions, continues tiresomely. They may be potential buyers, influential curators or a complete waste of my time, I just don't know. The reason I don't know is because the information channel that usually supports my interactions has broken down. S has disappeared. The situation rapidly deteriorates. A person who must be a guest of a guest says one of my pieces is 'beautiful'. A ripple of disdain emanates around their remark (we do not speak of beauty in art, we speak of the sublime) and I nod ambiguously and rock back on my heels with a dry smile to prevent embarrassing them as well as cutting off the conversation at its putrefying root. As if she has heard my ultrasonic whine of distress, Mother appears, slightly flustered – which is unusual for her – and elegantly hustles the low-grade crowd away and slots in beside me a group of Americans (likely buyers, Mother's clandestine wink tells me) so that I may pump their big strong American hands and point out pieces they may be interested in buying by talking about my technique, sources of inspiration and further assorted bullshit that this type of mob loves to hear. As I seduce the Americans, I notice S – poking her head outside the door of the gallery, looking left and right as if she's expecting a pizza delivery. Then she throws a furtive glance towards Mother who is busy charming the woman from the British Council, the Greek consul and other top brass. What on earth is S doing trying to distract Mother when she is clearly ensconced in business?

When I return my attention to the Americans, they have gone and I am left alone – a floundering foal separated from the reassurance of the fawning herd. I am adrift in the yawning white space and staring at my own work – a conspicuous disaster! The artist must at all times be surrounded by a clique of admiration and solicitations so that he may be distant and indifferent to them, above the fray. Yet the fray has inexplicably moved on and it has become impossible to be aloof, as I ought to be, because I am completely stranded – abruptly abandoned on a lonely dune, the tinkling of champagne flutes and erudite voices tantalisingly close by, yet out of reach. I cannot go to them of course, they must come to me. I feel woozy with rising alarm – I have to make a move. Where's Mother in this well-dressed crowd? She, too, has deserted her post – how has this been allowed to happen? I demand of the ceiling with its piercing halogens. I sense that the area round me has been steadily emptying for a while and it takes me several seconds to connect that occurrence with the gruff voices chanting '*Allahu ekber!*' outside. Relief agents flood my system as it dawns on me that my myopic appreciation of the events unfurling in front of me has caused me to become distressed for no good reason. I have been so completely walled off from everything – so totally enmeshed in the moment – that I failed to notice Mother, S and many others collecting like marbles at the main entrance.

I linger at my spot as others surge forward to see what the commotion is about. Then – a deafening crash and splintering of plate glass rips through the gallery. I hear screams and a lucid throaty roar of horror (Mother) as the Arabic mantra of 'God is great!' rings off the walls now that the whole front of the gallery space has been smashed to shards. I find myself walking towards Mother whom S is battling to pull back from the road, exposed as we are to the hooligans that have descended upon us. I help S navigate her away from the melee and charge her with calling a taxicab to get her safely home.

'Unbelievable!' Mother fumes. 'Religious fanatics on our doorstep – here, in Cihangir.'

Cihangir is an exclusive enclave of İstanbul well known for its costly real estate, private art galleries such as the SALT Galata modern art museum, and assorted antiquarian shops frequented by interior decorators. Strictly speaking, we are not in that area really, but close enough – details never overly concern Mother. Anyway, this is not the sort of place one expects to be attacked for drinking alcohol. It turns out some of the locals arranged a protest against the gallery for its long-running battle to serve drinks at private views when it is located within fifty metres of the famous *Yeraltı* ('underground') mosque, a vaulted Byzantine structure where savvy tourists can witness subterranean Islamic worship, should they so wish. It is a crude and unsettling attack that may or may not have been a portent for the whole country. The police arrive unhurriedly and the perpetrators conveniently vanish, leaving only a clutch of onlookers and, curiously, a couple of journalists already photographing the scene. The whole episode reeks of a pre-planned publicity stunt to consolidate the conservative votes at the looming local elections and to unsettle the liberal elite. Still, it might garner some good exposure for the exhibition as well. That is the spin I will put on it in any case, as part of my anecdotal debriefing when I meet Father, a meeting that fills me with existential dismay.

*

I make the obligatory pilgrimage to Father's region of the city across the Bosphorus on the Anatolian peninsula. In the morning he called me and wished to meet at his favourite eatery in Kadıköy, a thriving and eclectic waterside district bursting with markets, cafes, bookstores and historical edifices including a still-functioning Armenian church behind a high wall and solid metal gates. The weight of closely packed humanity on the tight pedestrian streets at the heart of the fish and produce market is overwhelming as I nurse a terrific hangover following a binge-drinking session at my hotel last night, which I spent alone and deflated after the reception of my work was met with what I can brutally describe as polite indifference. It makes my situation more desperate and I have to get my neurons into order so that I can fish out the idea that first germinated in London and is doggedly refusing to gestate satisfactorily.

We sit across from each other outside a Turkish coffee shop, enveloped in a miasma of roasted beans with our little cups of jet-black postprandial liquid and tiny biscuits to soothe our stomachs after my meal of chickpeas with rice and his one and a half portions of İskender kebab doused in sizzling melted butter. Watching him overeat – in the absence of his new wife who polices his diet zealously – I am moved to enquire after his health and he is happy to ignore the question whilst ordering more şıra, a fermented grape juice, as if the magical properties of the bitter beverage will dissolve the vast volumes of fat he has ingested. We speak of London, my non-existent love life (he hankers for grandchildren) and, finally and inevitably, about work. I start by outlining the content of my recent show – he was invited but demurred, although he promises to visit the gallery soon – then I move on to the sore topic of what I will create next. He has a half-smile dancing on his face. I pause, knowing that what I am telling him is of little interest.

'And what are you doing for money?'

Money. The only thing that holds any power over our jaded hominid minds. The mystery of money is mastered by only a few – the anointed few hidden behind the dark bricks of town houses, stucco and tinted glass. Because of this potent magic the rich are looked upon with awe. How much more awe does a stainless steel and lacquer Anish Kapoor generate when you learn its dollar value? Think about it.

'My agent Joseph is setting up meetings for when I get back to London,' I lie, having regressed to my adolescence when Father would ask over dinner how my studies were going and whether I would furnish him with a suite of A grades at the end of the year in order to justify his investment in a public school education in England.

'Agent?'

'Yes. For work in advertising.'

'I don't understand how you live, I really don't.'

'I get by.'

'I could never do it. If I was your age I'd be lost without a job. Utterly lost.'

'Well, art doesn't pay very well...'

'Art!'

Unable to shake the feeling in his presence that I am doing something unutterably wrong with my life, I fall into a practised silence. He does not fill it.

Father took little notice of me until I was, in his words, 'old enough to have a conversation with' and that turned out to be when I was old enough to realise that he wasn't much of a conversationalist. He is a man of unplumbed complexities, of secretive smiles and a mysterious inner domain of rich emotional depths hitherto only explored by one entity alone: himself. He has been and always will be a hermetically sealed unit designed and operated to keep everyone else out. His mind is a trawler's net, dredging the seabed of human knowledge and brimming with a multitude of squirming thoughts, historical trivia, aphorisms and snippets of poetry. Never does he provide attribution, context or dialogue. The flow of output is either in the 'on' position or the 'off'. He speaks and acts as though he were a triumphant machine from the Turing test, which has made a very convincing show of appearing to be human. I applaud his ability to be successful in life (three homes, constant travel and two wives) and I love him as only a son could love a father who has no known ability to express genuine affection.

He is an electrical engineer by trade and can hold an audience in thrall as he discusses, with real passion, the intellect of Nikola Tesla or neuroplasticity. For him, a true genius could only be a man of science, Leonardo da Vinci's work in hydrodynamics far superior in his mind than any of the polymath's paintings. His lineage is shrouded in mystery since his parents passed away when he was very young and there was no extended family that he was in touch with. He is a staunch secularist, the same as Mother, and also an avowed atheist who demonstrates a blind faith (the irony!) that only scientific investigation can reveal truth. In fact, some of his ontological hypotheses are otherworldly, verging on the pseudo-scientific spirituality of Saturday afternoon Discovery Channel programmes. There are gods, he attests, and they have created mankind in their image. But, he ruminates, they are not inchoate creatures residing in the firmament, they are super-intelligent beings who have created a simulation for us humans to live and die in, much akin to mortal human scientists who construct mazes and other testing environments for the laboratory rat. How he ended up marrying a woman of passion like my mother and how she ever imagined an exciting and fulfilling life with such an asocial character is, for me, difficult to grasp. Some sort of chemical attraction took over, I suppose, before they could get to know each other properly. For she is attached to life to the same degree that he is committed to deriding it. Perhaps it was their common adherence to secularism that bonded them. Who knows.

One night in the green suburbia of south-west London, our telephone rang. Mother was in the kitchen and Father was imbibing a glass of red wine, a Chopin piano concerto tinkling from the Bang & Olufsen stereo system. Mother rushed into the room, hands wet from washing up, and snatched the telephone that was barely a metre from where Father was seated in his favourite tubular steel and brown leather Wassily chair.

'Son,' he had said after Mother had left the room, 'remember that the telephone is not an alarm bell. There's no need to run when you hear it.' Immensely pleased by the fact that he had imparted this wisdom to a young and impressionable mind, he forestalled my follow-up question with a raised index finger and closed his eyes to listen to the music. Denied further enquiry, I remained unclear at the time what he meant by undermining Mother's reaction to ringing telephones. Was he saying that life was too short to risk injury whilst fervently trying to reach some arbitrary goal? Or was he criticising the Pavlovian conditioning response to the sound of a bell? I conjectured that my initial gut feeling was nearer the mark – that it was a willed detachment from temporality and thereby mortality itself. He had hardly any friends when I was growing up and anybody from his extended family who called him invariably asked for money. Therefore, he probably reasoned that anybody calling late on a Sunday night couldn't have anything worth saying to him. If on the other hand the call was for his wife, as was most likely because Mother was socially active and had many friends, then he would have got off his Wassily chair and interrupted Chopin for nothing. He knew that she would eventually pick up the call and she knew that he would rather suffer the grating chimes than move a muscle to give her any help. In the end, Father's self-coined maxim was nothing to do with imparting valuable knowledge gained from experience to his son, as it should have been, but a cloak of contempt for Mother's actions that disguised the guilt he ought to feel for his indolence.

A child has neither the wherewithal nor the motivation to unpick these scenarios at the time that they happen. These unsolved psycho-dramatic moments settle like sand at the bottom of our mental oceans, creating subconscious itches that cannot be scratched. They can only be resolved in later life as long as the memory is accurately retained and one has the tools to investigate the phenomenon. Luckily, I always had the vague idea that Father was in the business of acting out fatherhood as it appeared to him it should be performed rather than just being a dad. Maybe he was afraid that he would fail us in a similar way to how his parents had failed him – by dying young. Such clues as these can often lead to muddy speculation and the detective has to draw the line and admit defeat. In contrast to the murky depths of Father's inner life, Mother is an extrovert and made sure that I understood that I am carrying her genes and not Father's. The important ones, anyway. She is a go-getter and, by extension, I must be too.

Nevertheless, I strongly suspect that I might have been happier lolling through existence like an overfed cat slinking from one life event to the next if I had been without her guidance and constant affirmations during my formative years. It would horrify her to learn that, left to my own devices, I probably would have jacked in the art same as the filmmaking until finally my chromosomes met another's and I became responsible for feeding and clothing a mewling shit dispenser until such time as society deemed it appropriate for my fruitful creation to be released from my custody to gallivant in the world as I had done before it. I've asked myself whether I would be a good father – a paterfamilias in the sagacity-spewing and fine-wine-drinking sense. I'm certainly no macho alpha male creature hankering for chattels (subservient wife, obedient children) and have always found the matriarchal sphere far more comfortable a place to dwell. Perhaps that's why I was drawn to art in the first place. The arena of Art is quite feminine. She nurtures the lucky few who survive the test of early career mortality and dotes on them. She holds them tight to her heart and stirs the whispers of anointed gatekeepers – with the mysterious power to hold your future in their soft gentle hands – into a frothy nourishing brew of glowing success. Alas, due to the daily rigours of life, I am yet to transcend my earthly constraints and manifest the idea that has been lurking within. Each day, with every cycle of the sun and then the stars – fluorescent freckles on God's inscrutable face – it feels as if the idea that I had that morning in the cafe is slipping away from me.

My compressed ejaculation of memories and meditations over, I hurtle back down into the here and now – sipping coffee with Father in Kadıköy. A residual glow of warmth flutters like a blue flame in my belly from the nostalgia of days long past, that untranslatable emotion called *hüzün* that pervades İstanbul and the whole Turkish psyche and shrouds my soul. I am reminded squeamishly of the necessary love that must have helped in my creation and for a few moments I quell the recollections of a fraught upbringing and bourgeois preoccupations that spoil the bare fact that I am lucky to be alive. Then the feeling is gone when Father says, 'What do you want out of life?'

Surprised, it takes an uncomfortably long while for me to give an answer. I vacillate between what I want to blurt out – 'fame!' – and what I think he wants to hear. I have no idea what that might be.

'I want to be an artist.'

'Well then, forget about all this advertising crap,' he says, surprising me for a second time in as many minutes.

Conception

*

At my boutique hotel in Beyoğlu, a district where non-Muslims made their home during Ottoman times, I am left to contemplate my tomorrows in the wake of my conversation with Father the day before.

As for right now, I cannot decide on my next move. I have reached the white infinite wall, nose pressed up against it, searching for a horizon to lock on to and steady my mind. If a speculative collector – an evil and dangerous breed – purchases a swathe of your work then, far too soon, shoves them on to the secondary market (auctions) hoping for a quick profit then you have been 'flipped'. Galleries don't appreciate their art being treated like houses for sale. My work has been flipped before one too many times and that has threatened to ruin the taste in the buyer's mouth for my product. Maximillio would never say it to my face but I fear that the reason behind my present lack of sales is due to the effect this unspeakably vulgar practice has had on my work. A self-perpetuating downward spiral of devaluation can choke an artist's career and thereby deprive the chain of curators, gallerists, managers, agents, advisors and savvy art collectors of their lifeblood. The whirling dervish blinks, stumbles and the magic vaporises, as do all those lovely dollar bills. An asset class engineered out of such gossamer thin and perishable material as awe has to be protected by the amniotic sack of viscose language and the razor wire of cultural elitism. Art must remain illusive and immutably out of reach. Desirable. Valuable.

I must maintain a humourless core. Art is not funny. You can be as amusing or amused in person as you please, but when enacting the sacred process of creation alone in your writhing desperation to mock death you must be as serious as a cat. The cat does not doubt its purpose and neither can the artist. I don't go into a church and chortle at the sacraments, so one cannot enter my church – the art gallery, exhibition or museum – expecting levity of any kind. Your mind will submit to the spectacle of my utter conviction that what I have produced demands nothing less than your unflinching gaze of admiration or failing that, repulsion. Either way, you won't be laughing. If you are, then you will be exposed as a fraud incapable of comprehending your own ultimate destination to the dirty bowels of the earth where you will be digested and turned into compost. Yes, art exists to remind you of your mortality. I am merely the fleshy announcement of Death and accordingly I cannot take any inappropriate joy in the fulfilment of my grim and sober duties. Stressed by these thoughts, I slip into an escapist daydream:

I think of the hallowed white space and my prey: the gormless spectator hungry for the spectacle of meaning. He is obliviously wandering the gallery, gawping and frowning at the art arranged about him, art that is pulsating with a magical aura imbued as much by the emotive lighting and incomprehensible titles (*Wretched Blue, Dimorphic Embolism* or simply *Untitled*) as by the wilfully opaque work itself, his desperate eyes flitting nervously across a canvas here, searching vainly for significance, or a three-dimensional brass declaration of mortality there, his whole being straining to extract substance from it – the pattern-seeking *Homo sapiens* brain doing its ape-like work. If only he had the power to read the signs of his impending doom, unaware of the grip I will wield on his tiny fluttering heart – with my unforgiving claws and drilling feline gaze. Yes, he is alone and separated from the flock that are but mute shadows glimpsed in the yonder and now he turns to face me and I invite him in to worship. He is transfixed. He is staring Death in the face. By then I have a good chance that he is so mesmerised that he will invest large sums to divest himself of the crippling doubt and replace it with the certainty of money.

Relishing these sacred images of my apotheosis, I swell momentarily with the delectable sweetness of enjoying the certitude of ascendancy over and above the mediocre masses. All I need at this stage is my idea to fully form. I have the will to put it into action when it does. Having ruminated thus, I roll out of the bed stained with the by-products of the night's exertions and go through my wallet for the credit card that I will use to pay for this hotel and am struck by the weight of my impecunious standing as a struggling artist. A low growl of desperation rises from my throat before I am even aware of the fact and I hurl an empty glass across the room – a tirade of suppressed self-hatred spills out of my body, over and over, as I thump the mattress manically and fling my suitcase against a wall. It is a while before I perceive the urgent rapping on the door and a hotel employee shouting for me to open up.

'It's nothing – I'm fine... thank you,' I bleat gingerly.

*

I meet Mother in Nişantaşı, a salubrious and über-chic neighbourhood where she was shopping, and we jump into a taxi that takes us to the Hilton Hotel, sitting resplendently above Maçka Park with views of the straits, for afternoon tea.

She reminds me of our last discussion about my next project and the word that was flung out to haunt me. It had to be 'unique'. Somewhere between my *tarte au citron* and fourth cup of Earl Grey, I am holding forth on the thoughts that have been gnawing at me for some time:

'Over here people keep telling me that I am not a Turk, that I've been Anglicised beyond recognition and over there all they want is for me to act out their fantasies of eastern exoticism – I am torn, Mother – I am neither this nor that, a wraith cast in the wind...' And I want to go on and say that I wish I could quote song lyrics by Zeki Müren, stanzas by Nazım Hikmet, the prose of Orhan Kemal, Sabahatin Ali and Cahit Kayra – but I only know what I was taught and grew up with in a land far away from my roots, my heritage! I wish I knew the Turkish proverbs that others reel off to colour their communications and impart wisdom – wondrous phrases like 'no one can be a prophet in their own land', 'a single stone cannot make a wall', 'if watching makes one an expert then a cat would be a butcher' and hundreds if not thousands of others that speak of the acumen of a centuries-old culture that I am a part of yet somehow has been lost to me. When, from time to time, one of my irascible aunties leans across the sofa with melancholy in her eyes and a glass of tea in her hand and sings out a line from an Anatolian folk song to the reciprocal sighs of those in attendance I feel as dislocated and alien as a lonely asteroid streaking past the moon.

'What does Maximillio say, darling?' Mother enquires, calmly ignoring my existential cry for help – obviously trying to remain clear-eyed in the face of my unproductive emotional turbulence.

'What does Maximillio say? He says nothing. But I know what he's thinking – he's thinking that I am a bridge between East and West similar to this old city astride the Bosphorus that can claim knowledge of the centuries where civilisations clashed and melded... I don't know. I'm a rambling mess.'

'Let it out then.'

'Mother, I never wanted to be in between – I'm not blaming anyone for this, let me make that clear – but I was taken from the place of my birth and dropped into a foreign land and left to flail about, not knowing who I was supposed to be or where I was coming from. I am a rootless stranger oscillating violently between two alien realms – trying to fit into both and fitting in nowhere.'

'And out of this pain there will be something glorious, I feel,' she says with equal parts equanimity and sadism.

*

I leave the tea-soaked meeting with Mother and the word 'unique' is echoing in my head mercilessly like a Ramadan drummer in the dead of night. It's just not possible to be that distinctive any more, I whine to myself and curse Mother's Thatcheresque barrel vision – knowing full well that she has a point – as I stamp along the pavement like an infuriated infant. Perhaps I am a perpetual child, as all serious artists tend to be? Unable or unwilling to become an adult, which would mean leaving the pampered dominion of the household pet dog (another perpetual infant) that, with utmost seriousness, demands play and chases after balled up socks as if his very essence depended on it. The canine, evolved from wild stock to favour the cuteness of the puppy's characteristics, has one purpose alone: to facilitate the release of oxytocin in itself and its human handler, creating a positive feedback loop of devotion. A simple chemical trick to endear itself to those who feed it and provide shelter from the elements. A process not too far from how a child must endear itself to adults to secure their protection. Or how a working artist must gain the patronage of a benefactor. The right image has to be nurtured and projected just as the dog sports its floppy ears and babies possess squeezable cheeks. The artist has his or her impenetrable aura to attract fidelity. The artist's feedback loop once built up can sustain itself for the duration of a lifetime but must be constantly reinforced so that the illusion that his art is substantial and carries meaning is maintained. Some of these loops resonate over the ages, through generations, and the artists are rendered immortal: Degas, Matisse, Rothko, and the images they produced are preserved, gawped at and fetishized forever.

People sometimes use tired old tropes like if Mozart were to have been born in the 1980s he'd have started an electro-pop group and taken us all by storm, or if Leonardo da Vinci were alive today he'd be using the latest technology to blah, blah, blah – no he wouldn't. Da Vinci would end up most likely a computer animator responsible for the Hulk's left buttock if he were born today. Mozart would be crushed by the soul-destroying machinations of the music industry and be spat out after one hit. They would be spent before they could attain greatness of any kind. The awesome talents that shone during the Renaissance, when subjective human consciousness was only just emerging blinking from the Dark Ages, would weakly flicker and be snuffed out today in the blinding overdrive of competition; their talents and unrealised artistic potential taken to the grave. The light of Enlightenment is only blinding when it shines out of an inky blackness. Ah – that's doubt insidiously infesting my mind disguised as reasoned argument. No, I won't let myself down in this way. I must and shall bolster and buttress the ego so essential to my creative well-being with copious amounts of alcohol (as I have decided to give up hard drugs). The binge will hopefully return me to factory settings.

My last serious descent into hard drugs, when I left art college and entered the real world all too suddenly, had been mercifully swift but unfortunately quite debilitating, approximating the experience I imagine of being dunked underwater for three seconds to a depth of 300 metres. I fell into the diamond-rimmed hole of persistent cocaine abuse with an abrupt vengeance born of frustration at how much time I was spending asleep when I could be up being productive. Instead of lowering my alcohol intake, as I needed its effects to help lubricate my process, I decided quite logically to supplement the downers with stimulants. Caffeine was woefully below par as a balancing force and in fact seemed to overstimulate by nullifying the beneficial and desired loosening effects of alcohol. Cocaine worked perfectly with the booze and permitted me to fully embrace my ego – shedding the strictures of societal norms. Artistically speaking of course, since self-censorship is the artist's mortal enemy. Inevitably, due to fatigue from all the productivity induced by the chemicals I was recklessly utilising, I hit a wall and the cocaine became an end in itself rather than a means. Many close acquaintances of mine began to notice the change in me and they made it known that they were unhappy about it. An unfortunate side effect of moderate to heavy cocaine use is an unresponsive sexual libido. You know it's there but it can neither be roused nor tempted to satisfy the undimmed urge to attain sexual congress. My sexual partner at the time was understandably distressed by our lack of carnal coupling, whining that not having sex was the same as owning a four-by-four and never going off-road – quite the turn of phrase for someone so dim-witted. After many months of hiding the true nature of the imposed celibacy, I was caught red-handed with the nose candy, bent over a toilet cistern at my private members club, Home. I cut a melancholic figure, I thought, in that stall, scraping the white powder from my top lip and rubbing it into my gums. I abhor waste. I felt that it was fair to say that I had perhaps taken a few missteps in my sincere attempts to unblock my once fertile imagination. I also had a Ukrainian waitress in there giving me a blow job. My partner at the time had a different and far less quixotic appraisal of the picture before him and said something along the lines of, 'You pathetic little man.' The insult had come from the heart. He was much younger than me and, unsatisfied by the sexual component of the relationship, and frankly my sluggish career trajectory, and he left for greener pastures (a fashion photographer) but not before traitorously revealing everything about my drug abuse to my outraged mother. The spectre of a drug-induced death for her son was too much for her after what she had gone through with my brother. She wailed like a mourner at a Mesopotamian funeral and I had to confess to myself that my behaviour was damaging to her as well now and that was not sustainable. I couldn't do that to her. She had invested too much in me.

Yet I couldn't give up the drugs either. Addiction warps the mind and bends your will to serve its commitment to feed your overdeveloped cocaine, alcohol and nicotine receptors. The cravings can not only interfere with logical thought processes that conclude you are actively killing yourself but can also hijack the auditory circuits of the brain so you begin to hear its – the craving's – arguments against your giving up the drugs. The arguments are typically very persuasive indeed, intelligently worded and totally reasonable. The craving says, 'Well, look, you're suffering for no good reason and life is short. Go on, have a toot.' Or, 'You're not strong enough for this; it's not something you are capable of dealing with so stop stressing out – that's bad for your heart, remember. Have a drink and calm down.'

The cure came from an unexpected source. Father held the opinion that one was not actually alive and well unless one had a pension plan in place, robust health insurance and a job for life. It made my blood boil to consider the possibility that he was right and that I had wasted my life instead of doing what he did, which was to get an actual job straight out of university and start a family. Passing on the selfish gene. The drugs were not helping me to ease his distress as he watched me deteriorate both financially and in terms of general well-being. It was his usual disapproving face morphing into a sad disappointed face that finally tipped my brain chemistry into purge mode. I rallied against the self-medication that had spiralled out of control. The drug-taking would have to stop. As part of my creative process, the alcohol could remain in circulation and then I could wean myself off that as well. I had resolved to get back on track – to prove the naysayers wrong. A good enough motivation if you didn't have anything else to hang your hat on.

One of my previous efforts to disabuse Father of the notion that I was a failure came a few years after he had segued into another life with a new wife and her grown-up children and began to rarely interact with Mother and me. We had dinner at his apartment in İstanbul. I was in my late twenties and buzzing after receiving a hefty commission for a piece I had salvaged from an old art school graduate show and I was, relatively speaking, flush with cash. So I had bought presents for my new stepbrother, stepsister and stepmother for New Year's Eve. In Turkey, the occasion is celebrated along the consumerist lines of Christmas, complete with roast turkey and baubles on fake pine trees. You can even see men in Santa Claus outfits ringing bells in shopping malls. In fact, if some archaeologists are to be believed, the tradition of decorating a Christmas tree originated with the Shamanic Turks who adorned a white pine – indigenous to the Asian steppes – to celebrate the winter solstice. Anyway, these presents were items from stores that hadn't any branches in Turkey at the time; it was before the spread of global brands to all corners of the sphere.

The presents I lavished on them were, to my mind, beyond their reach and I was telling them that I had a better life than they had, that I could access the fruits of prime consumer-driven cultural centres like London and they could only scavenge for scraps in their 'developing' country. Yes, an insult. Their gaunt expressions of fake thankfulness as they accepted my gifts from Muji and Marks & Spencer told me that I had succeeded in making them feel small and I hoped that Father could see how much better his actual offspring had done in the race of life than these usurpers. As usual, his face was a mask of indifference and any smile or show of pride was limited to platitudes bookending our get-together. He had not been impressed by my munificence and the gesture had been rendered hollow. By the time the next year rolled round I was penniless and indebted. As the years go by, the gulf widens between us. I refuse to plead for his approval and he refuses to concede that I have not wasted my life. Mother maintains that this is because he is jealous of the fact that I am doing what I truly want to do in my life whereas he has forever been a slave to the system, incapable of breaking out of it and pursuing his dreams. I'm not so sure she's right. With a sinking feeling when I am at my most enervated and morose, I tend to believe that the old man is just worried for his son and doesn't want him struggling, foolishly, in financial dire straits for the rest of his life. So utterly defeating is this latter possibility that I prefer to adhere to Mother's view, painting a mythic tableau of father-son rivalry.

Despite the welcome distraction of these anxieties that fuel my procrastination, I am suddenly hit by the monstrous realisation that I am one missed rent payment away from homelessness as my return to the UK approaches. Sure, Mother would take me in but where would I work? How could I exercise my right to sink into the deepest funk in order to birth my next creation within sight of her stern and loving gaze? No, it is not an option. I must and shall hit rock bottom before the process of actualisation can begin. I must now enter a phase of total isolation – an intoxicated shaman on the Eurasian grassland whence my ancestors came on horseback, an inebriated cave hermit on the cusp of a revelation, an Aghori ascetic smeared in cremation ashes – before I can rise again from the abjection of my tenuous bodily existence as a prophetic revenant to shock and inspire awe in all those who look upon my work and despair.

I halt in my tracks, somewhat dazed, on the cobbled incline below the Galata Tower in the area that was once a Genoese colony, my musings having truncated the time it has taken me to get from the Hilton to the mouth of the Golden Horn on foot. The sounds of the street invade my ears. A battered scooter carrying two young men beeps me aside and off the narrow road. I look about, dumbfounded by the blur of human activity round me. Smells from *döner* vendors, corn-on-the-cob and roasted chestnuts sellers abound. Gulls squawk in the sky and a ferry blasts its klaxon at a passing tanker. I find myself smiling stupidly like a baby waking from an abstract dream. If my unrequited love for the bitch that is London is anything to go by then I must have a severe and lasting crush on this city of cities they named İstanbul. I am torn between disparate cultures – the tragedy of the émigré – and to conquer them both to me seems impossible as I gather my scattered senses and realise that soon I must fly away from here to another place I call home.

IV

So, London.

On the fourth day of a state of incommunicado, S knocks on the door of my studio continuously for forty-five minutes, as instructed. Through a haze of alcohol-induced slumber I pretend for a while that the staccato rhythm of her puny balled-up fist on the authentic early twentieth-century dockyard cast-iron-clad oak door is a laconic master builder lovingly restoring the antique door frame. Then I start to think she might call the police, or much worse, Mother. S had strict orders to protect my alone time for three days so as to facilitate the artistic binge from which I was currently emerging as though from a chrysalis. These commands included providing takeaway food and alcoholic beverage deliveries to my door so that I need not interface with another human being for the duration of my pupal stage. However, on this day I am to be roused as per schedule – kicking and screaming if necessary – from my tar-black pit of detached inebriation. Her actual name is Samantha, by the way. I hate the name but she looks the part and works hard. I would have preferred a Cadence or even Sienna. I refuse to call her Samantha or the androgynous Sam so I try to address her by name as little as possible, but once in a while she needs to be summoned from within a crowd in a hurry and I settle for a sibilant 'S'.

I unlock the door and throw the wrought-iron latch to enable her ingress. My faithful hangover is fading fast. It served me well, though, and during its tightest grip on my body when I was debilitated and laid out full of sickness, my mind was teetering on the knife edge between a roasting hell of self-loathing and a hard, hard place that defies description, a place where one is prepared to extinguish the flame of existence for the peace of oblivion yet, yet... I had (thankfully!) cracked through the seemingly impenetrable gloom of those hours stretched out into what felt like days of maudlin auto-flagellation, darkest despair and almost whimsical state of morbidity – when my chest could not rise to take a breath and my heart thumped along the arteries of my left arm in the throes of a pseudo attack. During these moments I had felt at my most like the flesh and blood creature that I am, that we all are but try to forget or ignore the fact because we choose to imagine that we transcend the ageing cells of our fragile frames and exist on another plane; that we possess an everlasting 'soul', which will magically continue to exist long after our earthly forms dissolve away.

Ha! What nonsense. You and I are made of meat and bone, the muscles shot through with tendons, nerves and veins. Can you feel your heart beating? How would you say it feels as it slows and grinds to a halt – will you panic or cry out in fear? Or have you never sat still with these meditative questions and just listened to your body working? Notice the pulsing artery in your neck, the distant pump of your cardiac muscle walled within the dank cave of your upper trunk, protected and safe behind a cage of ribs. It just flexes away for you – the dumb convulsive animal – shoving the oxygen-rich fluids down your aorta, keeping the life juice flowing through your undervalued, over-abused physique. Poor thing! If it could it would split asunder from your troublemaking, addiction-prone, error-ridden and hormone-controlled consciousness and live a happy, fruitful and long life, just *being*. Like a starfish or an African lion; doing what it does best, honed to near perfection over aeons of evolution; eating, fucking and making little future eating-and-fucking machines. Who needs 'the mind'? It's the cause of all the bloody trouble.

When the hangover was at its most keen, I could almost feel the meat threatening to peel from my bones as if I'd been slow-cooked in a Bedouin zarb for nine hours. This sharpened sense of dismal, painful reality struck me in the oily sump of my depression; it felt more real than anything I had experienced before (bar the raw agony of my botched circumcision) and there, barely floating in the inky blackness of a post-mortem blood pool, I had seen light.

Other people try to elude a good hangover as a matter of received common sense; automatically they go for the water, sucking it in desperately from the tap and pop this pill or guzzle that remedy. There's always some fashionable recipe for losing a solid hangover doing the rounds. Humankind is obsessed with neutralising pain and ending suffering – two profound benchmarks of being a human being. I, on the other hand, relish the hangover, it being a pain that convinces every cell in your body that it will never go away and at the same time is guaranteed to finally ebb, leaving little to no damage, save for a few million neurons sacrificed at the altar of creation.

S looks at me, her questioning expression double-framed by the doorway and her angular fringe of light brown freshly ironed tresses. She is clutching her folder to her chest trying to decipher the look I am giving her. Yes, the look says, I have emerged from my own private Dark Age of witlessly failing to make far-reaching creative connections. I have, without mercy, reinvented myself as an artist, having realised that the tools of my trade to date were now redundant, nay, dangerous to my core being. They were nothing but crude implements of an extinguished era that had passed its apogee long ago. In accordance with my new trajectory, I had – in a drunken delirium – snapped every single paintbrush I owned and squeezed each and every last metallic tube of oil paint into the now definitively plugged toilet. I am not sure if my countenance conveys all of this satisfactorily to S in that moment we stand together locking eyes. However, I haven't spoken in three days straight and I am not about to start now. After I beckon her inside, S waits patiently as I take a long, hot, intensely erotic shower then languidly dress in loosely fitting cotton *şalvar, yelek* and over-the-calf socks. Reminiscent of a Turkish samovar bearer on his day off, I then eat the breakfast of vegan sausages and fried eggs she serviceably prepares for me. We still haven't spoken yet and she knows very well that I am not going to signal the moment when the silence is broken. She begins to tidy up the pile of wood that was once my easel and stock of blank canvasses.

'I have it,' I finally say quietly across the expanse of my studio to S, who is stuffing a bin liner with the detritus of my extravagance of the preceding three days and three nights: pizza boxes, beer cans, various bottles of wine, vodka and, to my astonishment, melon liqueur (I do not remember anything about any liqueur). She gives me a sly look that confirms my long-held suspicion that she is attracted to me. My teasing silence may have turned her on and for an aching moment or two I think about having sex with her right there on the granite top of the breakfast bar, her legs splayed as I nuzzle her. But the image is fleeting – it does not expand into a storyline worth pursuing; nothing in its details awakens the concupiscence that necessitates these images transforming into solid, earthy actions. Also, I have a rule about sleeping with the help.

I let the bitter tang of dark roast coffee divert my senses to above my beltline and wave her over. She sashays across the room on her strange little buckskin bootees, bumping the black bag in her grip against the side of her knees. Her green eyes level with mine. I stoop on my Gino Bombo stool, which I remind myself needs replacing along with the others; they've gone out of style faster than they can knock them off in China. I fucking hate them actually. I make her write a note to dispose of said articles with a solemn instruction not to give them to charity. They must be taken to the recycling plant in Wandsworth by the grey sloshing Thames and dismembered, crushed and incinerated. She writes it all down in her folder (I abhor all handheld computer devices with touchscreens and have banned them) and then looks up, keen as a kitten. She has a way of looking straight into me and this stirs a direct primal connection with something I can't quite put my finger on right now. Can she read my mind?

I don't know. The vertiginous feeling passes. I swallow the last of my coffee.

'Sit down,' I say and she perches herself on the stool opposite. Something is amiss – I can't do this on a ghastly plastic and aluminium barstool so I kick myself off and stride over to my brown, weathered, thickly enveloping armchair and sink into it.

Annoyed by my own procrastination. I go on quickly, 'You're the first person to hear what my next piece is going to be.'

I let that sink in. She teeters on the edge of her stool, her feet turned inwards meekly and her delicate chin raised, eyebrows sitting comfortably atop her cleverish eyes and an attentive smile on her finely wrought lips. Our eyes lock, not for the first time today, and I realise that she, in a way, is penetrating me. I take a breath, disguised as a yawn, and let the feeling spill over me like a freshet from a thawing stream. Then it ebbs away and is gone.

'You should take notes,' I add, to buy yet more time because I am struck by the revelation that I can't say what I was going to say out loud in this casual mood. It requires a sacred solemnity in order for the exchange to be made correctly. This idea of mine, earned through acute anguish, is a potent spurt of human endeavour – it is nothing less than a historic moment to cherish. I can't risk the words I use to describe the thing not holding up in the harshness of daylight, that unforgiving radiation and cheery killer of the imagination. I need a crypt-like atmosphere of reverence and dread. Following my directions, she scurries round the perimeter of the open space and brings down shades and snaps shut the curtains. A cool, gloaming calm descends and allows me to breathe karmically and in control at last.

Deciding to stand fully erect, having found the comforts of the armchair too suffocating, I look S directly in the eyes and am impressed to find her contented mug without a hint of anxiety, boredom or impatience. She truly is a most valuable assistant. I open my mouth and the words simply refuse to come out. They hide behind my molars, some of them darting back down my throat and I gag and need water. Ably, she fetches me the life-giving, cleansing liquid. I drink away the dryness from my caffeine-addled gums.

'Are you okay?'

I nod, pause and say quite matter-of-factly, 'I will eat my own kidney.'

She is trying to interpret the sentence as if I have quoted her an aphorism in Latin. I continue, 'In front of a select group of invited guests at a gallery space to be determined.' I gaze at the dust motes, thick with purpose, in the slits of weak light infiltrating my secular sacristy. The weight of history – art history – snakes on to my shoulders and makes a home there. It hunkers down round my neck and whispers sly references to fame and tasting immortality. She takes notes without a trace of excitement. Had I been expecting a bigger reaction? I suppose her cool disposition is an asset and I congratulate myself for being an excellent employer who has trained his staff to the highest standards where work always comes before base emotion.

'I will have my kidney removed whilst I am fully awake with the use of a local anaesthetic. I don't think I can do it myself. It may be a physical impossibility – look up the procedure for it, please. Once removed, I will without delay – actually look up how quickly I can be active after the operation – I will

Özgür Uyanık

sauté and eat the organ, probably cooked over a propane stove or something. The event should be recorded on thirty-five-millimetre film and photographed – no video. The resulting stills and film will be presented as limited editions, signed by me, naturally.'

I look at her scribbling away. She finishes and says, 'Got it.'

Lapsing into cliché I clap my hands together to signify the end of a satisfactory meeting.

'Good,' I say, surprised and perhaps a tad let down by her sangfroid. Then I realise that she must be in shock. It hasn't sunk in yet, that is all.

'When are you thinking of doing it?'

'It's got to be ready for documenta.' The solidity of that goal makes my spine tingle.

'I better get cracking then,' she says jumping to her feet to go.

'Great,' I say. She abruptly stops in her tracks and regards me with a deeply befuddled look.

'But you're a vegetarian,' she says.

'Yes I know that,' I sigh.

She nods smartly, still stunned, and exits, dragging a couple of bin bags with her. I wonder what will happen when the numbness wears off and she grasps the full visceral reality of my design. Perhaps she'll be in line at a coffee shop taking delivery of some sugary concoction when it hits her and she'll swoon to the ground in delayed astonishment. I don't know. Yes, my lips haven't touched meat since I was a teenager and my project is all the more compelling because of it. I feel giddy with excitement. I dread this moment when my playfulness in the arena for imaging concepts has to wind down and my mind has to sit still whilst real world practicalities have to be

82

appraised and organised before I can begin in earnest. Now that thoughts have been transcribed into actionable words, the conception complete, the thing must gestate. The particulars of its anatomy must uncoil from a lumpy nucleus into a living, breathing artefact tangible inside the realm of the human. It will be tenderly held when it comes out into the world, or rejected by horrified faces backing away from it in confusion and terror. Either reaction is tantamount to triumph, although – being honest – I'd much prefer to witness the latter, more transgressive outcome.

Mentally and emotionally exhausted, I stretch out on the antique Anatolian *kilim* woven assiduously by Turkish womenfolk from some eastern province that forms the centre-piece of my living quarters and prepare to fall into a honeyed afternoon nap. Eyes closed, pupils darting about under my lids hyperactively, I think back on my life:

It was in my wretched, stupid youth that I squandered my precious early promise seeking a doomed career in the realm of the mediocre. Father insisted in his own pleasant and unremitting manner that I would be left destitute, alone and unutterably miserable if I chose art as anything other than a passionate hobby. Mother was in her deepest abyss of painkillers, beta-blockers and a cornucopia of depressive ailments that rendered her a mute witness to her husband's eager mission to have me invest my life force in the pursuit of settling bills, nurturing a mortgage and sundry other earthbound and tasteless tasks. I held out and rebelled by fleeing the parental home and holing myself up in a bedsit – on housing benefit – perilously near the oily, humming dust belt of the North Circular, a dual carriageway like a noose round my neck. I had chosen a subsistence lifestyle temporarily subsidised by Her Majesty's government coffers out of desperation.

This interlude of signing on at the Job Centre would, I hoped, give me the precious time to wheedle my way into the hallowed hippodrome of fine artistry and eventually global acclaim while plying my trade with intense bouts of productive work and longer periods of staring at walls and drinking heavily. Unfortunately, the memory of my twin brother's death always came back to empty me of all illusions, making me unable to delude myself, which is a disaster. My parents converged on me like thirsting wildebeest at a muddy watering hole and brought down upon me their redoubled attention. I soaked up their kindness and wasted no time in inuring them to the task of supporting me into my twenties and maybe even beyond. The guilt had gripped my heart then. Had I profited from the death of my sibling in some strange way? His mortality had furnished me with the material and fuel that fed my art – all those anguished canvasses thick with paint and suffering that had got me into art school! I was encased in a patina of rotten self-blame so I sloped back home wretchedly from N11 and succumbed to the job applications Father had printed out for me with irritating prescience. Mother preternaturally pulled herself out of the alcohol-aided self-absorption of grief and began to see me again as an individual rather than the remaining one of a pair. I stood before her as a rough-hewn marble block, the figure trapped within and yet to be revealed. She set to work on me as an all-consuming project. Father dwelt thenceforth with his circuit boards and electrical drawings and barely came home from his office.

Conception

My first successful job interview was followed immediately by my resignation on the first day of work. Mother did not subscribe to the notion that great art can be produced in tandem with receiving a living wage. Father was soon after cleaved fully from the already diminished and chronically faltering familial unit. It would take another few years of drawing my share of monies, pursuant to their divorce proceedings, for my work to get any attention. Mother never lost hope and she rejoiced when I sold my first piece to an illustrious collector, which launched my career. At the time it was as a waking dream; I was sleepwalking, notionally aware that my life had changed but scrupulously cynical about any continued success. That weakness of my willpower put me back several years. It kept me in Father's orbit far too long. It took me a while to spin away towards the unknown and make myself the revolving centre of my own universe. Now here I am, the peregrination of my quest for creation over, my strolls in the streets of London as a *flâneur* at an end, the bricolage of my cultural vacillations tuned into a coruscating beam of intuition, resolve and dire intent. I am going to eat my kidney.

Forgive me, brother, forgive me...

V

A snow-covered New York City greets S and me a couple of months later. I refuse to sit for more than two hours a day. My body has to be erect for as long as possible. Only societal pressure forces me to sit when the options are limited, for example when at a public dinner or an important meeting where someone higher up in the food chain requires me to 'take a seat'. I will comply under these circumstances as a diplomatic gesture of goodwill; however, I may also judge that it is possible to compromise by throwing a defiant leg over an armrest or something. This will be my chosen posture when I half-sit across from Maximillio Zvwark, a man more important than me at this stage of my career. He is a gallery owner, a gallerist with branches here in NYC, London and Paris. His father was the famous art dealer Sinfredo Zvwark who once sold forty Warhol Brillo boxes out of his dining room when he was slumming it in New York in the late seventies. Without Maximillio's showrooms my work is invisible to the buying classes. With these permutations of anxiety riddling my person, I enter the Zvwark Gallery on West Broadway on the southern tip of Tribeca, a stone's throw away from the 9/11 Memorial site. I nod to the demi-alien embodiment of haughty feminine allure seated behind a sheet of white lacquer at the front desk. As a well-informed intern, the girl recognises me and slips out of her seat to traipse over to Maximillio's office at the rear, beckoning me to follow with her glossed lips. Whatever happens I resolve to leave with my self-respect unblemished. I refuse to beg. It never works with these people, anyway. After a few minutes of poised banter (I abandon my leg-over-armrest position early on as the armrests are too high), I elucidate my stratagem to Maximillio and end firmly with, 'Let me be clear, Maximillio. The work will blow everyone away.'

'I'm intrigued,' he says.

'I need assurances from you that it will have your full backing when it comes to market.'

'But of course it will.'

'There will be a few expenses – trips to Turkey, the costs of the operation, the showing in London and of course the final manufacture of the artefact,' I say and my eyes are unblinking. 'As there is no precedent for what I am going to do, there are risks involved.'

I hold his lidded gaze perfectly. His glasses look heavy, thick-rimmed and gloriously expensive. I see the discreet gold lettering of Dolce & Gabbana. I sense the deficiency of ophthalmic bulk on the bridge of my nose and inwardly cringe at my rampant envy. His shirt looks freshly bought, unpacked and ironed by some underling who keeps a stock of them rolling in, if I had to guess. The collars are razor sharp and his suit jacket on the back of his chair has the look of bespoke tailored twelve-ounce merino wool, I surmise by the way it hangs. I imagine it drapes beautiful on Maximillio's broad muscular shoulders. Based on this sartorial evidence, my confidence in his ability to move my work overflows with an ecstatic joy bursting in my belly like ice-cold fireworks. I wonder if he holds the same confidence in me. It would of course be unthinkable to actually ask him.

'Do you remember the first time we met?' From me.

'Er, refresh my memory – when was that exactly?'

'It was at the hotel bar of the Majestic in Cannes. I was attending the Short Film Corner with a piece of shit film that I had made and you were there, tagging along with your wife who was working for the Fudowski Company at the time and we fell into a conversation over a pair of Kir royales?'

'And your life changed.' He smiles, fully aware of the power he has held over me from that day forth.

'I was drunk and depressed enough to pour my heart out to a complete stranger.'

'Ah yes. As I recall, you were quite entertaining.'

'Well, the misfortunes of others tend to be quite palatable when retold as comedy,' I say. 'And you told me then that I was barking up the wrong tree with the film-making malarkey. You told me to turn my stories into art – tangible objects that could be viewed in stasis.'

'Did I? I must've been drunk as well.'

'Maybe not in those words exactly – but suddenly my mind was opened and I realised that I had to go back to what I knew and loved.'

'And here we are.'

'Here we are indeed. You opened the door for me and I know that recently things haven't been flying off the shelves but I have something truly extraordinary with this one.'

'I know it.' He smiles. That's it. So I stand up to nod insouciantly and shake his weighty manicured hand in order to close the deal. 'Oh wait,' he says and delves into his desk drawer to fish out a sheet of folded paper. 'I wasn't going to mention it but then I thought – since you're here,' he says coyly and hands me the piece of paper. It is one of those clichéd ransom-note-style affairs where the words are made up of letters cut from newspapers and magazines. It's quite artfully crafted and I know in my gut who it is from even though it is signed, rather redundantly, as 'Anonymous'. It reads:

Dear Max,

This is to let you know that there is a snake in your midst. The Anatolian asshole that you represent is a phoney. Soon he will be finished. Don't go down with him.

Yours truly,
Anonymous

Smiling at Maximillio I say, 'Well, no one ever achieved anything in life without a few enemies.' He concurs and, keeping the note, I leave. As I walk out of the office, I see that S is waiting for me inside the entrance door wrapped to the gills with a thick knitted scarf, that folder of hers pressed against her breast like a shield. I must find another look for her – this one is too closed off in the wrong way. She seems vulnerable not aloof. In public she represents my persona and is an extension of my unapproachable detachment. I must help her to project the perfect note of pride and apathy. She does look cute, though. A warm wave of sentiment surges over me and then is gone.

'Where are we going for lunch?' I ask her as she pushes the door open for me and I glide out into the fresh freezing air feeling that most dangerous of emotions, hope.

'You wanted old-school Italian so there's Salvatori's on Mulberry?'

'Perfect,' I say and mentally punch myself. I'm with the Japanese with regards to things being perfect in that if perfection were attainable it would not be worth having and therefore I hate using the word in a lackadaisical fashion. I dismiss this line of silly self-criticism as I slip into the back of a filthy taxicab and, my eyes serenely shut, I breathe in calmly through my nostrils as S instructs the olive-skinned young man at the wheel to take us to Little Italy. Mindfully, I imagine all my hope inside a box and despatch that box down a fast-flowing river and away from me.

*

We filter through the south Manhattan traffic at a glacial pace, steam rising from the vents in the streets as if images from countless Hollywood movies have been brought to holographic life. I allow my mind to wander at the possibilities enthroned in the high-rise dreamscape that comprises this concrete pleasure garden for the sociopath, entrepreneur and seeker of glory.

With this new piece, this *Gesamtkunstwerk*, I can conquer this place, this third Rome, I feel sure. As a Turk I am prone to feeling wronged by a historically racist America that relishes the end of old empires and the beginning of their own hegemony. Formidable lobbies exist to besmirch all things Turkish, especially high-profile artistic or literary personas, unless a certain amount of ingratiating talk about the Armenians, to take a contentious example, is expended and the knee is bent for the sovereigns of haute commerce on Central Park West. You must have the patronage of this high net worth cadre who are rich enough to afford their own yacht with, at the very least, a replica helicopter on the helipad – even better if they are ultra high net worth and own an actual helicopter for their yacht or yachts. But they are within reach as long as one can circumvent the hidden racist voices peddling their Turk-hate! I am of course referring to the hatred of the one who wrote that ridiculous note – that Selim Mehmet who clearly wants to be a fractious barnacle on my brain as his way of attaining vengeance for my exposure of his fragile ego and lacklustre talents. He is a self-hating Turk projecting his fallibilities on to me; having come to realise the truth I spoke to him has utterly dismantled his undercooked thesis on art and his own validity as an artist. S asks me if I am okay and only then do I realise that I have been grinding my teeth and quivering with wrath.

'I'm fine,' I say, still bristling, 'Manhattan traffic tends to put me on edge.'

'It can't be worse than İstanbul traffic,' she quips and I wonder tersely why she felt the need to joke. Perhaps the strain I feel is contagious and she simply blurted out nonsense she thought was amusing in order to alleviate the tense mood.

Instead, her misguided attempt to ameliorate the situation has backfired and, in the metallic, glass and vinyl enclosure of the cab, I detonate like a small controlled explosion.

'What's the point of comparing a megalopolis of fourteen million people with this fucking island that, if all the Turks in İstanbul spat on it, would fucking sink?' I say.

'I was just...' she falters.

'You were just what? Joking? They've got a bloody grid system here for fuck's sake! Do you have any idea what a colossal labyrinth the streets of İstanbul are – that people die on those streets every day because drivers don't obey basic traffic laws or adhere to even a minimal level of common human decency?' I begin to dislike the bleating tone my voice is taking on. This makes me even angrier. Clearly, I am worried about something deep down and am taking it all out on S. In a way, of course, she is a human shock absorber and being bullied by me saves us from a far worse collision, I suspect, down the road on our journey together. Getting my aggression out now is a savvy move.

'I'm sorry,' she says.

That takes the wind out of my proverbial sails and the remainder of the jerky stop-start ride is completed in silence. In the peace, my mind grasps the root cause of my anxiety. I am regressing to my childhood when, as a newly arrived émigré in a foreign land, it was impossible for me to express myself in the native tongue. Our parents installed my brother and me in some 'international school', aged five, where we mixed with nationals from countries including France, Italy and Nigeria. None of us had a common language and most of our time was spent gesticulating, crying or pointing towards the toilets.

Özgür Uyanık

There were no classes to speak of – it was a kind of a cultural quarantine station before we could be implanted into the English educational system with as little friction as possible. The stinging failure to make oneself understood is traumatic – a psychologist might offer me a course of therapy whilst a psychiatrist would prescribe drugs to alleviate my symptoms. Yet I have always eschewed those sorts of avenues and carried the trauma shamefully with me to this day (shameful because I have not managed to overcome it.). The ignominy often manifests as a sense of inferiority and pops up spontaneously when I'm in a place where my foreignness is intensely tangible – like New York City. The fact that I'm aware of this pathetic foible gives me hope that I am sure to conquer it one day. It doesn't help that Americans are so blissfully unaware of the vibrant geography beyond their borders that their ignorance puts them in a state of impenetrable self-confidence. Unexamined stupidity allows nations to proudly parade cherished ideologies as the unimpeachable truth in direct contradiction to the weight of racism, corruption and plain evil violence that they perpetuate. Comparable to the Spanish conquistadors five centuries ago bamboozling the Aztecs with trinkets (winning their hearts and minds) to extract their gold in South America. If ripping them off politely stops working as a tactic, then hitting them with shock and awe certainly does. Every global power ends up abusing everyone else with blinkers on, resolutely unabashed by the evidence of their own evil. When I mention this to our taxi driver, a young man harking from Beirut who is lead guitar in a rock band from Brooklyn, he enthusiastically holds forth with a liquid Middle Eastern accent and the restrained passion of the habitually oppressed.

'Black gold is what it's all about, my friend, am I right?' he spouts as we trundle along past Columbus Park on a route that feels a tad meandering. I decide to give him the benefit of the doubt on that.

'They are constantly infiltrating cultures like some sociological Mendeleev,' I say by way of a reply.

'Sure, yeah.' His reflection in the rear-view mirror appears baffled.

The rest of the way to our destination is spent in silence as I take in the streets outside my window, impressed by how much of it I think I know based solely on what I've seen in the movies. The steam venting from the ground, those so-called 'sidewalks' and their hyperactive pedestrians disgorged from monumental skyscrapers – so clichéd, so thrilling. Had we had the time I would have liked to tell our driver about Abstract Expressionism. A cultural weapon nurtured and developed by the Central Intelligence Agency during the Cold War to fight communism. Don't let anyone tell you that Jackson Pollock, Mark Rothko, Willem de Kooning or Barnett Newman – influenced by Armenian exile Arshile Gorky who hanged himself aged forty-four after a lifetime of tragedy – came up with the movement out of a process of osmosis. No, it was willed into being by the state, a mash-up of European sensibilities of surrealism alongside the energy of the German expressionists, disavowing outdated figurative notions, averring their mission to rise above the machines that had taken over image production through photography to create something that no machine could reproduce – the very essence of being human. Or, more precisely, the very essence of being a white, middle-class and middle-aged male from New York when America was a rising superpower soon to dominate the globe both militarily and culturally. Such a robust contrapuntal force against communism's threat to the western world's biggest weapon – its very civilisation expressed via the artist's philosophy – could not have come about merely organically. By the way, that Gorky was exiled once before when the Ottoman Empire collapsed. He then changed his name, ancestry and nationality when Lady Liberty welcomed him to her shores where anyone could be anything they wanted to be – the good old American Dream since bastardised into a capitalist mantra. But too much liberty can be a very bad thing. You change your identity to suit the time and place where you find yourself and then, when you need it the most, the very thing that makes you you disappears. After his death, fake letters by Gorky were written to tie his art to a fervent nationalism serving the narrative of the Armenian diaspora. When it comes to your past, honesty is therefore the best policy, otherwise you are opening yourself up to being rewritten with no editorial control – a bit like history itself.

S and I walk across the 'sidewalk', where I see several oil splatters that remind me of Pollock's work, in fact, and enter Salvatori's. I am in a temperamental mood mainly because I loathe Italian restaurants. Being a gluten-intolerant vegetarian, ninety-five per cent of the menu is off-limits. If I have two slices of bread the ensuing build-up of noxious fumes in the room I happen to be in would strain credulity. The gluten, a gluey protein, coats the inside surface of my digestive tract and disables the healthy breakdown of nutrients with the by-product being copious amounts of putrid gas. I have been gluten-free for over a decade and started the specialised diet years before it became a fashionable trend for narcissists in

California whence it spread as Spanish flu did to capture the figure-obsessed imaginations of idiots everywhere, delighted to have something other than their own failures of control and willpower to blame for their state of bad health. Before I knew the gluten diagnosis and I was blithely consuming more than a typical student's fair share of doughy produce, having denounced meat, my art school peers used to joke that something must have crawled up my anus and died there. I am also lactose-intolerant, allergic to the ink used in newspapers and cannot stand the sight of my own blood, as mentioned. I am at least satisfied that, after all these years of worrying and tending to the erratic fauna of my microbiome, I have a good grip of what's going on down there and bar the surprise appearance of a parasite I feel confident that my digestive prowess, so crucial to my new endeavour, cannot be faulted.

*

'I'll have the *reni di agnello*,' I say and snap the menu shut.

The waiter asks me about starters but I ignore him. He has no right to impinge on my mental space. My assistant, elegantly fine-spun I notice for the first time (is she wearing a tighter fit of dress?), orders a modest Italian salad for herself and a jug of tap water with a slice of lemon for the table. The afternoon-crowded restaurant, with its ersatz bucolic decor and red and white checked tablecloths, makes me wince but this is as authentic as America is going to get.

'That sounds exotic,' she says.

'It's offal. Lamb's kidney,' I say and humorously add, 'This is a working lunch.'

'Right,' she says and dutifully takes out her folder from under the table.

'What have you got for me?'

'I've researched the areas you asked me about and a few other things that seemed pertinent,' she says and lays out some printed sheets of information she has obviously purloined from the Internet and takes me through the bullet points: the procedure is called nephrectomy and I'll need a qualified surgeon to perform it as the placing of the kidneys in the body makes it untenable for me to attempt auto-surgery even if I were to master the operation myself. One beguiling option that transpires from the preliminary research is to use a medical robot that I'd control remotely with a monitor to guide the keyhole surgery. Once the kidney is disconnected from the bladder and blood vessels, it is pulled out of a two-inch slit in the skin below the ribs towards the side of the torso. The angles are just too acute for a manual approach never mind the fact that I'd have to be heavily anaesthetised.

'Can we get round my sleeping through the whole affair by administering a local anaesthetic?'

She shuffles through her papers, googles (or bings) it on her laptop and says we'd have to consult a surgeon about that. She has a list of candidates prepared. The theatrics would last two to three hours followed by a recovery period of at least twenty-four hours. These were all ballpark figures as far as I was concerned.

'Legalities,' she begins as the food arrives. She clears the sheets from the tabletop and my eyes lock on to the plate floating swiftly towards me. It makes a perfect landing on the woven mat. Steam momentarily fogs my glasses and I delight in the delay of visual gratification. Once the condensation evaporates, I am disappointed to find the offal has been drowned in some sort of sauce.

'What's this?' I ask the smiling waiter.

'Lamb kidney in a thyme-infused red wine sauce with wild mushrooms...'

'It won't do.' I smile back at him. His professionalism falters and his moustache droops round puckered lips, denoting confusion.

'I would like to see the chef.'

'It is quite delicious, sir; a very fine sauce and very delicate flavours.'

'Does it taste of offal or does it, as I strongly suspect, taste very much like thyme-infused red wine with wild mushrooms?' I say with a pleasant lilt in my voice to put the creature at ease. He is as tense as a racket string, still gripping S's Italian salad in his paw.

'Perhaps I ought to have been more vigilant when ordering. However, I did not notice a clear enough description next to the *reni di agnello* that referred to anything resembling the item I have here. The chef can see me now?'

In my peripheral vision I detect S shrinking into herself; she has witnessed similar conversations before. However, it is not my duty to make sure that she is happy and comfortable at all times. I stand up and gesture for the waiter to lead the way. Bamboozled by my genial yet unyielding manner, the man acquiesces. I flap my hand at S to follow. In the rattling flame-spluttering kitchen I can see – the waiter did not have to keep telling me – that the staff are busy tending to the lunch-hour rush. I hail the chef with a firm yet respectful stock phrase. Baffled by my intrusion and assuming that I am someone important, he spares me his full attention as I grill him regarding the restaurant's lamb kidney dish. I tell him that I want to see one raw. A kitchen hand is dispatched to fetch a sample.

Moments later, several kidneys are brought from the cold storage and laid out in a row on the steel counter – giant glistening beans. The humdrum moan of the working kitchen begins to fade into the background as I take one in my hand and, although repulsed by the cold watery pink liquid seeping out of the squashy lump of dead meat, I keep hold of it for a closer examination. I bring the kidney tentatively closer to my face and detect the faint but unmistakable whiff of urine. The organ has a gelatinous dark red-brown membranous tissue encasing a soft, dark red interior, all cupped in what I assume to be gristle – dull white and rather inflexible like petrified rubber. All of these accoutrements have been pared down ahead of their arrival at my table, I note, for I can only recall a nondescript soft blob of flesh, of uniform texture, underneath the coating of sauce. The raw organ is lightly marbled with tendrils of fat trailing off and laced with a multitude of blood vessels and sits snugly in the palm of one's hand, no more than a couple of inches across. Sweat begins to bead on my forehead and I realise with a start that I have been holding my breath for some time. I move my kidney-holding hand away from my face and suck in some air through my nostrils, having turned my head away from the offending smell but hiding my motives by glancing at S who is standing by with a look that tells me she is both fascinated and overwhelmed by the activity surrounding us; the kitchen pulses with concentrated franticness and I can feel the throb of the chopping, slicing and cutting pounding at my temples. I tune out the extraneous cacophony and take a breath.

'Is it possible, Chef, to cook this as plainly as possible – no sauce, no onions and so on? Just the kidney itself?'

'It can be fried or even grilled but the flavour is a bit too much for most people. But me, I adore offal – the liver, heart and lungs,' replies the chef and goes on with a pleasant smile, 'and sweetbreads – the pancreas, thymus gland...'

'This odour,' I manage to say without gagging. 'It is urine, is it not?'

I look at the floor as the chef speaks so that no one can see my eyes watering from the stench of the fucking dead thing in my unwilling hand, some manner of jellied organic fluid dripping through my fingers. But I have to be strong and persevere so I force myself to look at it again, to keep a hold of it. A belch of protest rises from my belly but I keep it down. I fairly feel my innards lurch and swoon as if they know, independently of my consciousness, that one of their kind is going to be singled out, torn from its warm homestead and slaughtered in a bizarre ritual they could never hope to comprehend like an innocent child about to be sacrificed to the gods at an Aztec ceremony. I remember then that the human gut has millions of neurons embedded in it, the same number as a domestic cat's brain. It has a kind of rudimentary intelligence, a mind of its own, and it interfaces with the brain proper via the vagus nerve, which is the longest one in the human body. These half-recalled factoids keep my mind from being overrun by the flight response – at least for the moment.

'Yes, well, you have to make sure to cook that out. The smell. We also peel the membrane away – and the gristle – which is very tough, very chewy,' he goes on.

'Membrane?' I say in a blasé fashion and have the illusory sensation of a boil bursting in my mouth, its hot liquid contents streaking down my oesophagus. It takes a supreme mental effort and delicate control of my diaphragm to halt the gag reflex in my gullet. I finally plop the lump of meat back on to the table as nonchalantly as possible. It slides out of my wet palm like an oyster. I must have dropped it from a bit of a height because little flecks of the viscose bodily liquor splash on to my shirt arm and I faintly utter a curse in revulsion. I must not throw up. Concentrating on breathing calmly, I feel my nostrils flaring rhythmically as I look at the chef's feet – his black workplace-issue shoes marking him down as merely a cog in the wheel of this culinary machine – and then I plan to raise my head and offer him a grin of gratitude before I make my excuses and exit. But the seconds draw out too long as I feel an acute nausea rising in my thorax. Finally, after a protracted silence, I look up and form a faltering smile on my quivering lips. I must look deranged.

'Are you okay?' asks S and I respond with a strange wave of my hand, a gesture that could mean anything right now although I suspect it conveys some form of intensifying panic.

Waiting for my next move. He must think I'm some high-powered food critic – possibly drunk – even though by the way the waiter is archly regarding me I am prepared to wager that he has his suspicions by this point. Then someone hands me a towel. It may have been S but I am too deep in a tunnel-visioned reverie to fully notice. My visual field has markedly shrunk in the claustrophobic and hot environs of the galley. I wipe the sticky residue away from my hands and fold my arms, pondering what I have learned as best as I can in the infernal heat where not vomiting has become a real hardship.

The chef, as I expected, mirrors my pose by folding his arms too and leaning ever so slightly towards me. This sort of behaviour indicates that I have succeeded in arousing his curiosity as well as an unspoken comradeship. I am about to ask him another question when I glimpse the stainless-steel work surface unaccountably flipping towards me with merciless speed.

*

I open my eyes and find myself on a stretcher surrounded by an ambulance crew, S and several rubberneckers outside the restaurant on the pavement. The staff must have panicked thinking that they had poisoned an important gastronomic figure and overreacted by calling an ambulance. My forehead hit the steel countertop and knocked me out. I am clear-thinking enough and capable of taking myself to the hospital to be checked for a concussion and when they insist on loading me into their ambulance I persuade the paramedics that they have more urgent errands than mine to attend to. They let me off the stretcher, my forehead expertly bandaged.

My real identity remains a mystery with the restaurant staff, who are wonderfully attentive and, after vague reassurances that I will make no mention of the incident in any professional capacity, we walk away from Salvatori's. S links her arm through mine as a steadying force on our way to the waiting taxi and I humour her by not withdrawing the limb even though I am totally capable of walking unaided despite my leg muscles feeling slightly less taut than usual. I calculate that the close proximity of our bodies would give her much needed reassurance that her boss is as real as the sky above her head, that I am back on my feet and ready for action. Who am I to diminish her morale as we continue on our path towards perhaps my greatest work of art?

*

On the flight back to Heathrow I ask S if she has any questions for me thus far with regards to The Process. When she looks at me her face abruptly crumples up and she starts to weep. Is it the Xanax I gave her for the journey? I can't be sure and I do not want to offend her by ascribing her emotions to a drug-induced body chemistry imbalance so I ask her why she is crying.

'What you're thinking of doing... it's just so... it's nightmarish. I thought that you'd, I don't know, have filed it away among the other rejected ideas by now but when I saw you in there with that kidney in your hand, I realised that you were serious.'

'Nightmarish? You're exaggerating,' I say.

'You looked like a ghost with that kidney in your hand and you think you can just bury your feelings and go ahead with this stunt and get through it?'

The drug has loosened her tongue and she is on the brink of a hysterical episode. I have never seen her this way before and I have to take evasive action.

'Do you know why I cannot stand the sight of blood? Why it makes me nauseous?' I ask with an engaging frown.

I need her to shift focus from her hardships in dealing with the mental and emotional strain of being part of my working life and instead pivot her centre of attention to my needs. I bring out my notebook, pull back the elasticated band and open up the pocket at the back that holds scraps of paper, ticket stubs, mementos and so forth. I fish out four pieces of lined school exercise-book pages that have been folded and re-folded to fit the snug pocket, covered in spidery blue ballpoint pen ink. The pages are gossamer thin now and textured smooth by years of handling.

'I want to read this to you now. Are you ready?'

She nods and dabs a tissue at the corners of her eyes. When I see that I have her full awareness I begin, 'I was thirteen years old when I wrote this so you'll excuse the grammatical errors.' Then I read to her the story of how I was seven years old and wrested from my burgeoning life of assimilation into Anglo-Saxon society and dragged back to a clan-like netherworld of initiations, dark religious rites and excruciating agony. It is the story of my male genital mutilation whilst on holiday in Turkey. I had been tricked into it. My parents both kept silent about the true nature of my journey and in their collective wisdom had decided they were only going to tell me that I was going to be circumcised once we got to İstanbul. They told me on the eve of the operation and said that it was 'traditional' and that all young boys had it done. I asked why. Mother and Father supplied several platitudes regarding its virtues – even though one was a non-practising Muslim and the other nominally C of E – and the medical advantages of having one's foreskin removed. My twin brother had died a few months earlier so I assumed that there was an element of ritualistic currying of favour with the gods so that their second son would not be taken away from them as well. It had upset me that this had clearly been planned well in advance (I imagined that you couldn't book a hospital procedure of this magnitude overnight) and that I had not been treated in good faith. Nevertheless, I acquiesced since apparently I'd be the only uncircumcised man in my family if I refused and that seemed a cowardly thing to do. To my horror, all of my relatives would come to 'celebrate' the occasion afterwards and I'd be given lots of presents. I became confused when I was taken to a clinic masquerading as a harmless shopfront at the ground level of a block of apartments. I had seen Turkish *sünnet* ceremonies on TV and they involved a lot of blaring music, drums, cheering and the wearing of crowns, robes and other carnivalesque components. Inside there was no cheering and the only costume I was to wear was a hospital gown. They gave me a local anaesthetic and hung a white towel between my head and my bits on armatures when I was laid out on the operating table. I recalled, aged thirteen at the time of writing, how I could feel blood gushing through my engorged member and how I could see the silhouette of the gloved hands and their instruments as shadow puppets cast on to the towel. The surreal atmosphere was enhanced by the anaesthetic, which kept me in a fine mood but when I reached home, the drugs wore off and I started swearing at anyone who came near me. A kindly cousin with a gift-wrapped present I knew was shit was taken aback and appalled when I told him, in the English playground language I had recently mastered, to 'fuck off'. The pain to my nine-year-old brain was exquisitely, diabolically torturous. The gauze covering my wound was black with dried blood by the time my bladder needed urgent relief. The women – I can't recall who exactly – took me to the humid bathroom and a plastic bucket was placed between my legs. As the gauze was fused to my genitalia, the urine could not escape cleanly and pressure built up at the tip of my penis as if a new hole would erupt from it when the hot stream of piss found the usual exit point plugged hard with coagulated gore. I felt that the people I trusted the most had violated me. I could not process how they were treating me as if I was being unreasonable – with my swearing and screaming – when to me it was perfectly clear that I had been wronged on a biblical scale.

I carefully fold the sheets of paper back up and observe with satisfaction that S's eyes are closing as the Xanax and my palliative vocalisations make their therapeutic repairs to her bruised and shaken psyche. She still manages to add:

'You wrote that when you were thirteen?'

'Yes. I'm afraid I was rather precocious. Do you understand the point of the story?' I ask as her eyelids droop. 'Those I trusted violated me and I lost my innocence. It's also why I cannot stand the sight of blood – especially my own,' I say, looking S squarely in the face – her slack, sleepy face. I continue, 'That is why I need to do this and why it needs to be done. I am an artist and my life as it goes on must and shall be an ever-fuller expression of me. Nothing else. I have two kidneys and one going spare, so that is all the soul-searching you need do on the subject.'

I slide my notebook back into my pocket and turn back to S. 'Is that clear?' She is soundly asleep. I then pull out Selim's note to Maximillio, tuck it into the seatback pouch next to the sick bag and close my burning eyes. S has aggravated me at 30,000 feet and I must make sure not to overshare with her in future – she simply cannot handle it in any meaningful way clearly. I put that to the back of my mind and turn my thoughts to how to handle telling Mother that I am going to eat one of my own kidneys.

VI

S never says another word from the moment she wakes up as our plane taxies to our gate to when we part ways outside Earl's Court Tube station, thick sheets of grey rain falling upon us. I trust that she will continue to hold it together as I cannot countenance a weak link at this stage. She is good at her job and I shudder at the thought of having to interview, vet and train a new assistant. I need someone I can totally rely on.

I put that to the back of my mind and turn my thoughts to how to handle Mother, who isn't exactly going to fall in love with the concept of me re-enacting the death of my twin brother from kidney failure (as she will interpret it, I am sure). She will probably do everything in her considerable sway to dissuade me from going through with it and, failing that, stop me through some ingenious method of sabotage that I will never be able to prove was her doing. I could just keep her out of the loop on this one but the idea of her eventually discovering the truth troubles me a great deal. She did after all handle most aspects of my career. She would have to be told about the deal with the Maximillio Zvwark Gallery so as to be able to handle the legalities, for example. It would also be perceived as a betrayal of trust. No, I have to share it with her and face the consequences.

*

I choose a neutral spot to meet with her that is public enough to undercut the possibility for any spontaneous dramatics. Not too public, of course. The new branch of my private members club, Home, is located in a plum location far from the old artists' haunt of Soho, an area now overrun with the desperately chic but close enough to the Old Street region that is a bridge to where London's most earnest practising artists often reside these days, Bethnal Green. But it isn't so near to any one particular location of fleeting fashionableness that it could be too easily accessible by the unsavoury hangers-on of the art bubble, such as bankers, city traders, financiers, estate agents and self-made millionaires. The self-made were the worst, the nouveau riche – the moneyed poor. Old money was okay because they knew how to handle themselves round creative people. Not too eager so as to smother you with their flattery and not so overawed that they act all bolshie to cover up their lack of confidence in their own knowledge of culture.

We order champagne. 'Mother...'

'Yes, dear – oh, I hope you've been thinking about documenta.'

'That's why I wanted to speak to you.'

'Here? Why did you drag me to the bowels of East London to tell me something you could have told me at home or at the office?' She blinks copiously to underline the absurdity of what I have done to her.

'This is hardly East London – but never mind. Please listen.'

'I'm all ears,' she says and peers at me expecting something extraordinary to issue from my lips.

'I propose to remove and consume my kidney. In public. Well, to a select gathering. The piece will be recorded on celluloid with a limited print run plus stills, also limited edition.' I drink my fizzy beverage and hold my breath.

Her soundless stricken stare into the middle distance denotes, to me, genuine surprise and possibly disbelief. This is good. This is not going to be a simplistic act of auto-cannibalism but a wilful deed of Duchampian intellectual vigour. The same whiff of urea ran through his seminal work that immortalised him and my own planned piece – I feel a tremor as the tectonic plates of my consciousness shift at the thought of this profound connection with the father of conceptual art, binding our legacies as though a steel cable were stretched across the chasm of historical time and space. I feel a buzz, I am elated – chemicals surge through my brain announcing the wonderful news – and suddenly mankind is one and I open my arms to every man, woman and child to embrace them with my profound love for humanity. Even the Americans are welcome to the party!

'It is stunning, isn't it, Mother?' I say with bottled-up glee.

I wait for her reaction. She slowly puts her champagne flute down and lays her palms flat on the polished mahogany table that separates us. This is a heart-stopping moment for me. The initial reaction is the authentic one and Mother's instincts are raptor-like in their deadly accuracy.

'Sorry, dear, I drifted off there for a moment – I thought I saw Gwen,' she eventually says, much to my chagrin. I know she is only just digesting the information I have imparted, perhaps with too much excitement to react immediately. I wait some more, now aware of rainclouds of misgivings blighting my horizon.

'Darling,' she says and stops.

'What do you think?' I say, debasing myself with the stock phrase utilised by people who do not know their own mind. I am teetering on the tip of my ridiculously low-slung red leather chair. Mother levels her piercing blue eyes at me and I wilt somewhat, expecting the worst. I curse myself for getting carried away on my own riptide of unregulated optimism.

'Gwen, darling,' she says into the space behind my head.

It is Gwen approaching, a well-respected curator at the perfectly credible minnow gallery that smells and acts like a museum, The Shoreditch, in the East End of London. Compared to the mega-galleries including Gagosian, White Cube or Haunch of Venison, The Shoreditch feels more as if it's a public service institution with its educational programmes, workshops and events for children. Gwen had favoured my work in the past and was a dear, close friend of Mother's. I even stand up to greet her. She air kisses Mother then me but refuses to sit down as she is, she says with urgency, en route to the office and just wanted to 'say hi'. She reminds me of a skittish llama who has wandered out of its enclosure, her handsome neck accentuated by a low-cut blouse and pearls.

For a staunchly English woman with the received pronunciation perfected in Cambridge, the Americanism 'hi' clashes with my sense of her as a doyenne of the East End's down-and-dirty artistic scene, where she has a reputation for discovering young and interesting emerging artists and oversees a fascinating course on collecting contemporary art aimed equally at bored millionaires and fantasists. Mother, notwithstanding my belief that she has not processed what I have told her, asks me to relay to Gwen the concept for my next piece. Having regained the mindset of the poised artist on the cusp of something extraordinary, I break the news to Gwen, as a wave attacks a sandbank.

'I plan to consume myself, Gwen. As protest. As manifesto. A declaration of intent – without art there is no true meaning to life,' I announce to her, the doubt crushed, desiccated, dissolved and cast away like so much flotsam.

'I couldn't agree with you more,' she says into her finger-tips. 'To metaphorically consume oneself—'

'No, darling – literally to consume,' interjects Mother.

Gwen consults her memory banks before asking, 'Who was that fantastic Mexican artist – drained off his own fat with liposuction and cooked meatballs with it – served it up at a dinner party?'

'It's on the tip of my tongue,' I lie automatically, vaguely aware of the pun. I have to be able to marshal all reference points or at least appear to have given it considerable thought with knowledge of comparable works. This broadside about some Mexican who sort of consumed a part of himself is an interesting if weak association. I make a mental note.

'I think that's a different case, Gwen, darling,' Mother reacts swiftly and accurately. 'My son is to eat his own kidney. It's a far broader scope – it's not just a cheap stunt. It's real and potent.'

'The resultant artefacts – the recorded images of the piece – will live on, of course, after the performance,' I add, somewhat apropos nothing.

'Well we won't get into details now, Gwen, but I will of course invite you to the performance,' Mother assures her, before Gwen leaves, saying that her head is spinning. The idea has dazed her. Mother falls into serious thought.

'I still don't know what you think, Mother,' I say, needy, after a long silence. Her eyes are slightly asquint with lively intelligence. She says:

'At first I was shocked, then... I realised the shock felt old. Out of date somehow. Shock is yesterday's news. Then I shuddered at the thought of the disparaging headlines, you know – "Kidney Kebab Anyone?" The usual to-be-expected nonsense of course.'

'I... I suppose so but there's more to it than that,' I stumble as I realise she is right. Who can be shocked nowadays? How far do you have to go before people say it's too far? Some Chinese artist ate a stillborn human foetus and photographed it. I guess that's too far. Or is it?

'I don't want to be pigeonholed with the Turkish label either, Mother,' I add peevishly. 'I prefer the Turco-British label if there has to be one.'

'But that's what they'll say. Turkish. They're going to find a Turkish angle whether we like it or not. Perhaps it's best not to fight it but to embrace the orientalism – neutralise it by accepting it.'

'How so, Mother?' I ask.

'I'm quite certain some members of post-colonial society will project their own guilt on to you, a Turk with his own heritage of empire, first chance they get and cave in to some lobby or another.'

'And award me a Nobel Prize,' I scoff.

'Quite. You mustn't become a pawn in their narrative,' she says glumly, fidgeting with her napkin. 'You must earn your place without their intervention.'

'Yes, of course. Even if they did, I'd reject it the way, er, Brando rejected his Oscar,' I say brightly, hoping to steer our collective energies back towards the positive.

'Wait a minute,' she says, squeezing her napkin inside her fist. 'The whole thing with the film and the photographs – it's so old hat. You're not an "installationist" or whatever the hell they call themselves, darling. No, you are a bone fide artist with a deadly solemn message. It has to become an artefact to behold, an object – do you see?'

'What do you mean?' I say, somewhat apprehensive that she's going to suggest I pickle my kidney and display it in a jar instead of eating it. Could Mother make that much of an error in judgement? I dread to think.

'The procedure has to be holistic – from start to finish, the whole process must be included. What's that word the Germans use? Starts with a "g"...'

'I'm not sure I follow, Mother.'

'You eat, you digest and then you...' she prompts.

'I metabolise the food—'

'Don't call it "food", darling.'

'Sorry – the organ – and it goes through my digestive system and comes out, you know...'

'As shit,' she says with devilry.

The word 'shit' sits there with us at the table, ready to join in the conversation.

'Shit?' I squeamishly repeat.

'The final artefact, yes.'

'How do I, I don't know, preserve it afterwards?'

'Darling, let's not talk about it any more. Talking could hurt it, do you understand?'

'Yes, Mother. You are absolutely right.' I pause to consider the so-called elephant in the room. 'Mother, are you not troubled by my choice?'

'How so, darling?'

'I mean, you know, the kidney thing...' I say and she takes my hand.

'It is a tremendous memorial to him. It's as if you are sloughing off the guilt of not being able to give him the gift of life.'

'We weren't a match, Mother – I couldn't have donated my kidney even if I wanted to.'

'The devastating irony of it won't be lost on anyone, my boy.' She smiles reassuringly.

With that issue out of the way, I feel it is a good idea to sleep on it for a while rather than rush in blindly – the third eye, the sub-conscious must first perform an initial sweep over the concept and, after a nourishing period of not thinking directly about it, allow, tentatively and with utmost seriousness of mind, practicalities to be considered in the cold light of another day. However, the cat was out of the bag with Gwen now aware of my plans so it was a matter of honour to follow through. Failure is not an option, nor is changing my mind. I'm stubborn like that.

*

That night I dream that I am opening myself up as if I am a tin of sardines and pulling out my wet glistening kidney, which flops about like a dying mollusc. Curiously, the organ is attached to my innards with a pseudo-umbilical cord made of intertwined plastic cables. Then I plunge a skewer into the squelching kidney and stick it over some hot coals. I am wearing a fez, curly slippers and sporting a huge waxed moustache. I stand cooking my kebab in a vibrant Ottoman bazaar whilst western tourists line up to taste my wares. Maximillio, Gwen and Joseph are there, applauding enthusiastically. S is a stolid smudge at the periphery, livid and judgemental, standing next to a seven-year-old phantom – sad blank sockets where his eyes should be staring me down. My dreams are rarely subtle, as I've said, and the meaning of this one did not fail to dawn on me at once. I was warning myself not to become something close to De Quincey's 'Oriental dreams', a horror show to be fawned over by the approving West desperate to lose themselves in the abstraction of the Other. Every American, European and Brit would love to see me incorporate frivolous elements that they are inclined to be deeply interested in, thanks to their own superiority complexes confirming their righteously held prejudices regarding the Turk, that nineteenth-century synonym for the feared alien culture lapping at their borders like a deadly unstoppable algae bloom. No doubt, many of them entertain the idea that I ought to weave in some commentary about my immigrant status alongside the main dish of shish kebabs followed by a dessert of Turkish Delight! Well, fuck that.

How swiftly the West chooses to mask its own disastrous history of tyranny by condemning the Turk as being the Sick

Man of Europe, denigrating our successes and culture by siding with lobbyists who jealously salivate over the promise of the resurrection of the Treaty of Sèvres. One day, many dream that they will finally be able to dismember the invisible Muslim empire with its heart yet beating in İstanbul. They forget that Turks are foremost a pragmatic people and that their original ancient religion of Tengrism shapes them more than the Arabian one ever managed. The terrifying Turk remains aflame in their nightmares ready to huff and puff and blow their houses down – sitting astride the straits of the Dardanelles and the Bosphorus, waterways that remind many of extinguished power, the Roman dream dead and buried forever. I refuse to be defined by their terms – I refuse the label of immigrant and outsider or anything other than what I choose to say about myself. This mental manifesto sparks a frothing indignation that convulses my stomach and culminates in my punching a door after I accidentally pour the last of my morning coffee on to my lap where I thought, mistakenly, that my cup was resting. It is at this moment, my brain chemicals hopelessly variegated, that Joseph chooses to place a call to me. I am already talking before I pick up the telephone so that Joseph catches only the final part of my manically caffeinated sentence, '—and really I'm very close to breaking point, Joseph, to be honest with you.'

'Sorry,' comes the lamely predictable answer.

'Oh, what is it, Joseph?'

'Great news, I've got you a meeting at Mercile and Mitchum ad agency.'

'Oh?' I say and calm pools back to my centre as innate professionalism kicks in, smothering the panicked child within who disappears to his room and now, quietly, closes the door so the adults can speak.

'Yes. Three o'clock Friday, at their offices in Shoreditch.'

'Right. What's the pitch?'

'It's right up your *strasse* actually – a Turkish jean brand is trying to crack the ol' UK market and they want an online ad campaign, you know, a viral thing.'

' "A viral thing"?' I say with naked derision.

'Yes...'

'Alarm bells are ringing already, Joseph.'

'It's worth a meet-and-greet, no? To brainstorm.'

'Don't use that word Joseph, I beg you.'

'Sorry.'

However, an excursion into the tasteless arena of working for money could be a useful distraction at this point, I reflect. The creative mind often needs to be wrested forcibly from its prime objective in order to regard the true work of creation askance. To embolden the subconscious and have it participate in a fulsome manner – a muscular way crucial to the artistic process, without fuss, without undue concern for the outcome and yet as deadly serious as that outcome is and must be. I agree to the meeting – who am I kidding? I need the money! Sales from my solo show in İstanbul are woeful and my new idea is the only thing keeping the hope – 'the bread of the poor' – alive that I can one day in the not too distant future pay off my alarmingly widening collection of credit cards.

'I'll be there – text me the address,' I say and hang up.

*

After a joyless self-inflicted orgasm that serves only to deepen my apathy for the upcoming meeting, I set off on my forced mission, leaving the stillness of my flat as a cat might slink unwillingly from the cool shade of an overhanging tree. Moreover, I have to prove to myself that I have the total awareness of the fully functioning artist. To test my instinct in the realms of pornography (what is advertising but the mendacious promise of repeatable gratification?) and make a bit of money while I am at it – that most distinctly human of all foibles. Maybe the dalliance with the almighty dollar will help me to return my feet to the ground so that I can let all negative energies flow out into the earth – be utterly normal for once. How refreshing that would be!

As I sit in the gently rocking carriage of the Tube I begin to hone my creative pitch, delving into my consumer-lust lexicon with an appetite, to toy with lesser, more curtailed minds who make such a big deal out of their ersatz creativity. I am not looking forward to this 'brainstorming' session where the 'creative' director will follow instructions fed to him by the dominant ideology of the time, from coffee-table tomes on think-methodology and second-hand images sourced from photo-predators who have deduced how to point and release a shutter.

'Viral.'

The word is a hackneyed lie – it's a cheap sell to tight-fisted businessmen who believe that the Internet can provide unlimited word of mouth for free. Already, I am closing myself off to the concept of accomplishing anything meaningful in this meeting – I must stop being so neurotic and just enjoy the experience, I am saying to myself (it could be fruitful fodder for future projects!) as I walk with Joseph into an old tea warehouse on the terraces of Bethnal Green, the last bastion of the London artist. There they sketch and paint and sculpt and starve within a fixed-wheel bike ride from the shocking reality of the soul-crippling commerce and masculine mayhem that is the City of London. The moneyed encroach surreptitiously also on the flanks of Hackney, nibble daintily at the fringes of Dalston and press their luxuriant nouveau riche locks into the armpit of Islington. So-called gentrification (absorption of the barely solvent into the ranks of the consumer debt-droids) is making the sight of struggling artists in greasy spoons, swathed in their comfort blankets of self-delusion, quite rare. Storefronts once home to cheap booze in tight stacks of multi-hued bottles casting a stained-glass glow of salvation from suffering on to the blotchy faces and engorged fatty livers of the sub-creditworthy are refurbished today into zones of comfort-browsing – 'pop-up' shops proliferate like pustules. Even that experience – the physical act of shopping for goods – is drifting into the misty past with clever plastic, connective pulses and gesture-recognition taking over in cyberspace from the old-world charms of crisp twenty-pound notes, brass and zinc. They are going the way of the barter system. Money is shuffling off its mortal coil, rendering itself invisible, unaccountable and even trickier to fathom.

Feeling pleasantly nostalgic for the fading analogue realm, I cut a swathe through this open-plan office of angled wood, teetering lamps of industrial provenance with original patina and reflective video screens scattered atop 'hot desks'. The walls are dotted with bright drills of colour, slick copy blares out and glossy logos demand my precious attention.

There are people here too, but I blank them out – they are reduced to fuzzy silhouettes of haircuts and beards in my peripheral vision. I approach the big office at the back of all of this visceral visuality, led there by the shuffling gait of Joseph – who, by the way, has not taken on board a single one of my sartorial suggestions and is, I'm sure, wearing the same slacks I saw him sporting the last time we met. Through glass doors we go and, once in, twinkling glass trophies glare at us from glass shelves. My hand makes an assured arc through the chilled air as tailored shirts approach me warmly and our palms dock together in the confident mode that promises willies are to be produced for the purposes of waving them about the boardroom table that is shaped – appropriately enough – like a giant vulva.

Had the 'creative' director of the agency begun with words along the lines of, 'I love your work,' or, 'I managed to catch the last day of Frieze and was astonished by your latest piece.' Had either of these sentences been spoken ahead of what came first out of his balm-greased lips, then perhaps I would have taken the trouble not to stand up from the office chair where he had parked me with his chunky hand swipes and plucked eyebrow work as soon as I had entered his crystal crypt, his mausoleum to mediocrity, each prize certificate, plastic plaque and engraved cup or Silver Leek or Platinum Onion attesting to his industry position as top scum-sucker in the evaporating pond of his profession. This is what the moisturised cavity said:

'You know – I was telling Joseph when he called me – that I would've directed this video myself. But, as it happens, I'm completely slammed right now.'

Joseph knows of course what is going to happen next. His face seizes up and a pulse of panic beams from his skull, pings out and bounces like a radar signal from every shiny surface in the sarcophagus of this pinstriped prick. It bounces off the edge of a Golden Potato Award for Best Use of Masculinity in a Post-Watershed Infomercial or whatever the fuck – it ricochets silently against the fake brushed steel of a plaque that celebrates a win for Best Use of Clever Metaphor in the Field of Ophthalmology and it goes shooting past the poor secretary's ears, making her eyes pop open. Finally, it veers and loses velocity at the matt coffee table clustered in front of the artifice of the man's architecture of hair, creamy neck and cuffed wrists until it comes to rest in a dissipating pool of groaning echoes on the laminated parquet flooring. That's what I feel and imagine, in any case. Then I envision kicking him as I remain seated, toppling him from his chair and dropping him to the ground where I would pummel his massage-soft back and gym-toned limbs, so tender and unaccustomed to being bruised after all his years of avoidance, hiding behind chairs, lawyers and other human furniture until he frothed and choked with his own anaemic blood.

Once my split-second fantasy fizzles out, I concede that a physical assault would be out of tune with the moment. Instead, I turn my sights elsewhere and, through example, hope to paint a tableau of medieval horrors that await this man, or anyone else, should they attempt to insult me in this manner ever again. So I attack Joseph. With a searing look of pure opprobrium, I tell him all he needs to know. Then I say softly something along the lines of:

'You fucking asshole.'

I catch a reflection in the window. It is a crimson countenance aflame with rage and flashing eyeballs. It is me, of course. I flee from the suffocating, airless room, slamming the glass door behind me, although annoyingly its pneumatic mechanism thwarts my attempt to make a loud noise. I tunnel furiously through the office, down the emergency exit stairs (the alarm sounds to my intense satisfaction) and evacuate myself out on to the street, the ringing reverberating in my skull. The piano-key pavement blocks flap beneath my feet, cars lollop by like bucking broncos and the sky churns, spins and collapses on top of me.

*

It is Joseph's sweet, worried face that I see first as I open my eyes to the glare of diffuse sunlight. A crowd of interested parties flick their eyes at me as they pass by my supine body. Joseph helps me to prop myself up against the wall of the building I had just collapsed in front of.

'Joseph,' I say, my tongue a dehydrated slug peeling from the corrugated roof of my mouth, 'I'm calling it a day.'

'I understand,' he says.

'I'm not sure you do understand, Joseph,' I add, 'but let me say that what just happened… was as if someone had injected a small but concentrated amount of this city's sewage straight into my heart.'

'I'm sorry about that,' he says and cracks open a plastic bottle of water. I drink. It seems that my credit card collection is going to be expanding further because there is something inside me that spasms frightfully against the conformity inherent in the act of violating one's self for the almighty dollar. It is self-destructive and perhaps an act of sabotage that I will one day regret. However, for now, I am dedicated to the road I have chosen and, whether that road leads to hell or happiness, only time will tell.

'Joseph,' I say with a smile that I hope conveys a deep sense of gratitude. 'You're fired.'

*

I rally my troops. That is, I contact S and ask her to set up an appointment with the surgeons on our list. We hit problems almost immediately. These surgeons all have varying degrees of ethical compliance at the forefront of their slavish minds and S strikes out with every single one of them when she tells them what I want done. Soon enough we realise that complete disclosure is counter-productive and it makes sense to leave out our ultimate purpose following the proposed surgery. Having eliminated the bulk of our candidates I am left with a handful further down on the list. Competent doctors, no doubt, but not the cream of the crop as far as the medical trade is concerned.

The second snag is going to be the theatre of operations itself. There is no way these men are going to set up some battleground temporary surgery room in a gallery space. That would of course give the game away. I wonder why there are no players in the invasive surgery business who can put aside their initial misgivings about this type of work and become at one with the spirit of enterprise driving all human endeavour to greater heights. It would be too risky to let on to the remaining candidates the truth behind my request to have my kidney removed. It is somewhat similar to voluntary amputees; there is actually no law against having a doctor cut off your perfectly healthy arm or leg if that is what you want.

There are people out there who attain lasting happiness through the surgical removal of a limb. They have one advantage over me and that is they are considered to be medically in need of the procedures because they are often so unhinged that they will attempt to self-amputate which can lead to horrific injury, necrosis of the tissue and sometimes death. It is a preventive measure dealing with mental health issues manifesting in the patient that could lead to serious and life-threatening self-harm. I, however, have no practicable way to remove my own kidney save for slashing at my torso with a razor and digging it out with my own hands. A feat that I contend would challenge and ultimately defeat any human attempt to do it.

The matter is simple. I am going to eat my own kidney and how it gets out of my body is unimportant. The original plan to include the surgery in the performance piece was rightly abandoned. I will submit to the procedure in the normal way at a designated and fully equipped surgical theatre. The kidney will be stored on ice as per the usual method of preserving the organ before a transplant.

The thought has occurred to me that the act of wasting a potentially life-giving organ is callous and inhumanely selfish but that is weakness of spirit talking in the face of a commanding superego. Learned morals that have no reliable basis of fact; if people have the right to destroy their internal organs slowly over time with the use of freely available tobacco and alcohol – rendering them useless as donor organs – then

I have the equal right to destroy mine in the manner of my choosing. The discussion is over and so is the possibility of ethical stalling. The human body is constantly consuming itself inwardly anyhow as dead cells are digested and expelled. Even as I outline this line of argument to myself as being sound and unassailable in its logic, I know deep down that there is something I can't talk about that has a bearing on the whole exercise – I'm getting myself ready to assimilate it, but not yet. Not yet.

*

When Duchamp signed a urinal and declared it to be art, it was a defining moment for the twentieth century and now, in the twenty-first century, I want a similar moment to be forever associated with my name. I want there to be a class of human on this planet – the elite who hold the power to write history – that keeps my name alive. Forever. My genes can be lost for all eternity but my name and the things I have achieved must live on. I will do this by forcing everyone to face the parasitic nature of man head on. I must confront humanity with the horror of the truly abject. As auto-cannibalism and other body-shock activities that involve the ingesting of human body parts, waste products or vital fluids is abhorrent to those dwelling in mainstream society, the shock value will allow the concept to percolate down to those who do not usually engage with high art. I stand compliant and naked at the altar of the highbrow with a deep commitment to conceptual art. This is the only way for my work to have the resonance required to carry my name through the generations. Otherwise, my name will only live on for as long as it persists in the fallible and mortal memory banks of surviving relatives, old friends and acquaintances who, soon enough, will themselves turn to dust and be forgotten forever.

I remember some of those friends and the life decisions that have led me to this moment. Back in London during the nineties, I was scraping by on a subsistence lifestyle, having failed to cleave from Mother entirely as she continued to support me, and keeping the art dream alive by doing group shows and selling the odd piece to odder collectors with the pulsating excitement of the BritArt scene promising almost everyone fame and fortune. It did not turn out that way for most but I was too busy attending private views and exclusive parties for the best part of the nineties to care about my contemporaries falling by the wayside. Becoming jobbers. That period of partying with the rich and inebriated was a heady time and I long to be able to recall precise details about what actually happened. Alas, the alcohol and various drugs I was taking at the time that helped me so much in enjoying those moments ironically took away my ability to retain them as memories. My reminiscences are supplemented by the recollections of others who were there and that is one of the reasons why I keep my roster of friends as intact as possible. Polaroids and sketchy journal entries are not enough to bring back in gleaming clarity the japes that I enjoyed on those long, deliciously degenerate nights.

Isn't that what friends are really for? They help you define who you are by reminding you of the things you have done. I am often taken aback when a friend from art college tells me how I took off my shirt and danced on a table at the Freshers Ball. It sounds so unlike me to be totally out of control (no matter how much alcohol I have imbibed) that it adds an edge of dangerous unpredictability to my already well-rounded set of personality traits. Sometimes a friend or acquaintance will tell me something that I said at a dinner party that was hilarious and it's as if I am reliving the moment from their point of view and can feel the frisson of excitement I evoked in them at the time.

One such friend appears in front of me, as is often the case actually, on the London Underground. She has three children now and is married to an ex-soldier who likes to beat her up, she tells me. She is miserable, poor and her teeth are turning black. I can see the dark rot through the translucent enamel. All I can do is stare at her teeth as she gabbles away at me on the escalators at Piccadilly Circus. A chance meeting that has her going over every single memory she has of us being together; at a party ('I got locked in the bathroom and you got me out'), during a lesson ('without your notes I was definitely going to fail') and at a friend's house when we unwisely copulated on the living-room carpet whilst the others slumbered (this episode had no dialogue and consisted only of hungry looks, moans and tamped grunts). The slew of recollections is like an assault as I can barely recall anything other than the carpet capers, which had kinaesthetically carved an indelible memory groove because I had burned my knees on the abrasive pile. As we step off the second mercilessly lengthy escalator, I feel the cold blast of central London ready to embrace me but she is not finished with her orgy of remembrance. From her intimate and warm manner towards me, I feel sure that there must have existed a friendship between us that she gave more value to than I had done. Perhaps she is on medication and cannot stop talking. I can't be certain, but I have to think ahead to the inevitable moment of polite exchange of numbers when we part ways above ground. I look at her front teeth as she smiles and I wonder how long before they dissolve to reveal the foul black pestilence within.

'Are you on Facebook?' she says. Relief floods my upper torso and my shoulders un-bunch and I started to breath normally again.

'Yeah, sure. Look me up,' I said and waggle my watch to get a good glance at its face to indicate that I am late for something. Her smile freezes on her face, criss-crossed with laughter lines, crow's feet and other euphemisms for encroaching decay. Her three children have sucked her dry. The decay is coming to the surface through her teeth, evoking steamed Chinese dumplings with a filling of black worms. I shudder as I walk in completely the wrong direction to where I should be going just to avoid another step with her by my side rattling off her memories, consolidating her past in readiness for some sudden and decrepit demise. Maybe she has a death wish or a premonition and she is desperately trying to scream for help by connecting with me afresh but my ears are dulled to that kind of oblique cry.

There are other people with whom I've kept in touch via social media, our friendship cryogenically frozen; my inseparable partner in crime was a girl called Trudy (who later changed her name to Kitty and, I conjectured, would become a slatternly singleton by her forties, whom I met when I was moonlighting in a call centre flogging a free business magazines to managing directors across the land. It was a job that required nothing more than the ability to talk animatedly on the telephone about a monthly corporate periodical that we were pressing on to the highest-placed manager we could get hold of. We weren't even asking for money. The magazine was free and sustained by advertising. Even so, most people we rang up were suspicious right off the bat and the bulk of each call would comprise our attempts to disabuse them of the concept of there being 'a catch'. It was mundane, soul-crushing work that was made almost bearable by the banter of the real salesmen who populated a desk right behind mine – aggressively flogging. Their job was to sell advertising space in the magazine that I was trying to give away for free and frequently not managing to do. It was in such an environment that Trudy shone, in my eyes. She was a complete professional when she had that telephone cradled on her shoulder softly murmuring into the mouthpiece to seduce whoever she had managed to hook at the number she was calling. She sat one desk away and faced me so I could hear her mellifluous tones wafting across the desk when the sales oiks weren't shouting at each other – or making lewd jokes in between calls to establish dominance in their musky male hierarchy. During breaks, she was bursting with joie de vivre and always had a tale of weekend mischief to share. I was taken by her energy, yet her penchant for dying her hair blonde with ugly black roots, a nose ring and an insatiable appetite for costume jewellery rendered her an unattractive proposition. Sexually. Nevertheless, we hit it off when she found out that I went round calling myself an artist and we arranged forthwith to attend a private viewing in Swiss Cottage that very evening. As an art school graduate, I had some contacts in the field but she knew the actual collectors whom she had met and charmed at parties and events where she peddled a sideline in Reiki massage. Aside from Trudy, cocaine became my loyal companion at these soirées where to be sober was to be ostracised. One simply could not keep up with the *bon vivants* and generally alarming excess of drug-assisted vitality without the help of something chemical. If cocaine was thin on the ground then speed was substituted or if that made one sick then one would have to take an ecstasy tablet or stoop to downing copious amounts of taurine and caffeine-enriched energy drinks with an uplifting spirit like vodka or gin mixed in.

Trudy would cartwheel into rooms and demand piggyback rides to the Tube station and it was exhilarating to be within her orbit as she introduced me to other artists and important collectors. Once we ended up in a penthouse suite at the Hyde Park Hilton and drank champagne, snorted coke and watched a whacked-out pair of prostitutes simulate sex on the glass coffee table with our mercurial host writhing about underneath the glass with a video camera barking instructions. Although I had little inclination to do so, Trudy took me back to my place that night. I told her that my flat was in a state of supreme untidiness and she replied:

'I'm not interested in your flat, I'm interested in your cock.'

It would have been churlish to turn down sex with Trudy after that remark so we went at it in an alcoholic tangle of limbs. I discovered that her nose was not the only part of her anatomy she had deigned to pierce.

What will these old friends of mine think of me after I eat my kidney and pass the metabolised tissue through my gut and discharge it out of my body ready for the next stage of its transmogrification from the abject into art? The whole idea of it – their reactions of disbelief, shock and hopefully awe – just thrills me to bits.

*

Mother wants to call the piece *My Rectum is Full of Gold* with a vague nod towards the folkloric goose that laid the golden egg. I baulked at first as it smacked of sensationalism, which is old hat – however, it is growing on me. I am going to shit out my masterpiece. Literally. Once the stool emerges (hopefully sufficiently voluminous) it will be dipped into a flask of liquid nitrogen with a temperature of around minus 190 degrees Celsius which will instantly solidify the faecal matter long enough for it to be very carefully, as the frozen excrement is extremely brittle and could shatter if improperly handled, polished. Next, it will be delicately sealed with layers of gold leaf by Italian artisans in Tuscany, thus imbuing the turd with the aura of impenetrable mystery that is a prerequisite to it becoming an *objet d'art*. Producing a single artefact would be a far more elegant manner in which to transcend the limits of what had been originally conceived as a performance piece recorded for posterity on thirty-five-millimetre film. A clumsy and unoriginal way to proceed, I think. Mother's genius for perfecting my nascent instinctual process of creative cognition has always delighted me and my respect for the connections in her brain that could allow for such leaps of cogitation continues to grow exponentially. Art and shit have a distinguished history together. For example, in the 1960s an artist sold several dozen tin cans containing his own shit, allegedly, and called the work, pleasantly enough, *Merda d'artista*.

Of course mine wasn't shit for the sake of shocking anyone or passing cynical comment on the relationship between art, the artist and the art market or some other intellectual gymnastics that have been done a million times before. The avant-garde has aged badly and has been fully assimilated into the cloying mainstream. The gilding process I have chosen to perform is the only sensible way to produce a tactile artefact to denote the existence of the event itself; a natural end product of the artist devouring his own body, the collocation of precious metal and worthless shit. Pure profligacy! Putting thousands of dollars – I will ask my gallerist to front the expenses – of gold to use like that is a debauched thrill and I feel the long-dead souls of Nero and Caligula stir with amusement at the delectable (deplorable) prospect. It is unadulterated decadence and all decadence leads to degeneracy, decay and dregs. The fall of Rome followed by the Dark Ages. My heart quickens at the notion that I'll be written into history for this, perhaps as an augur for the approaching apocalypse.

S is suitably impressed by the new proposal but the logistics at her end have not changed and she is very down about how she might pull it off. We still have to settle on a surgeon to remove the kidney in the first place and to date no one has agreed or even considered it. It looks as if no reputable person will and I am loath to go underground for the procedure. Organ trafficking is rife and for all I know my kidney could be halfway to Canada by the time I am roused from my anaesthetic slumber. I have thought about employing security guards as S would be no good in a confrontation and the whole thing is spiralling out of control and turning into a bad reality television show. This has to be done right. It needs gravitas and the solemnity of a death ritual. Funerals have always fascinated me by their tight regimentation, whatever the religion.

The details vary enormously between cultures; however, the central theme of a dignified exit that we would like to guarantee for ourselves is key. The thought, even to an atheist, that one day we will drop dead and be thrown out with the garbage to rot in some landfill, no better than a discarded lettuce, is still potently unsettling, even though most people would agree that once dead it seems rather a silly waste of resources to make a meal of one's internment. Ha! A meal is exactly what I am going to make of my own mortality. The pun is apt. The layers of meaning in the work will be multiple. Satisfied by the weighty feel of the project I go to bed without a drink for the first time in perhaps years, and fall into a dreamless sleep only to awake the next afternoon to a worrying development that, due to a voice message from S, threatens to insert the proverbial spanner in the works.

*

S and I discuss my dwindling options. Not one registered UK surgeon will accept my offer. I even increased the remuneration and made assurances that there are no legal impediments. We had consulted with top lawyers on the topic of 'aiding and abetting' a person to self-cannibalise. I would naturally sign a waiver and they would be unidentified if they so wished.

At the louche coffee shop near my apartment on the cobbled streets of lower Rotherhithe, I look at S across the table, both of us thinking through the problem in concentrated silence. It strikes me that we have to throw the net wider. I suspect the task of removing my kidney may be easier in a so-called Third World country, a place where ethics are perhaps more elastic?

I pose this as a question to S, aware of the racism that may be implied.

Turkey comes to mind but then I am reminded that, as a NATO country, Turkey is very much of the First World. However, if the United Kingdom's inflexible laws aren't going to oblige me then I will go where the parameters of health and safety legislation are still being established. That's not racist, it's a fact of life. I make no judgements. However, I do hope – and I let S know my feelings – that there will be no actual illegalities. I am repulsed by the greedy degenerates who profit from corruption. I am merely exploiting the collectivist nature of human endeavour that flourishes in my home country where people are willing to bend the law a little in order to help a person out. With that in mind I am confident of finding a qualified surgeon with an impeccable record and top-notch facilities who doesn't mind removing a human kidney for no other reason than to earn a tidy sum of money and – perhaps – in the noble pursuit of art. S is taken by the idea and we set our sights on İstanbul. The iced organ will have to travel the 1,500 miles back to the London premiere but that is a suitable compromise, as I will need the time to fully recover before the event itself.

Talking about the nitty-gritty has done wonders for S's attitude. She is smiling again and every time I see it, it warms my heart. A happy helper is what I need right now. A miserable state of mind tends to scoop out one's innards leading to the vacuum being filled with anxiety about the meaning of it all and, before you know it, you're trying to stare down Death itself and – be assured – it never blinks first. Instead, I've got rather good at repressing thoughts of death altogether and I believe that I have trained S to do so, too. We are on a mission to eradicate it from our lives – by ignoring it. Loneliness, I find, is a similar affliction to death anxiety. It is a kind of living death where you are there but not present and it gets more debilitating the longer you try to face off with it, with loneliness. You have to put it out of your mind or it will eat you alive. One does not have the capacity to stand up to it because it holds all the cards. You cannot win an argument with something that knows you better than you can ever hope to know yourself and it has no mercy or sense of compassion either. Its whole *raison d'être* is to crush your spirit so that you curl up and die. Loneliness is nature's way of separating the weak links out of the gene pool. It's crafty, loneliness; it is a sharp tool evolution wields to cut away gangrenous flesh from the rest of the organism – the pulsating populace of humanity – so that the species may survive. Feeling somewhat shaken by the direction my train of thought has propelled me, I invite S to have dinner with me. She says she has other plans but I persuade her that we must continue our line of enquiry without hesitation and after some thought and a few text messages she says she has to send – to whom I have no idea – she agrees.

*

Over a light supper of lobster tail, rocket leaves and a chilled Sauvignon blanc in a quaint brasserie near Sloane Square, we discuss S's past. Perhaps incredibly, I have never asked about her personal life and if I have, as a courtesy during the interview for example, then I don't recollect what she told me. I am astounded to learn that she is fully four years older than

I had estimated her age to be. She has the taut skin and fine invisible pores of a young woman not yet past her twenty-fifth birthday. Her straight brown hair – I take especial notice of her features now upon the revelation of her age – has a healthy bounce and shine to it. She shrinks into herself and I can't help but feel the deepest affection for her shyness.

She is modest, too. Evidently, I only lightly scanned through her résumé because I couldn't bring to mind any of her work experience or training. She tells me of when she decided to pursue a serious career in the arts at a city college, I forget which as soon as she tells me. I drift back to the moment I settled upon her as my new assistant. Only a few images remain of the meeting. Her green eyes, the glossy hair and her legs demurely tucked under her seat. As my focus returns to the present I realise that she has finished talking and I am staring at her with my stupid mouth open. I close it. She is actually quite beautiful. I banish the mawkish thought from my brain. It must be because I am very tired from the lack of alpha-wave sleep recently; I am haunted by a panorama of offal in nightmares that keep me awake half the night.

S goes through her notes then pauses. With a pensive look she asks me whether the parameters have shifted too much for the undertaking to be satisfactory. She is getting hung up on details. The bottom line is that I am going to eat my own kidney. How it gets out from my body and on to my plate is superfluous to the concept of the piece. She reminds me that the aforementioned Manzoni's *Merda d'artista* has recently been acquired by the illustrious Tate Britain and still courts controversy. The ninety sealed tin cans individually sold by the mischievous Manzoni, labelled as containing thirty grammes of his own faeces, were later asserted to hold bits of plaster. The artist was dead at the tender age of twenty-nine so it was a case of getting a can opener and destroying the art to prove whether or not he had lied. As I furrow my brow in thought, S comes – finally! – to the point and says, 'Why does it have to be your kidney? Just stating that it is your kidney will achieve the same aim, no? Manzoni did that, didn't he?'

'And what would that be? The aim?' I say, pursing my lips as anger washes over my head like boiling water.

'To subvert the concept of conceptual art by forcing the market to stretch its credulity without ever paying off its need to know the veracity of our – I mean, your – claim.'

Claim.

I become fully enraged. Heroically, I fight to check my emotions. My face, however, must be betraying me as I feel the blood flooding to the surface capillaries, no doubt rendering my countenance a deep shade of Qatar red. I know that I have lost control when S jolts back in her seat and straightens her back like an alarmed alley cat.

Where had this come from? She is so circumspect and spare with her intrusions. The mistake is mine! By asking her to talk about herself I have lowered the invisible force field that protects me from people invading my sphere of authority without explicit permission. I have never asked her what she thought about the work or how I should go about it. She is an enabler, a facilitator – no more – and my fucking employee. How dare she spout this Art History student bullshit. Her age and relative lack of experience is no excuse either, as she isn't even as young as I thought she was!

'Did Marc Quinn lie when he said he used nine pints of his own blood to make his frozen head sculpture?' I ask her rhetorically.

When she tries to answer I lose what little cool I had remaining and she is already standing up and backing away. I can hear my hectoring voice as if someone else is shouting the words at her, pumping my jaw feverishly as if I am a ventriloquist's doll.

'Did Marco Evaristti lie when he invited his guests to eat meatballs fried in his own liposuctioned fat?' Her face crumples up and she runs away. 'Did Zhu Yu use special effects when he cooked and ate a stillborn human foetus? No!' I yell after her as she darts away and I fancy I can hear her choking back tears of shame.

'They're selling picture frames made of human placenta and you want me to fake it?!' I add as an afterthought to highlight the unshockable nature of this post post-modern consumerist era. She is gone by then and my audience of polite strangers do their best to totally ignore my outburst but I can see that I have infected their timid minds with a virulent idea that will, in the best minds that are most receptive to original thought, one day flourish and set them on a new path away from the ordinariness that they joylessly and listlessly call their lives.

Things are turning in on themselves and swallowing all meaning with it. I can't lie about what I am doing and there is no way to simulate something that relies on pure integrity for its very existence. I am not a magician tasked with entertaining the hoi polloi who are ready to be tricked as if they had unknowingly signed some irrevocable compact with all magicians, saying that they are willing to believe as long as the conjuror dutifully pretends it is real without slyly winking at the audience and ruining it for everyone. This is art and it has to be honest, gut-wrenchingly real and embarrassingly authentic. The whole point is that it isn't fake or playing with the idea of what constitutes authenticity. I am not going to be teasing the art aficionados with an impish piece about the meta-narrative of art history. No! I am going to rip out my kidney and eat it!

Then I am left there, my chest falling and rising, sly eyes monitoring me from other tables in case I lunge at one of them randomly. My fingers go up to my temples and I note that my hands are trembling. She has irked me. This isn't some Dadaist stunt where I am commenting on the meaning or value of conceptual art. If she is thinking about my well-being then she is letting her personal feelings get in the way of her job. How can I rely on her to get the work done right if deep down she has serious reservations and could possibly, even subconsciously, scupper the endeavour? I have lost my trust in her. This is a disaster. The phenomenon is similar to the disrupting instinct of the likes of Seb and Chifre who had coalesced into one personage, a self-procreating (or not in fact) hermaphrodite entity more akin to plant life than human. They, too, subconsciously worked to destroy what they were excluded from, similar to the anarchic youth gangs frozen out of mainstream society; they would wreck, riot and pillage righteously and only be vaguely aware that their main drive was less about rebellion against an unjust system and more to do with their own failings over which they had zero control and which they could not remedy despite the motivational myth that hard work always pays off. They were simply born to the wrong parents in the wrong place and at the wrong time. Why couldn't people accept that their situation in life was ninety-nine per cent pure luck? That way they'd take their seat at the poker table with the knowledge that the hand dealt to them is what they have to play with and strategise accordingly. When Einstein talked about dice and how God doesn't play with them, I'd like to have replied, over a glass of frozen vodka with Marilyn Monroe sitting next to us, her sultry eyes boring into me – I'd have said:

'True Albert, very true… and that's because God *is* the dice.'

The unsatisfactory curtailment of my evening with S would have to be addressed at some point. She had abandoned her post, leaving me adrift in a cold sea of my own doubts and internal monologues. I don't want her to be another Joseph and it is too late in the process to switch collaborators – her emotional exit needs a sense of cathartic closure, I feel. Perhaps the wine is to blame, exacerbating my already heightened emotional state. No, I need to put a lid on my self-examination and return to the business at hand. I order another bottle and wonder who will book my flight to İstanbul.

*

As I am allowing for a break in communications between S and me whilst the dust settles, Mother uses her travel agent to get me on the next available flight to Turkey. After take-off I peer out of my porthole at the River Thames that shines in the flat grey light of morning. An older woman sitting beside me is scribbling something down into a palm-sized notebook. When I ask her what she is writing, she tells me it is her 'book of blessings'. How very quaint, I think, and such an alien concept to the atheist. She is an American, from Denver, and her buoyant mood and naïveté compels me to engage her in some further light conversation.

'Were you in London long?' I ask.

'I was in Scotland mostly – such a beautiful country – my ancestors are from there,' she burbles adorably. 'Quakers.'

'Well, that's wonderful that you're reconnecting with your, er, heritage,' I offer, trying to cement her belief that she has one. Then I experience a sinking feeling but I don't know what is causing it.

'Oh yes, my father's family were from Aberdeen.'

'It's good to know where one comes from, isn't it?' I say, feeling queasy.

'I felt such a connection to the land – amazing. Where are you from?'

'I'm originally from Turkey,' I say, 'but I was brought up in London.' A stab of pain in my stomach.

'That's amazing – how wonderful.'

'Thank you,' I say, not sure why. My gut twists in pain and I think back to what I ate earlier today but cannot recall anything suspicious.

'I'd like to have seen more of London – so much history.'

'Yes... yes. In fact, if one were to remove London from the equation,' I muse, trying to divert myself from the turmoil in my gastrointestinal tract, 'England might as well break away from the British Isles – leaving Scotland and Wales standing proudly in the North Sea with their Irish cousin – and drift away into the middle of the Atlantic; a sad little country coming to the end of the process of shedding its past splendours, settling down to retire from the global stage and looking for a comfortable place to watch the world go by.' I rush out the sentence in a panic of prickly heat and realise with relief that my innards have suddenly calmed down.

'Wow – you know, I've never really thought about it like that,' she says and turns to meditate on her book of blessings. Something about that notebook of hers vexes me terribly and my insides are afflicted afresh. I need to keep talking.

'I'm sorry to say, you'll be lucky to maintain the kind of longevity that the British Empire enjoyed. Everything is simply moving faster. But America is driven by psychotically ambitious and delusional maniacs so there's plenty of hope for them to keep swinging.'

She looks at me, nonplussed. So I go on:

'By way of comparison, Turkey had its own empire and a big powerful one at that with plenty of positive contributions to world history – taking in the Sephardic Jews during the Spanish Inquisition, keeping the peace in the Middle East, introducing coffee to Europe when the retreating Ottomans left behind their supplies at the gates of Vienna where the first coffee shop was opened, inspiring the West to develop the jelly bean when they tried to copy Turkish Delight and, of course, forcing the accidental discovery of the Americas by blocking off the Silk Road… to name a few.'

'Wow.' She beams with genuine interest. 'The jelly bean – my gosh! I never knew that… I love jelly beans. And coffee!' she adds and chortles with abandon.

'Have you ever had any Turkish Delight, by the way?'

'I can't say that I have but I surely will try it when I get there – is it very similar to the jelly bean?'

'The jelly bean is an inferior confection,' I say bluntly and am amused to see her purse her lips and frown, disappointed to have never had the opportunity to make a direct comparison. I continue to tamp down my bowel-centred anxiety with more words:

'For me and others like me who bridge vastly different cultures between the, if you will, jelly-bean West and Turkish Delight East, it can be very confusing; one minute you hanker for good old fashioned Anglo-Saxon no-nonsense know-how then suddenly you feel like rejecting their haughty prescriptions for a life "well lived" and ache to be part of the vertiginous discovery-in-motion that is Turkish culture – bounding from one delectable crisis to another... in flux; in jeopardy. Incredibly exciting in equal amounts to being intensely maddening. Once exhausted by all that toing and froing, you're suddenly coveting the simplicity of the American Dream.' Her eyes go wide and her vaguely smiling lips, I note, are stretched over a perfect set of North American dentistry. I go on:

'Then that all starts coming off as futile – an unattainable dream – the clue is in the name, right?' I chuckle pointedly. 'So you begin to crave the down-to-earth Britishness you so admire, then that starts making you depressed – it's so fuddy-duddy – and you yearn for the centuries-old Turkish way, living by the seat of your pants, and so the merry-go-round spins and whirls and turns your brain to jelly!'

'Or Turkish Delight,' she says with unexpected wit. I smile and nod sagely.

'Yes. That's right,' I sigh and am, finally, out of things to say. Somewhere over the English Channel my row companion goes to the toilet as I pop a soporific pill into my mouth, my head aching after all that enforced chitchat. I try to settle down to enter a hopefully vacant slumber but not before I reach an epiphany of sorts. I am dreadfully aware of the infinite yet incapable of ever comprehending it; a speck on the wheel of time, desperate to imbue my existence with meaning come what may – living with the delusional belief that my accomplishments will allow me to stretch beyond my physical lifespan. Others, equally delusional, imagine that parenting will allow some part of their selves to live on in their offspring. Some seek everlasting life through membership of a religion and its collective mirages of heaven, resurrection, reincarnation and all the rest of the diverse packages of comfort available. I prefer my less selfish choice – why drag another being into this mess? It also seems to be the most contrary – to live on in one's work, eschewing the easy route to immortality, thwarting my basic urges, denying my animalistic humanity. Then my consciousness succumbs to the sweet liberation of a dreamless sleep...

*

When I awake above Bulgaria, I see that the woman from Denver has, strangely, not returned to her seat. I hadn't even got round to asking her why she was going to Turkey. As for me, the flight had streaked past in pharmaceutical oblivion; a much-needed interlude for my soul (whatever that is exactly) to find its bearings and rest so that I can face my next – boringly practical – challenge. Perhaps I have been a shade too impatient with S and this trip will need her calm presence after all. Then it hits me – the pain in my stomach was envy. I was envious of the woman from Denver with her book of blessings and her love for a land far away she has come to call her own; no doubts about her origins or where she belongs or what she believes. Certainty makes her invincible.

VII

When we land at İstanbul's Atatürk Airport, I am reminded of the previous trip I had made here for medical purposes. It was to have my foreskin removed. That time I had been tricked and taken advantage of by the people I had trusted. Now I felt as if I was in charge.

Once checked in at my hotel, I walk through the old city of Pera, opposite Seraglio Point where the Sultans lived off the Golden Horn (that romantic promontory that flows into the metallic navy-blue waters of the Bosphorus Straits) where long ago the infidels inhabited this part of the capital of the Empire. When all but a handful of them were forced to evacuate, they left behind handsome apartment blocks, churches, synagogues, arcades, trams, luxury hotels like the famous Pera Palace, the first ever underground train service (a one-stop affair built by the French) and the last stop on the defunct Orient Express at Selimiye. Today it is a crumbling relic of past glories, the central metropolis of luxury restaurants next to traditional Turkish eateries and upmarket bars reserved for the relatively wealthy that are perched atop the decaying cheap dives for the poor, who are being pushed out to make way for boutique hotels and vegan cafes. This part of town is still steeped in romance and mystery and it is the only part of İstanbul I actually enjoy. It is European in its looks, inflected with the Orient, and full of foreigners either visiting or living here. You can feel their collective effort of will to go back in time to an age of Sultans. The past seduces us all.

Doctor Avni's clinic is on the top storey of a terraced apartment in what used to be an upmarket Italian district. Its steep cobbled streets now host basement workshops full of illegal immigrants, cavernous antique shops, slick coffee houses and numerous tawdry estate agents. Transvestites roam the streets in the less salubrious enclaves looking for trade at night and by day a quiet disgruntled populace goes about its business with tourists happily weaving through the native human flow, spoiled cats and the scrupulously tagged street dogs, snapping shots of this peeling edifice stained as if dragged from the seabed or that bygone-era, be-costumed street seller flogging sherbet or *Osmanlı macunu*. It is also one of the few places in İstanbul where you can hear the ding-dong of church bells amongst the five-times-a-day calls to prayer from loudspeakers. There is something to be said about the pleasantly singsong Turkish style of rendering the Arabic call to prayer – it adds an aural spice to the oriental mix as it wafts through bazaars and over hookah pipes that I'm sure the tourists thoroughly enjoy.

I step into the cramped elevator retrofitted to the insides of this hundred-year-old building and my mobile rings. It is Father. How did he know I was here? Like Darth Vader, he has some sixth sense that alerts him to my presence. I wasn't planning on visiting him as he has a habit of extracting the truth from me irrespective of my best efforts to hide it, and I did not wish to tell him anything about my upcoming piece, as he would undoubtedly try to stop me, using his powers of persuasion through the medium of guilt. As a father, he would be ashamed and traumatised in equal amounts by my undimming artistic ambitions to make a name for myself rather than settle for the type of life that he had envisaged for his son – a life that would provide grandchildren for him in his dotage. What could I possibly gain from such a risky enterprise when I could be earning a proper living with a normal job like everyone else? What was the bloody point of it all? he'd plead. As the phone continues to ring I have all of these mini imaginary confrontations swirling in my mind. His voice is in my head already and I haven't even picked up. No, I have to dismiss these made-up conversations and ignore them. It was not Father talking to me inside my head but my own self, the superego that wants me to adhere to the rules and conform to societal norms whilst my primitive id squirms – a prehistoric fish in the mud of my consciousness, ever eager to satisfy its urge for dopamine, endorphins and other chemicals of pleasure ignited by the use of drugs, the taking of stupid risks and other activities 'normal' people refrain from doing so they can be wholly responsible for the task of passing on their genes like good citizens of their race. The poor ego stuck in that mental maelstrom is constantly negotiating between the id and the superego trying to find a middle ground. That is how the struggle to stay sane works. If you're not careful the ego will shut down, unable to cope, and to all intents and purposes you become a basket case. My legacy will be my work and not my offspring so the sooner he internalises that fact the better.

'Hello, Father,' I say.

'Where are you?'

I bristle at this. It is the first thing he always says. Where am I? What does it matter where I am? You have me on the telephone so speak and I can speak back and we can have a decent conversation but you start with that faintly accusatory tone and you want information from me just so you can have the upper hand, well... I have to stop this voice inside my head. It is getting me down. All I have to do is play along. He is an old man; stop reading so much into it and allow your throat to relax.

'I'm in İstanbul,' I say and there is a pause. The silence is reproachful and a little confused. 'I was going to give you a call in a while – it's been very hectic lately.'

'Come over for dinner,' he says.

'I don't know if I'll have time. Can we meet for a coffee instead?' I say, a little peeved by the unexpected arrangements I have to make. He agrees. I hang up, feeling silly and trite for the internal conflict that has underscored the brief telephone exchange, and make my way into the clinic ready to be charming to the woman behind the reception desk.

As I wait sitting on the ersatz leather sofa, slowly sinking into the creaking foam, I feel the pleasant yet unwelcome fuzziness of an afternoon nap warming the back of my eyeballs, radiating cosy pulses of sleep. Yet I want to be fresh for this meeting and not in a post-catnap stupor. My body is snapping into some old memory of a waiting room and it wants to dream itself back to when I was a child and doctors meant a strange hypnotic state where I would be a helpless kitten caught on the cold metal table and utterly at the mercy of the giant adults round me. All doctors have soothing voices and that soothing voice is coming back to me now and lulling me into a state of childhood calm. No, I must not be a child today. I have to be the adult with the serious purpose he has set himself.

I ask the receptionist if I can have a coffee or something. She calls down for a Turkish coffee (medium sweet) and I sit there as the minutes drag and I feel ever more vulnerable to being intimidated by the man I am about to meet. I want him to remove my kidney and he needs to know that I am a fully cognisant being who will not take no for an answer. I feel weak. The coffee is taking too long to arrive and I close my eyes for the briefest moment. I fall inwards into the folds of the traitorous sofa and sink into a honeyed snooze.

When I resurface from my doze and see the cold coffee on the table, at once I become hugely irritated. Surely, I must have been waiting for more than half an hour by now. As if in answer to my distress, the receptionist indicates that I can go in. In a minor panic I slurp down the cold coffee for the hit of caffeine, get the fine grounds in my teeth and have to get a cup of water from the cooler to gargle the stuff out of my mouth before I can confidently enter the doctor's office.

He bids me to sit down then peers at me over the desk. S briefed him on the telephone in English but he wasn't quite sure if he understood her meaning, as his English is a little rusty, he says. I look him straight in the eye and tell him that I want a surgeon to perform a nephrectomy and hand over the resultant organ to my care. After a pause, his face takes on a disapproving look. He is positively scowling in fact but the edges of his lips are turned up in a simulacrum of a polite smile.

'I do not wish to be involved, sir.'

'But Doctor *bey*, I am at the end of my tether and I was told that you were the person to speak to about these sorts of operations.'

'"These sorts of operations"?'

'Yes. There are so many protocols that inhibit my gaining access to the kidney after it has been removed that it makes it nigh on impossible for me to have the operation done by a skilled technician rather than some organ thief in India. I cannot take that risk even though I am willing to take any and all risks to actuate my art. Look at me, I am a desperate man.'

There is a long pause as the good doctor absorbs the information.

'Art?'

'Yes, didn't my assistant tell you? This is an art project.'

'A student project?'

I chuckle immodestly – being humble is a mark of weakness here. 'No Doctor *bey*, I am a working artist. You can look up my credentials on your computer if you'd like.'

'The girl said something about a project but I thought that was code for something else. I do not approve of organ sales, sir. And if this is some front for that I will ask you to leave. I have never condoned it and I have never been involved in those kinds of activities.' The doctor's eyes are beginning to bulge and I imagine his throat is tightening as his pitch gets higher with every word. By the end he is pounding the table with his fist. I notice he has a gold wedding band and a fading tan that has turned the hairs on his fingers almost blond. Why is this man being so grandly outraged? Does he think I am wearing a recording device and that this is an undercover sting? Is the idea that an artist would do this so ludicrous that only the police or perhaps a transnational investigative journalist can have dreamed it up? My work is once again being implicitly compared to a fucking prank. I rise from my seat, chin jutting out with offended dignity and I look down at the doctor with what I hope is a measured contempt for his accusations in my flaming eyes and with as little blinking as possible I assure him that he is barking up the wrong tree and that I am deeply offended by his jumping to conclusions and also that his attitude is indicative of the poor cultural education he had received. He stands up too and shows me the door, jaw quivering.

This man who has just ejected me from his clinic must be guilty of something. Maybe he does traffic stolen organs on the black market and that is why he agreed to meet me in the first place but when he saw across from him a type that did not fit his usual clientele's profile he became suspicious and even afraid and lost his composure. I speed-dial S and fill her in. She is astonished and denies that the man she spoke to on the telephone had a poor grasp of English. The good doctor was clearly hiding something, we both agree. In any case, the interview has been a washout. On the steps outside the apartment block I darkly ponder my next move. I am going to see Father the day after tomorrow but in the meantime I am at a loose end. I do not have any friends in town but I toy with the idea of calling an old acquaintance. Just then, the doctor appears behind me. I stand my ground but immediately notice that he is in quite a different mood, relaxed and even a bit timid. He has, he says, looked me up on the Internet, or rather his receptionist has. Apparently, she recognised my face from somewhere and tipped off the doctor that I wasn't trying to mess with him. He sort of apologises but adds that a man in his position has to be very wary of shady operators. Others had tried to inveigle him before in the trade of organ harvesting for wealthy clients and he was disgusted by the prospect even though it would have been extremely lucrative.

I thank him for coming after me and presenting his frank and honest explanation. I am glad I have not offended him, I add, and we graciously shake hands. He then surprises me by recommending someone else for the job. He gives me a name on a scrap of paper and an address situated in the Turkish Republic of Northern Cyprus. Bemused by the elastic principles of the man, I thank him and go in search of a Parisian-style cafe to jot down some notes. I am feeling positive and alive after the confrontation followed by the unexpected resolution at the clinic; this is progress and my mood lightens considerably. I call S again and ask her to drop everything and come to İstanbul. No reference is made by either of us regarding the debacle of our dinner together in Chelsea. We are, after all, professionals. Our journey is going to take us to Cyprus, I tell her, then, once I hang up, my body lurches at the flash of an appalling memory hitherto suppressed. I feel a tug in my abdomen and am sucked into another realm to observe reality through a thick, undulating veil.

*

S arrives in İstanbul within forty-eight hours of our chat and installs herself in a cheap hotel down the road from where I am staying. We must preserve the professional distance between us. Also, my expenses are being defrayed by the Zvwark Gallery so I have to be careful not to, as it were, take the piss. I tell her to freshen up and that I will meet her after my lunch with Father. I have requested that his wife does not come along. It's not as if I dislike her but rather I dislike the person he becomes when she is around. He play-acts to please her by being a fraction more animated than his natural rhythms normally dictate. I do not blame him for it. She is a fine Indonesian woman, brought up in Canada by her adoptive parents, and she takes good care of him. At the restaurant, in an air-conditioned upper-class mall – if that isn't too much of an oxymoron – near Father's office in the district of Levent on the European side of İstanbul, Father seems genuinely pleased to see me. As I take my seat, he waves the waiter over as he is in a hurry to order. I roll my eyes and say weakly:

'I haven't even looked at the menu, Father.'

'Have you eaten already?' he says, po-faced. Another stock phrase denoting that I am still the child and he is the adult in this relationship.

'No I have not.'

He acquiesces and tells the waiter grumpily to give us a few minutes and does not fail to mention that it is I who am not ready to order. Father is a man so unaware of his mocking tone that it is amazing to me that he has never been in a physical fight his whole adult life, as far as I know. I, on the other hand, was already fighting in primary school – my tolerance for playground banter was very low. I try to tamp down the lugubrious mood I am heading into and think of good things that make me consider my life a blessed one and dismiss the bad. Otherwise it is more than likely that I will end up loathing every single breathing human being on the planet and murder the cook with his own kitchen knife between the main course and dessert. Father is just a man with his own foibles and he can't affect or control me any longer, I tell myself forcefully, recalling a declamatory paragraph from a self-help book entitled, *You Are Not Your Father*.

'How's work?' he asks.

He knows full well that the word riles me because he doesn't mean my work as an artist but rather a 'job' – something he knows full well that I do not have. I show that I am rankled by slackening my features, letting the lids of my eyes drop down to slits. Unhappy, disapproving slits that scream, 'Don't pretend I have a job Father, don't make me tell you that my idea of work is not your beloved notion of a nine-to-five with fringe benefits. You baby boomers had it all – jobs for life and proper pension provision. That's a world that does not exist any more!'

'Fine. It's going well,' is what comes out of my mouth. The waiter sets a plate of complimentary olives, butter and some bread on the table. I can see a mini ciabatta, focaccia and seeded rolls in the basket. I can't touch any of them, on account of the gluten. Father rips open a ciabatta, lathers butter on and eats it in one frenetic movement of hand-to-mouth action and clomping jaw-work. Why did I agree to come to Vitrionni's in the first place? I could only safely eat the *risotto ai funghi*, so that's what I order. He goes for an antipasto platter with smoked salmon, smoked chicken, roast beef, chicken liver pâté, cabana sausage, mozzarella, full-fat goat's cheese, further unidentifiable cheeses, more olives, tapenade, rocket pesto and tomato chutney followed by *tagliatelle alla carbonara* – the most calorific items he can sniff out. He will most likely have room left for a dessert, a double espresso and, conceivably, a shot of grappa. The platter is listed on the menu as 'for sharing' but I know well enough that it will remain firmly on his side of the table. My father is a corpulent gentleman, fond of his food, wine and cigars – but only when his wife isn't around. Amazingly for a man of his age and eating habits he has retained his thick dark hair, elastic complexion and well-formed musculature that has not wasted in his advancing years despite doing no exercise whatsoever.

The father-son relationship is a sacred one in Turkish society and all hints that Father is disappointed by my achievements are tough to take. His opinion counts for something in society and therefore in my own heart that is programmed to respond to what others think. Am I so perfect that I can make myself immune to the thoughts and feelings of others? No – are you? Childhood coding is a powerful thing. I try hard to think of the past as a happy place where we had shared many father and son moments. However, as I stare at the menu blindly I fail to come up with a single moment of bonding or camaraderie. I feel wronged specifically because he was never a violent man, a loon or a drunk, so his sober decision to not hang out with his sons, like other dads did, when he had the chance to mould them at their most pliable life stages hurts all the more. Perhaps he had too many other things to do. Perhaps we were boring. To break my internal cyclone of fruitless conjecture I reflect for a moment with a tinge of shame that perhaps I am being too hard on the man – after all, how many fathers are ever given credit for being good at post-modern patriarchy in an age when masculinity is in decline or at least widely under hostile scrutiny. Even the Y chromosome, I read somewhere, that only the male of the species carries, is destined to shrivel to nothing within a few million years, surplus to requirements. My father's father – captured by the British in Gallipoli and interred in Malta – was a man who abandoned his family for another life and that particular wrong was all that my father could talk about when it came to describing my grandfather. I never met him but I assume that there was more to him than that. It strikes me that this abandonment issue is what drives our father-son relationship in that he requires of himself nothing more than to not abandon his family in order for his fatherhood role to be a complete success. In that regard he painted himself as having achieved his aim when Mother pressed for a divorce and so it was never by his own volition that he left the family to fend for itself.

Mercifully, the waiter brings the drinks at this point so that I can take a sip of water and stop thinking. We talk about my 'work' although I think he just wants to make sure I have a proper health insurance policy. I make it sound as if I am adequately covered by the British state. I know the NHS is free but I have no idea whether I am eligible for a pension – I will assume I am until further notice. I know he does not want me knocking on his door one day for handouts. He retells the story about how difficult being old is and how he has money squirrelled away for a rainy day. Health care is expensive in Turkey and one unforeseen procedure can set you back tens of thousands of lira, he elucidates, not bothering to sugarcoat the subtext that I have to be more financially responsible as I age. He's right, of course. I have no respect for time or money and I live in a bubble of sweet delusional bliss where ageing is an illusion and death a myth – a rolling horizon that is always there but never reached. As a functioning artist I have to remain above the fray of pecuniary preoccupations and obsessions of mortality, otherwise I will, I feel quite sure, go totally mad.

'Son, if this art thing doesn't pan out, what is it that you have in mind? What is your plan "B"?'

I feel the familiar pangs of defensive chagrin rising up in my gut, constricting my breathing, and I tell myself that being a son is difficult and that's the end of it. Just stop thinking so much, eat your Caesar salad and just be with your father; a father who dutifully paid all the household bills and kept you at arm's length. Old-school father – the British might label the type as Victorian. The curse of every son is to compare himself to his father and either be afraid that he will end up resembling him or be afraid that he will not end up resembling him. What a bind.

'Father, there is only plan "A",' I say with a dead-eyed smile denoting, I hope, a comforting sense of confidence.

'I simply do not understand it. I don't.' He shakes his head. 'How do you live, for God's sake?'

'This is who I am, Father, don't expect me to change,' I say, and prod the flabby mozzarella – a locally made and inferior replica. Father sucks up the last of his carbonara.

'Nonsense. People change,' he sneers at me. 'You have to think about your future – it'll soon be too late – what have you done with your life?'

'What?' I say, taken aback.

'Nearly forty, no family, no job. You have nothing,' he says with so much feeling that I think I might be about to be publicly humiliated again like the time he took umbrage at my adolescent forearm tattoo (a beautiful haiku in Japanese script), calling me 'a fucking thug' in a cosy little pizzeria on the King's Road full of families enjoying their Sunday lunchtime as Father, a wounded oil tanker spilling its poisonous cargo into the unsuspecting surroundings, exploded at me. That time Mother had been there to shut him up but now I am on my own, without allies or the know-how to navigate these treacherous waters.

'You're not like anyone else I know. None of my friend's kids sit round all day doing – whatever the hell it is that you do. What do you do? Tell me,' he blusters, a fleck of cold white sauce on his top lip.

It is as if he had been stopping up his mouth with food; plugs of antipasti and pasta had delayed this outburst for the duration of the meal. Now that the food is gone, he lets his anger flow freely out of the fleshy chute he had – moments earlier – satisfied with bread, creamy sauce and other comforting fare including a carafe of Sauvignon Blanc.

'You lost your flat, you're up to your ears in debt and, what was that girl's name, she left you because of it,' he spews. And then the killer blow, 'You've wasted your life.'

Stunned, I stay silent but behind and above my Adam's apple the muscles of my throat are contracting, pulling at the roots of my tongue, my gullet constricted and in pain. I am involuntarily suppressing my breathing and tightening my stomach muscles. I feel light-headed and dyspeptic, enraged and belittled all at once. I have nothing to say to this man who thinks so little of me. It occurs to me that if Celine had been here, things may not have reached their current conclusion and I regret excluding what would have been her suppressive presence. He wouldn't have dared to be so bold in front of his wife. She might have judged him poorly behaved, his splenetic performance inappropriate to the occasion. I stand up to walk away and he says under his breath:

'Or I wasted my life.'

That stings even more. He definitely wouldn't have been that candid with Celine around. So, I say to myself as I stand frozen beside the table looking down at his broad shoulders and neck hunched over his plate, either I have flushed my life down the toilet chasing some impossible dream like an idiot or he has wasted his life by going to the trouble of producing offspring who have both disappointed him – one by dying and the other by wilfully shaming him through his very existence.

'You have a talent for zeroing a person's self-esteem,' I manage to say.

'Yes. I do,' he smirks.

Deflated and, I feel, soon to be tearful, I storm out of the accursed Italian eatery wondering if his initial warmth when I arrived was simply the glee of imminent unburdening that had now taken place to devastating effect. I stomp along the polished floor of the mall; every single shining shop window, bright plastic plant and lighting fixture mocks the darkness that has engulfed me. I think about the safe harbour that Mother represents; despite the distraction of her alcoholism, she always kept us boys at the forefront of her thoughts and pushed my brother and me to excel. She wanted more than a humdrum existence and she saw in her children, especially me, reflections of her own ambitious nature. Why would Mother want to expose her child to ridicule at worst and broken dreams at best by lifting expectations to the stratosphere by organising an exhibition of her child's scrawls at age nine?

'Be hugely ambitious' is her message and Father is saying 'don't bother, you'll never make it'. That's the kind of mental clash that can tear a person's psyche apart. By the time I burst out of the suffocating structure, I am drowning in my own internal monologue. I stride without purpose through the tree-lined streets of Levent to the concrete and asphalt intersections of Gayrettepe and it dawns on me pleasantly that I didn't tell him what I was working on. By not telling him I feel empowered, somehow. This is the tiniest crumb of comfort I can extract from what I have just experienced and, for the sake of my art, I must focus with laser precision on what I am doing and take comfort in the notion that nothing worth doing is ever easy. I bristle at the cliché and walk on.

*

Next day, I invite S over from her hotel to have breakfast with me at mine which, being more expensive, offers a perfectly edible open buffet consisting of Turkified continental breakfast as well as a menu of other options. I regard her through my black frames as she tucks into a *sucuk* omelette with sleepy eyes. She sips her black tea from a traditional thin-waisted glass. I prefer a mug. She is interested in doing things the native way whilst she is here – just like a seasoned tourist, I expect, who fancies themselves as more of a traveller. S has combed her hair, still damp after a shower, and is ready for work, her clipboard poking out of her faux Hermes bag next to her feet shod with the ubiquitous babettes.

'Ever been to Cyprus before?'

'I went to Ayia Napa once.'

'I mean Northern Cyprus. The Turkish Republic of Northern Cyprus.'

She shakes her head and sips some freshly squeezed orange juice. I am drinking freshly squeezed pomegranate juice. It is sharp and somewhat bitter and feels as if it is doing you serious good. I have to say it is one thing I love about Turkey. The pomegranates are plentiful and cheap. You can't get a tall glassful of this in England for under five quid. Here, it's less than half that. On the street, vendors sell it for pennies. S has been talking for a few seconds and I try to catch the meaning of her sentence from the fragment that I grab after I tune back into the moment.

'—personally I would have loved it,' she says, nodding and chewing. Bits of parsley are stuck on her front teeth and I have no idea what she is talking about so I wait, feeling like some would-be artificial intelligence attempting to mimic human behaviour. Teeth. Those strange units of enamel and dentine with their pulpy cores attached to the jawbone in our moveable heads – grasping, shearing and crushing for sustenance, processing our food so that we can extract the nutrition better than the mud-sucking toothless organisms that eventually went extinct. A shark has teeth in its skin, I heard on a podcast once. Skin teeth. Strange fishes. We evolved from those. Then S's blurry visage comes back into focus and she is presenting an amused confusion on her face to me. 'What?' she says. 'You drifted off.'

'Nothing,' I reply. 'Carry on.'

'I was just rambling on about the hen do in Ayia Napa. Maybe I need something stronger than tea this morning.'

'Did you get enough sleep?'

'I think so. I don't know, sorry, you were going to tell me about this doctor?'

'Doctor Shipley. I do hope he isn't going to waste our time the same as the other one.'

'Doctor Avni got cold feet, I think. He was very much on board when I spoke to him,' she says, prompting me to debrief her on the meeting.

'I don't mean you did anything wrong but sometimes you have to be sensitive to the way people misrepresent themselves – in case they're missing out on some big opportunity – but then when push comes to shove they fall back on excuses,' I say, then continue, 'It's a subtle art to spot them, of course. Just remember that propaganda is king here, not communication; persuasion is out and cocksure arrogance is in; intelligence is never favoured over simple animal cunning.' She nods along as I continue, 'And cunning isn't some cute word either – it means to deceive and evade to achieve your purpose; even if it means wasting someone's precious time and finite energies. A vicious circle of dogs eating dogs.'

'But he's a Brit,' she begins. 'Ex-army. There were complications—'

'What's nationality got to do with it!' A piece of toast flies out of my mouth and I continue, 'Brit, Turk, Cypriot or Chinese – corruption has no ethnic identity. It is the place and time that corrupts.'

'Sorry.'

'Why're you apologising?'

'I made you angry.'

'You didn't make me angry. This situation is making me angry.' I take a calming breath and try to concentrate on the mission. 'I am under a lot of stress and I thank you for noticing. You're a very smart girl but I don't want you to buckle, okay?

If I'm losing it then just ride it out with me. It comes and goes. More tea?'

'Yes please.'

'I'll get the waiter,' I say gallantly and wave my arm at one. There and then, I decide to be totally truthful with her and say:

'I am more than a little stressed about Cyprus. You see, I've been there before – many times – as a child. And the last time I went I was still a teenager and it was not a pleasant experience I can tell you. To say the least.'

I then become uncommunicative and she understands that the silence is not meant to be disturbed. After a pause I add, 'So. Let's get in and out as fast as humanly possible. The island, as far as I'm concerned, is cursed. And what "complications" did you mean?'

'What?' she says, frowning.

'This Shipley and his early retirement, et cetera?'

'Oh, well… he was caught in possession of contraband and dismissed from the forces.'

'A drug dealer?'

'Cannabis. A few pills. Nothing serious.'

'Perfect.' I smile then add, 'Awareness is everything. As long as you are alert to the underlying malignancy that lives here, we'll be okay.'

'You make it sound very dramatic.'

'I am totally serious.' I fix her with what I hope is a stern look tinged with genuine horror. She must fully comprehend the dangers that lie ahead.

VIII

When, a few days later, the landing gears touch the runway at the small strip at Esen airport in the Turkish Republic of Northern Cyprus, I feel my stomach pitch. My skin crawls as I unbuckle the seatbelt. I sense that desolation – that sinking feeling of hope receding as I take in the scrubby brown panorama of this little half-island with its unending poignant despair.

Was it the teeth of fate pulling me back here for further punishment? I have had nothing to do with the machinations that led me to this place again and yet I have not resisted the journey and feel a fierce mortal enemy raise its smug head again. Doubt. I doubt my own courage to face the past. What I had merely hinted at to S in İstanbul is at the forefront of my mind, having poked its ugly head out of the sublimated depths of my consciousness. I look at S and she smiles at me with reassurance, as if she has it all in hand and knows what I am going through, with a remedy at the ready. I hope that she isn't feeling sorry for me in any way and if she is then I have to nip that in the bud so I say, 'Are you okay?' to deflect attention away from what my body language might be divulging.

'Fine,' she says. 'You?'

'Great to be here,' I say wistfully, as if rocked by an agreeable nostalgia, but an involuntary eye roll betrays me. With her head drawn back and a tired smirk on her face, I can tell that she doesn't believe me but is happy not to pursue the point.

Passport control take their time letting her in even though she possesses the erstwhile coloniser's own British passport. All I need is my Turkish identity card because this entry point is officially Turkish territory. What S doesn't know is that this place with its casinos, brothels and delightful beaches is the site of my first and wholly uninvited sexual tryst. It had been an innocent young man who had landed in the mid-nineties with his parents and a damaged non-virgin who took off a fortnight later after an otherwise perfectly ordinary family holiday in the coastal town of Girne where once Muslims and Christians lived side by side. Several drunk soldiers enjoying a weekend break from a British army base on its own precious sovereign soil nearby – still in existence today – had lumbered into my teenaged life.

In retrospect, I feel I was a sort of walking monument back then to the pain and humiliation of the conquered, a radical living art piece divested of choice and forced to carry the psychological burden of the colonised during the process of inculcation that they excelled at – I know because I am a product of it; assimilated as I was into the English culture I grew up in despite Mother's best efforts to keep my Turkish heritage intact. However, this concept of representing something greater than myself did not reveal itself to my adolescent mind. At the time,

I simply was not cognisant of the noble notion of suffering as art and did not deal particularly imaginatively with being violated on a warm moonlit beach where I was collecting items from the ground for a school project. In fact, I retreated into cliché and kept the knowledge of what happened to myself – a dirty shameful secret. Later, I began to experience this trapped trauma as a fecund well of pain providing the unrefined fuel that fed my first stumbling forays into making art. It took me years of abjection and failure to turn my spluttering greasy oil lamp into the sharp lantern of a lighthouse, sweeping across torrid seas of self-doubt to lead me faithfully home through many a tempest.

I had left the clinking cutlery and comforting murmurs of dinner on the hotel restaurant's veranda to pop down to the sand, seeing how bright the moon was that night. I could see the shimmer of the waves washing over the sand and I wanted to walk in the surf and hunt for stones and shells. I must have walked a fair bit because when I turned round to look at the hotel it was a small splurge of brightness on the curve of the bay and my hands were full of relics gifted by the eastern Mediterranean. My brain was abuzz with stories about where the beach debris had come from; flotsam from a doomed pirate ship or the ancient fragments of a giant sea turtle. I heard them laughing and joshing amongst themselves to the discordant musical accompaniment of clinking bottles in that English banter-tone I'll never forget – later shuddering with dread recognition at the sound when we moved to London and I heard the same masculine repartee in the first pub I ever went in to. By the time I saw them they had already seen me and begun a friendly conversation rendered menacing by the fact that they were mostly in silhouette – I counted three muscular bodies – whereas I was exposed in the moonlight from behind them. I became trepidatious when they wouldn't stop asking me to come over and hang out with them where they sat on a rocky outcrop beyond the sand. One of them let out a mighty groan of pleasure as he urinated and another, blond hairs standing out on his thick arms, came up to me swiftly as he talked – about what I do not recall – and grabbed me by the neck as if trying to give me an amiable hug but I could see the intent in his eyes and the set of his jaw. So I ran as hard as I could. They got me and dragged me back to the rocks. It wasn't a unanimous decision and I recall a dissenting voice and a few disgusted remarks of incredulity. The owner of that dissent stalked off. But there was the core pair of alcohol-soaked individuals who formed a quorum, briefly debated and then passed the motion. It was all very democratic.

But I digress. In the taxi from the airport to the capital Lefkoşa (Nicosia if you must) we zoom along empty highways with casinos lined along and set back from the main route through the seemingly deserted scrubby landscape, sitting squat at the end of long driveways, painted black with their dead neon signs, quietly awaiting nightfall and the arrival of gamblers from Israel whose flights are so short that as soon as the aeroplane has stopped climbing it begins to descend. A kind of twilight lawlessness suffuses the humid air. The city is steeped in melancholia. The natives schlep along, the tourists seem tense and people cross back and forth via a military buffer zone to visit the sites of the Christian south or Muslim north. There have been massacres here, I reflect. Then I banish these tragic sagas from my mind and concentrate on the task at hand. S and I settle into the same hotel with adjoining rooms. There is a casino next door attached to the main hotel but it is the offseason and the place is not crawling with the usual debauched clientele.

In the evening over a dinner of the island's famous *köfte*, more potato than meat, I drink one too many glasses of *rakı* and tell S about my teenaged run-in with the British soldiers. She is, rightly, mortified but I rebuff her overtures to console me and go to bed in a state of regret, having got her to swear to never bring up the topic again.

*

Doctor Shipley is an older man with tanned skin and thick white eyebrows. He reminds me of some colonial from a Graham Greene novel. He exudes confidence, bonhomie and, particularly crucial for a surgeon, indifference. As he gives me a tour of his clinic's modern facilities, we speak.

'Your assistant was quite coy about why you wanted this done but I am given to understand that this is something akin to an art project?'

'Yes, doctor, I am an artist,' I reply.

'How fascinating.'

'You will naturally be invited to the event in due course. I would be delighted if you could make it.'

'Wonderful. Where will it be?'

'London.'

'Well, er, I would love to attend if I can get away.'

'It will be quite a show, I guarantee it,' I say.

'Tell me, I am curious to know how the, erm, art project will make use of your kidney?'

I tell him. He barely acknowledges the information and continues to smile politely.

'Well, well. That is fascinating,' he says. 'We'll get you X-rayed after we have completed the tour to make sure you've got two kidneys. I don't want to go digging around in there without being sure. It's a small chance but you never know. Some people are born with a solitary kidney and never know it.'

My heart sinks at the possibility that all my hard work may be ruined by a genetic defect.

*

We wait apprehensively with S in his office. When he comes in with the film he is happy that I definitively have two kidneys and it is full steam ahead. That night my body processes blood with a full set of kidneys for the last time. We have dinner on the terrace of the hotel. A depressing open buffet that reminds me of the meals we used to have with my parents in Girne with one of their arguments still ringing in my juvenile lugholes. The catastrophe of witnessing two perfectly intelligent human beings who had once professed their undying love to one another, had committed to a lifetime of togetherness and shared the trauma of losing a child but yet found it impossible then not to vociferously hate each other in spite of the presence of their one remaining child – it strikes me now – is a scar wrought so deep that I fear my whole being has been crushed beyond repair. The idea of affection and warmth turning so swiftly into cold, hard contempt must have broken my heart and I carry that lump in my chest today. Irrespective of my desires, I cannot see myself enjoying the sort of companionship that others seem to delve in and out of – salmon in a gushing river, striving upstream no matter what.

*

Under a general anaesthetic I am relieved of my left kidney in under three hours – a record, I am told by the nurses – and when I awake in the hospital bed, encurtained for privacy, S is cradling a re-enforced Styrofoam box labelled 'Human Organ. For Transplant.' That's when I break down. S gently places the box on a table and sits beside me. She holds my hand tenderly as my body is convulsed by reverberating sobs and hot tears run freely down my cheeks. I try to say something along the lines of 'I'm being silly, please forgive me' but instead I produce a string of incomprehensible moans, snivels and lip-sucking whimpers. She tells me I have to rest and after a while my crying abates, leaving me exhausted, and I fall asleep like a baby.

By the time I awake again it is dark outside. S is still there, her shoes off and her legs dangling over the edge of the armchair she has been sleeping in, judging by her puffy face. I try to slide up in the bed and let out a gasp of horror as I experience my freshly sutured wound splitting. S jumps to her feet to call for the nurse who ascertains that it was my imagination. The wound is intact. S stacks the pillows up behind me and, upon my asking, tells me that it is three in the morning. I tell her to go to her room to sleep properly. She takes this as a kindness but I am really thinking about her being *compos mentis* the next day as our work is only just beginning. She brushes some sweat-matted hair from my brow and brings me a cup of water. She tells me that Doctor Shipley will visit me in the morning and that everything has gone well.

'I remember crying,' I say and glance at where the box had been.

'I put it back in cold storage. I wanted you to see it when you woke up' – said with genuine contrition – 'it was stupid of me. I don't know why I did it.'

'Don't be silly. If I could have got up then and left with the box we'd both be on our way but...'

'The anaesthetic knocked you out pretty good.'

'That's why I got emotional. Because of the drugs,' I say too quickly. 'Like you said, you know, it has strange effects on people.' She nods and smiles. I think she knows I am lying.

'You know how my brother died, don't you?' I say after a pause and her eyes tell me to go on. 'I was seven at the time. He'd been on dialysis for three years waiting for a suitable donor. He had a very rare blood type and none of us were a match. That was the first time I cried for him, after all these years. I suppose the sight of the box... it reminded me of how once we had such high hopes. It seemed so unlikely that he would die. It never crossed my mind that in this day and age a child could die from kidney failure. But he did. I suppose I felt guilty that it wasn't me. We were fraternal twins; two different eggs, two different sperm. That's why our blood types didn't match.'

'I'm so sorry.'

'I never grieved for him, you see. And I don't know why,' I manage to say before blubbering again. Every time I open my mouth for any length of time there is a release of endorphins.

Talking is getting me high. Either that or the crying is pumping out toxins accumulated over decades of buried guilt. S holds me as I cry myself out, shivering and shaking in her arms like a grateful puppy. Once it is over I feel something bloom inside me – a warm draught of air filling my chest, melting the hardness, with something approaching hope; a very dangerous emotion. The bread of the poor, as we Turks say. I know that the days ahead are going to see me attempt my greatest work of art. I had to be sure that I believed this whole-heartedly otherwise the enterprise would fail. I have to believe that it is the anaesthetic that has played havoc with my emotions and not some other deep-seated reason that I have been avoiding. These emotions have to be strangled at birth or my work will suffer. What is my life worth if my work, what I produce, has no value? This realisation hits me like a bucket of iced water and I calmly extricate myself from S's arms – her warmth goes with them and I feel more myself again. She smiles at me but I avoid her gaze. I can't be tricked into reciprocating in this moment of sharing. It is too intimate, a potential emotional drain that I cannot afford, and so I push the feelings away as a wise man turns down one final drink before the long journey home.

*

A few days later, on the flight back to London via İstanbul, I slowly come to the horrifying conclusion that I am in love with S... Sam... Samantha. Clearly, a part of me must have died on the operating table and I no longer care about documenta, accolades or what the bastard critics and collectors think. It is a scary feeling. The ambition that has led me through thick and thin falls away to reveal... me. My hitherto robust ego is exposed and in real danger of dissolving away. If I do not keep my wits about me and suppress the emotional attachment forming like scar tissue round my heart for this young woman, then my life's work will be lost! She sits there next to me oblivious to the turmoil she has caused. I begin to resent her for putting me in this position and it takes all of my strength and courage to deny myself the indulgent pleasure of fantasising about loving her – holding her naked in my arms or waking up next to her in bed on some fuzzy Sunday morning to gaze and reap the rewards of letting go of selfhood to combine with her in a miasma of oxytocin and mutual smugness. She knows by now, surely, that my feelings for her have changed. She must be aware that my attitude towards her has softened and I am quite certain that my looks and body language in her presence are betraying me. Here, then, is an opportunity for us to be together but she has to know that the project comes first. This isn't about sex – or is it? Even though I would be breaking my cardinal rule not to sleep with the help I am willing to do it so as to puncture the tension and get on with our work. These unchecked urges are potentially lethal to my ability to be productive. I wonder if we might adjourn to the toilets for a quick one but my wound is not yet fully healed. It would not be practical to attempt anything too athletic at present. It will have to wait for a more opportune time and so I shall continue stoically to ignore my emotions.

By the time we touch down in İstanbul I have barely spoken to her and I remain aloof throughout the three-hour stopover at the airport where I assiduously erase all references to my calling her Samantha and she becomes S once again. I imagine she has confirmed in her own mind by now that my nervous breakdown in Cyprus was not a gateway to a relationship as she had perhaps expected, but a discrete lapse brought about by the effects of anaesthesia. The showing itself – the culmination of all of this humdrum human activity, these emotional shenanigans and whatnot – is next on our schedule and I can't wait to board the plane back to Blighty. It is going to carry me, my faithful condor, into the fuggy yet exhilarating atmosphere of London, a London – my first true crush – that I am going to set alight with brilliance and controversy. I smile to myself as these thoughts course through my mind and S sees it and smiles back. The poor innocent fool.

IX

Mother was of course kept abreast of developments and had organised a selection of potential spaces for me to view. The date is set and invitations are being sent out to the custodians of the art world, the collectors, critics and curators (the venue to be revealed only at the very last moment). There soon follows a ripple of excitement in the press and a lively debate on the social networks about what I am going to do, with many proclaiming that contemporary British art is about to eat itself. Others remain more sanguine and reserve their comments pending the conclusion of the event. Some apparently believe it to be an elaborate ruse to hoax my way to fame. Despite the provocations I keep my own counsel and refuse to make any forays into the media sphere, staying scrupulously incommunicado. I have to seal myself off from the blather to keep fresh and untainted, as an expensive cut of meat has to be sealed over blistering heat in order to keep in the precious juices.

Out of the several options Mother presents me with, I settle on the refectory of an abandoned school soon to be turned into luxury apartments on the salubrious riverside in Battersea, south London. The concept of transformation is key and the setting I have chosen is able to add resonance to that. S beavers away as usual in the run-up to the showing and a select list of confirmed invitees is coming together. Key figures in art such as the gallery owners, art historians, journalists and, of course, several collectors are to attend, plus our partner-in-crime, Doctor Shipley. My kidney is being kept on ice in a medical-grade deep-freeze unit at an undisclosed location. This is more for show, really, and I think that it might smack of overkill but there it is. It could just as easily be stored in some bog-standard freezer unit like any other piece of meat. I shudder at the sound of the word 'meat'. It makes me feel as if a strip of my flesh is being carved out from my torso with a sharp sculptor's tool; chunks of blood-gorged body mass scooped out to expose the membrane of pink epidermis over a layer of soft white fat then the muscle, still warm, red raw and alive. I have been having bad dreams most nights about it as I am not allowed to drink myself to sleep with alcohol, in order not to overtax my now solitary kidney. The nocturnal visions are of a hallucinogenic quality that I have not experienced since childhood; vibrant pulsing colours, three-dimensional wraparound fantasy landscapes of purple hills, blood-red skies and fluorescent neon faces – a psychedelic light show. My off-line brain, undampened by booze, simply goes into overdrive and my overstimulated visual cortex becomes hysterical with outbreaks of vivid and detailed images of the nephrectomy. When I wake up I fancy that I must have had an out-of-body experience during the operation and these are actual memories! Memories of how my skin was sliced open with a razor-sharp scalpel and how the kidney was carefully detached from the ureters, veins and arteries (which are tied up at the end, neatly, like ribbons) before the surgeon scoops it out lovingly with a white latex-gloved hand, as if delivering a tiny premature baby.

I throw up several times in the mornings during the run-up to the event and begin to eat less and less, feeling nauseous at the mere mention of food. My internal organs are jostling in panic to evade a similar fate to that which has befallen their comrade, the kidney (left side), and they are moving about, vibrating and flexing in fear, making my insides churn, stretching the elastic of my gut and snapping it back like a rubber band – my bowels twist and squirm – how could I eat, for God's sake?

S is worried that I will be too weak to go ahead with the showing but I tell her that I am simply expurgating my internal demons. That's how it feels to me – as if I have wrested back sovereignty of myself from the invading forces of human mediocrity that have held me back for so many years. I have transcended the state of being a mere artisan and have become art itself, no less. The sensation of alternating phases of terror and elation, as the showing approaches, is hard to describe. One moment I feel as if I am doing something near suicidal, base and immoral – I fear God's wrath in my nominally atheist heart – but the next moment I am floating above the trivial trappings of humanity as a demiurge, split from the mundane reality of everyday earthbound life. A psychiatrist might propose that I am in fact having a psychotic episode; however,

I am with the Scientologists when it comes to their dubious trade built on peddling pills for Big Pharma. Moreover, creatives make strange and unsettling connections – creativity sits on the cusp of mental unwellness after all – that at first sight may seem like the ranting of lunatics until that sweet epochal moment when they become magically digestible to the masses and, upon reflection, most right-thinking people end up agreeing with the lunatic and he is transformed in their eyes to become a genius. These musings are, as the fateful day fast approaches, vented audibly for all to hear and Mother weighs in to calm me in conjunction with S's gentle prodding to not lose sight of the challenging practicalities ahead. Mother presses upon me some beta-blockers from her personal supply, which I grudgingly accept, and S encourages me to take up physical exercise to agitate my appetite as I have not eaten a meal in days. I reject S's offers of cooking or ordering hot food for me. I also refuse to leave the apartment or talk to anyone except for her and Mother. S weeps several times as she tells me that I am killing myself but I have never felt more alive! A glance in the mirror does show an emaciated frame and sunken features but that is okay, for how am I to pig out when the act of eating has become, for me, something that eclipses the simple process of satiating that most basic animalistic instinct, hunger? Hunger is no longer a physical warning signal to fill my stomach. Why should I denigrate the piece by using my mouth, throat, stomach and intestines to simply acquire fuel to live? Eating has become a vulgarity.

The day of the showing, before I know it, is upon me. Father heard about it eventually and is trying to contact me on a daily basis to talk me out of it. He is threatening to have me committed if I do not end my 'hunger strike', as he calls it. He finally, childishly, resorts to the argument that I am denigrating my brother's memory with this stunt. I tell Mother. She says, quite authoritatively, that the two things are not connected and that Father is simply jealous of my pursuing extraordinary life goals that he was too cowardly to contemplate for himself. What does he want me to do at this stage, anyway? I am not about to have the kidney put back after all. The rate of natural cell death means that any organ removed and not transplanted within hours is no good to anyone. I tell him this and other things, almost begging for his approval (in my debilitated state I cannot keep my emotions in check as I normally would have done), but he is determined to withhold his support. So be it.

*

It is going to be a noiselessly solemn affair. The old school refectory is dimly lit by low-wattage freestanding lights, normally to be found on building sites, that throw shadows hither and thither. The distant hum of a diesel generator in an adjoining room adds to the industrial effect. Two security guards are stationed by the door dressed in black and have been hired for their square jaws and height more than their expertise in the field of security. An official-looking letter signed by Doctor Shipley is hanging by the entrance for inspection, framed with platinum in order to draw the eye. It confirms that he has removed my left kidney. I say nothing when I enter the room and the whispering stops. Instructions regarding conduct during the showing have been passed around and indeed stipulated in the invitations. I am not nervous and the thought that someone might sabotage the showing has not entered my mind but there is an interlocutor who has somehow secreted themselves into the hand-picked crowd. She has a placard that screams the slogan 'Meat is murder'. She is obviously being ironic and in due course, to no one's surprise, turns out to be a first-year student at the Chelsea School of Art. During the kerfuffle – as the security men amateurishly grapple with her – my eyes adjust to the gloom and I see that Celine is here, lingering by the exit door – my father's spy. I put him and her and everybody else out of my mind as the clownish security team finally manage to eject the art student – at one point I can hear one of them urgently begging her to comply after much fruitless faux-intimidation – and the desired reverent hush returns to the grubby refectory. I light a propane stove, unfold a newspaper that holds the thawed-out kidney (noting with some disappointment that it is the sports pages of a daily free rag). My exilic kidney is about the size of a child's fist and all at once paints for me a poignant portrait of homesickness and mortality (I must remember to use that phrase in future interviews). I try not to look at it as I melt some imported Turkish butter, sourced from a village on the Aegean coast, in a seasoned cast-iron frying pan. It is too dark for me to clearly make out most of the faces in the shadows but there are several people holding their chins, which I am happy to see. Heads are thoughtfully angled to one side and only the hoarse whisper of the propane burning can be heard. The fat starts to sizzle and I slide the kidney off the newspaper and into the pan where it begins to cook. My kidney. It is absurd that this lump of now steaming and browning flesh was once an integral part of my own body. It had unfailingly and diligently filtered my blood and sent the waste to my bladder for almost four decades along with its partner and now I had ripped this one away and cast it into the fire and for what? It is of course far too late to back out now, even though I feel a complete fool – exposing myself to ridicule, pity and judgement. The next moment this negative emotion flips as a magnetic field does and I feel purified by my forthcoming potential humiliation and an emotion develops within me that is closer to... otherworldliness. That gorgeous sense of transcendence, powerful enough to sear itself into my consciousness like a bolt of lightning is, alas, also just as fleeting. The field flips again and with a deeply sad clarity I can see that Mother is wrong and Father is right. Soon I will be revealed and reviled for the tasteless monster that I am. With that devastating thought, I start crying. I am whimpering. My chin is quivering and tears roll down my cheeks. I can taste their salt. I moan, suppressing the utter shame of my failure – I am reminded horribly of a school play when I was alone in the spotlight, primed to deliver a simple few lines of dialogue and my mind had gone blank. The theatre audience, including my parents, was silent in an agonising state of embarrassed empathy.

I glance up, my vision clouded by my pathetic tears. Is that Joseph standing there amongst the crowd? His foppish presence vexes me only for a moment as I fleetingly wonder who may have invited him. Mother is near one of the lamps as if to make sure I can see her features and she looks worried – this is not part of the act we had rehearsed. Or maybe it is a look of deep concentration? A muted ripple goes through the crowd – a Mexican wave of concern – but these people are as invested in this performance as I am and none dare to interrupt the sanctified process or intervene, as if held back by centuries of theatrical tradition – the fourth wall breaks but one way. Deep down inside me I want someone to stop me by heckling, rugby tackling me to the dusty floor or turning all the lights on; destroying the carefully constructed atmosphere and jolting me back to my senses. My kidney sizzles. No one makes a move. I let the tears dry on my face, refusing to wipe the evidence of my frailty away.

The dank environment, the propane and the absence of my father now ignite a fresh recollection. The many camping trips I had conducted in our back garden alone. Only Mother had made the slightest effort to entertain my childish fantasy, through a haze of alcohol, by providing sound effects as I huddled in my homemade tipi. She howled like a wolf and scratched the outside the tent as I giggled within, gripped by an ecstatic terror. Now here I am, a grown man trying to impress a crowd of strangers, and the veil of hitherto unchallenged delusion that allowed me to get this far is whipped away like a curtain inside my mind and I stand there feeling totally naked. I wish pitiably that I was that child in the tent again and that everything was make-believe. A stupid game that I was losing, that I could just call off to lick my wounds in peace. But no, this is my actual life and I am teetering on the precipice of a giant fall into the unknown where I may actually end up losing my mind.

By the time I snap back to reality, my kidney has shrunk to about half its original size and a strong odour of urine is wafting through the air, a sharp smack to my olfactory system. I see that the kidney is cooked and it is time to proceed to the next step. I thought that I would flinch as I push a fork into the kidney but I feel nothing. This is a lump of meat and it does not have a phantom connection to my body any longer, as I had subconsciously feared. This yields some relief from the dismal trajectory of my emotions up to this very moment and I set the kidney down on a plate with some confidence that I am going to get this done without throwing up. Somebody out there in the darkness leaves quickly, his or her heels clicking on the bare concrete floor. It might be Celine, I can't be sure. A muffled female cry infiltrates the space as the person who has left reveals their discomfort at what is happening to an unknown second party outside. A few others are murmuring now – probably affronted as I am by the squeamish interruption – or perhaps commenting on the smell or my crying or both. I see S's lithe silhouette dart outside to deal with the situation as I return my gaze to what's in front of me.

There it is sitting on the white ceramic school-dinner type plate, some dark juice oozing out of it. I sit down at the table after extinguishing the stove. The stillness is dead air all around, pushing down on me, squashing my skull from all sides. I feel the pressure in my sinus and my temple begins to throb; a vein is pulsing up there and pain is building up at the back of my neck. I am tensing up – a fresh cadaver entering rigor mortis. My stomach has been empty since yesterday and I had an enema an hour before I began the showing to allow for a clearer thoroughfare for this kidney which is to be the only matter to pass into my body to be digested and thence excreted in due course for the completion of the work. All of that careful physical preparation had been done without enough consideration for psychological preparedness, I realise with a sinking feeling. Yes, I have been stupid in allowing multiple errors to be committed on the precipitous road to the here and now. I am entering some sort of cerebral circle of anguish, regret and sheer terror. Annoyingly, time chooses this insufferable instant of doubt to crawl to a dragging halt – a perpetual moment of presentness – the air is sucked out of my lungs and a rigid sphincter of pain encircles my gullet. Just like the time I was about to give my best man's speech at a gay Jewish wedding in Manhattan. At least then I had been drunk and coked up. Now it is just me.

I pick up the stainless-steel dinner knife and ask myself why the blade isn't serrated. Another unforgivable oversight. I suppose that the unexamined and horribly simplistic theme emerging is something to do with school dinners, given our location, and this has overshadowed the practical considerations of eating the kidney with the blunt tool I hold in my hand, lacquered in sweat. I push this nonsense aside as best I can and hold down the piece of dark brown kidney (the urine smell has dissipated by now) with the fork and cut into it swiftly. I feel a collective gut-clench gripping the crowd as they realise that I am going to do it after all. I take a mouthful and gag. It is very chewy and I suspect a little undercooked as cold juices run out of it and I fight the urge to spit it out. That would be a complete disaster. My jaw works and grinds down the piece of rubbery offal for what seems to be an age. I close my eyes and try not to contemplate the fact that I am eating one of my own internal organs. However, the lizard brainstem rebels against my conscious efforts to quash the unsavoury actuality of what I am doing and insists on firing nerves in my abdomen that made me feel as if tiny little teeth are inside my body cavity, where my left kidney had been, gnawing out my insides, hungry for my liver, intestines and spleen. Minute pulses of repulsion tighten my belly muscles and the imagined sensation of being operated on without anaesthetic takes me over. As it had done in my dream memories – the cutting, the tugging at my gaping lesion, Doctor Shipley's latex fingers sliding in, my shiny trembling organ trimmed with scissors, connective tissue snipped, blood vessels severed, freeing the kidney from the warmth where it had been living quite obliviously with its twin for as long as it had ever known. Actual memories of my dead twin assault me as I continue to cut, fork and chew then swallow several more mouthfuls – the kidney now quite cold. A mighty throb of revulsion, starting at the base of my pelvic bone, shoots up through my torso like hydraulic fluid – I fight valiantly to stop my stomach from going into involuntary spasms. My unsophisticated primeval mini-brain, a crude limpet lodged at the top of my spine, is detecting distress in the prehistoric depths of my psyche that forbids cannibalism and, clearly, I have not taken proper precautions to deal with that either, I chide myself mercilessly. This is after all virgin territory for my body, the animal parts of it, the bits that can't appreciate 'art' or recognise 'self-awareness' or indeed accept the oft-cited supremacy of the civilised mind over it. Its most unsophisticated, visceral recourse was the one that it preferred to enact now, betraying my ego in favour of the id.

Expulsion.

The human body can and usually does vomit more often than it actually needs to; when it is car sick, seasick, hung-over, lightly poisoned, dizzy, afraid, shocked, surprised, repulsed, suffering from vertigo, has had too much exercise and a host of other piffling reasons. This is because the brain makes mistakes. The only good reason to generate vomitus is if you have ingested a life-threatening poison. My kidney does not qualify as a toxin and I refuse to yield to the dumb sub-brain that, at this precise moment in time, is bent on making me expel the contents of my stomach. Having had no real practice in controlling my retching responses, I hope for the best and recall that most of the impetus to puke is agitated by the epiglottis – that funny dangling pink punching bag hanging in the throat at the root of the tongue and just ahead of the tonsils. Having thus visualised the area inside my neck where the gag reflex resides, I concentrate on my breathing and relax. This works a treat. After this necessary pause, I note with satisfaction that the room is transfixed by me and so I continue to eat. Feet shuffle in the room as bodies shift from tense absorption to anticipation of closure – only a few more bites remain. My eyes have fully adjusted to the lighting conditions and I can see and recognise individual faces. There is Mother with that inscrutable expression, clearly sensing my internal battle but not giving it away to the assembled eyes, and S is next to her biting her lip, less able to hide her distress. I swallow another rough morsel, starting to feel deflated by the amount there is yet to consume, and very nearly heave as the pulped cold meat slips down my throat like a slug. Stomachs tend to be their own masters and I am still nervous that it will reject its fellow flesh if I lose concentration even though I have avoided the immediate peril of spewing thus far.

If my body behaves itself and my gastrointestinal processes advance satisfactorily then I will have no further jurisdiction over what it does next, I muse. The shitting part is going to be a blessed autonomous ride in a self-driving car compared to this part of the journey. All I'll have to do is wait it out like some smuggler detained at border control. My mood lightening considerably, I pause and sip water from a tumbler – vexed for some reason by the school-dinner trope it implies – in as casual a manner as I can. I would have liked, upon reflection, a lovely glass of *şalgam* to wash the lingering metallic aftertaste away. Oh well, I may have some later if I can track any down to aid my digestion. The oppressive dusky ambiance is beginning to suffocate me. By the number of people walking out, I judge that I am not alone in my suffering. I consume the remainder of my congealing kidney in a determined rhythm of slicing and grim mastication. After what feels an indecently long time for a human being to be observed by a rapt audience performing auto-cannibalism, I am all of a sudden chewing the last of it. I stand up too quickly and have to take a moment to steady my dizziness. It is over; my plate empty but for a puddle of brownish liquid. I feel a giddy sense of complete mastery as I swallow the final mouthful and amble out of the room in a dignified posture of poise; not rushing it as if I am running away from the restaurant table without paying the bill.

As I step out into the chilled night air with its back-alley smells of uncollected garbage, I am close to fainting – the blood abandons my skull and rushes to my midriff where it is most needed. A car with a driver is waiting. I slip into the back seat – my sensitivity to smell overwhelmed by the brand-new leather upholstery – and the blood flow returns to my head with a heavy dose of adrenaline. My heart pounds and my ears strain for any perceptible reaction from inside the building I just vacated but all I can hear is a triumphant pulsing in my ears. I take a deep breath and belch. The thoroughly briefed driver neither comments nor flinches when I let loose another, louder, burp that shakes my eyeballs. I must have pushed down a considerable amount of air into my stomach as I was eating. The car pulls away with a luxuriant bass note from the exhaust and a few minutes into my silent journey alongside the Thames, past the decommissioned Battersea Power Station, an unpleasant thought constructs itself like that iconic Art Deco brick megalith in perpetual refurbishment. Was my po-faced egress just now not exactly the sort of thing a cheap street magician would have done?

*

There had been a strict 'no cameras' rule – having abandoned the crass notion of selling any recordings of the work that would have cheapened the impact of the completed artefact – and the happening was not chronicled visually. It is part of the mystique that those who were present are witnesses who can only recount what they saw, analogous to a great theatre production written into history as text – ineffable and impossible to recreate. The work of art is to be embodied wordlessly in the final concept itself, too abstract to communicate adequately in any other way. My gold-encased excreta.

By 2am I am terrifically hungry and yet it takes no effort to not eat; I welcome and cherish the growling of my angry innards. It feels wonderful to disallow my primeval instincts. I am astonished by how the body becomes so bent on making you eat. You feel nausea and pain at the abstinence; it feels as if your body is cleaving from your mind and becoming a separate entity accusingly indicating that you are trying to murder it.

Conception

Denying my base needs, mine makes me imagine that I have conquered the inherently vulgar nature of the perpetually feeding organism. Shovelling nutritional matter into a hole in one's face is the ultimate failing of the humanoid anatomy. We do the most sanctified thing possible via that aperture; we communicate with each other through it and use the wonders of language with it and, incongruously, we also use it for the biological imperative of nourishment, as crucial to life as shitting, sweating or ejaculation. I would prefer a discrete (and discreet) orifice for ingesting food. Perhaps it is the next stage in our human evolution when we transcend the requirement for eating through our mouths since, after all, the close proximity of the human oesophagus and voice box that allows us to be able to speak is also the number one reason why many humans choke to death in their prime. Let the fish and our other vertebrate cousins keep their millennia-old design that has served them so well in the oceans and wilderness whilst we migrate our eating apparatus away from our lips to another location on the body – perhaps employing something similar to the jawless opening of a hag fish or lamprey. It may be repulsive to imagine a new gaping orifice situated, say, on the torso nearest the stomach; however, it wouldn't be long before we all got used to it. Eating would become a simple utilitarian activity of feeding nutrients into our bodies, the hole equipped with taste buds to make sure we know what we are ingesting and a new era of gastronomy would no doubt ensue – as well as new forms of dinnertime conversation with our mouths freed up to adapt and improve its function as an orifice for ever more sophisticated forms of communication.

I am, of course, joking.

*

By morning, after a sleepless night peppered with maddening and hideous flashbacks to the evening before, every cell in my body screams for sustenance. My body is building up its resolve to betray me but it is impossible for me to satisfy its cravings. However, when I manage to divert my attention away from my rumbling insides, my mind finds a peaceful blankness to settle on after the exertions of the previous day. I resist the urge to pop a beta-blocker in case it interferes with my bowels. The work is so very near completion but I fear my intestines will rebel against me and instead of the smooth voluminous stool I desire I will be presented with a diarrhoeic mess.

I fall asleep watching television that night and all the next morning the tension mounts as my bowels refuse to move. The telephone rings seconds after the time period I had insisted I should be left in complete solitude. It is Mother.

'No, nothing yet, Mother. I prefer to wait a little longer before resorting to anything else,' I intone as she suggests the use of a laxative. 'I want the end product to be unadulterated.'

Mother thinks I am being too much of a perfectionist and wrings an assurance out of me that should the stool not be forthcoming by day's end I will make further arrangements to hurry it along. Otherwise, she contends, the bolus might compact and refuse to move at all. I tell her that I will not countenance the risk of constipation and hang up. Here I am, the expectant man-mother. I have consumed my own kidney in an unholy act of metaphorical insemination and now my body is converting those pulverised and digested cells into a new form, which I can cherish and swaddle in gold for posterity. I feel archetypal – the modern-day child of Aphrodite and Hermes. There are some trans people out there who can speak with much more authenticity on the topic, I am sure, and although I am rarely shy about my ability to empathise and inhabit anybody's psyche whatever their gender, sexuality, age or race – currently – I will not go there. Future commentators will no doubt make similar allusions once the work is put on display.

Then I remember fortuitously that tobacco carries something of a purgative property and so I sniff a cigarette to induce my gut to start up and then I stare with longing at the vintage glazed stoneware chamber pot sitting invitingly in my bedroom.

And lo, there is movement.

X

Tuscan artisans, as previously described, duly process my excrement. I enjoy watching them meticulously execute my every command in their dreamy workshop, a converted barn housing an assortment of craftspeople beavering away on a variety of art works from artists round the world who have outsourced the actual making of objects to others. The concept is king. The result is in keeping with the original idea, if a little underwhelming in its bulk. It seems that a human kidney once digested yields poorly, volumetrically speaking. It was quite a surreal journey for my excrement from chamber pot to Italy, smuggled in an airtight container packed with ice that was stowed within my luggage in case it caused too many questions going through the x-ray machines. I make some time to visit nearby Florence and imbibe the centuries-old stage of the Renaissance and Medici intrigue.

*

From Tuscany I fly to New York via London, the finished article this time nestled in my hand luggage like an exquisite heirloom, and arrive with a sense of increasing pride at Maximillio Zvwark's gallery. I have to admit to myself that he draws out the child in me – the part of me that craves approval and validation from an authority figure no matter how ersatz or contrived that authority might be. He greets me warmly at the reception desk, some new swan-necked intern craning to see who I am past his sturdy shoulders, and we glide purposefully towards his office.

'I'm very excited,' he says with a half-smile of intrigue.

'It's been quite a journey, Maximillio, let me tell you.' I smile back and hand over an envelope that contains receipts for expenses and an invoice for services rendered by the workshop in Italy. He curls his tanned fingers round the envelope and secretes it in his desk drawer with aplomb.

'The show went well, I hear – only four walk-outs!' He laughs with his baritone that never fails to send a quiver down my spine. The tasteless business of money out of the way, I retrieve from my leather bag the unprepossessing cardboard box that contains the work. It is an underwhelming moment and I want to get it over with as soon as possible so I say, 'Shall we see it *in situ*?' He stands up smartly to lead the way.

He has reserved for me the Ovoid Room that had formerly been the basement storage area and staff toilets. Now starkly white and evenly illuminated, it has lost all vestiges of its old life hosting buckets, mops, crates and boxes. The Gilded Turd, as I fondly called it in private – although Mother did not approve – was to be presented without a label. I hate the sight of earnest art lovers bent over descriptive cards on walls instead of engaging directly with the art itself. They are spoon-fed its meaning, rendering the whole exercise rather empty and dripping with condescension. Maximillio agrees with me and expounds on the power of withholding information. 'Signposting is so twentieth-century,' he says and we both have a good chuckle over it, followed immediately by solemn silence. Any right-thinking person can deduce something from what they see before them, surely, and that very act of trying to interpret the work is the point of conceptual art in the first place. The working title of *My Rectum is Full of Gold* has therefore become too much of a put-on, a prank, and a pun too far. I liked the playfulness of it; however, I am no Grayson Perry. My art is ponderous and thought-provoking and has to have appellations reflecting that essence. Even then, a title for the work suddenly feels a defeatist measure – a superfluous gesture serving no purpose other than to situate the art when it wants to be above temporality. Besides, by refusing to name the piece, I am modestly reflecting on the impossibility of delineating my work and thereby transcending the fruitless quest for meaning that so many billions waste their unutterably dull lives trying to acquire. Unless I am compelled to do so by something as delicious as an epiphany – or as odious as market forces – the piece shall be untitled. And no, there won't be a label attached to the wall next to it that reads 'Untitled'. That sort of thing makes me nauseous.

*

A few days later, some major international collectors as well as the usual riff-raff of painfully chic pretenders attend the private view. I hadn't ever truly doubted that it would be a success but the buzz round the work is truly astounding. It is sitting in the middle of the room on its minimalist podium behind a protective glass box on a small purple velvet cushion (modelled on the casings that hold the Crown Jewels and manufactured by Parisian jewellers Boucheron, founded in 1858 at the height of the Second French Empire). The turd weighs 114 grams, gold and all. The price is going to be in the region of $550,000 although the market will dictate the true monetary value of the work based on the metrics of desire and fashion. If a buyer agrees in writing to bestow the art to a museum upon their death and never let it appear on the secondary market then there will be a hefty discount of course, as art destined to be held by museums increases the artist's value, and hence the price of their future work, immeasurably. 'Museum quality' is the *sine qua non* of everlasting fame and fortune for a living artist. Such are the machinations of the art business. However, I am realistic about my standing and expect only that Maximillio will studiously vet every prospective collector based on his or her seriousness and reputation. Flutes of champagne and macaroons circulate amongst the guests as my gallerist and his assistant work the room. I, as always, remain aloof yet courteous at the approach of individuals who may or may not be purchasing my latest piece. I know that the list of people allowed into the showing is an exclusive one and therefore I am more relaxed than usually, effusive and charmingly generous with my time. Nobody asks me anything about how the piece came about or its beauty or any such ignoble nonsense. Mother and S are here too, of course, but only as guests who are here to enjoy the occasion, relieved of their normal duties by the professionals at Zvwark.

Then an old flame, Alex, creeps up on me and tells me that he is still struggling with his own work. He is part-timing it so he can earn a living as an English teacher, and has come to me many times in our past for guidance and help, alas to no avail. He simply doesn't have what it takes. He didn't have it in London and he doesn't have it in New York, having relocated following an unexpected inheritance. But I am too selfish to advise him to give up because I rather enjoy encouraging him along on his road to failure. I had helped him throughout art school in exchange for sexual favours (I considered us strictly fuck-buddies), which he misinterpreted as the makings of a lifelong romance. Then a minor tiff allowed me a graceful exit from his depressingly low-achieving life. That was years ago, of course. Over fifteen years in fact, yet somehow, through all the alcohol and drugs, he has managed to maintain his slight frame and boyish good looks. I have a quick word with Mother, who is having a great time singing my praises, and I leave with Alex. As I am going, S has a strange look of urgency on her face. She hurries over.

'Meet Alex,' I say. 'You okay?'

'Hi, I'm Samantha—'

'My assistant,' I say and clam up.

'Nice to meet you, Samantha.'

'Alex is an old friend and fellow struggling artist.'

'Well, a bit more struggling than you are, I'd say – I mean, look at all this – it's a great success.'

'Please don't jinx me, Alex,' I laugh then look at S with the expectation that she will make her excuses and let us go. But no.

'What sort of work do you do?' she asks, infuriatingly flirty with Alex. If only she knew.

'Traditional painting, you might say. Strictly representational,' he says a little tipsily as if he is pretending to be drunk for her benefit. I have no idea what this is but it's making me uncomfortable.

'Well, best of luck with it. Can I have a word?' she says to me with a fixed grin.

'Yes, it is mostly luck, isn't it?' I say acidly at her.

'We make our own luck – from the hand that life deals us,' Alex offers and I want to tell him that an inheritance is indeed a massive piece of luck but abandon the thought so as to concentrate on why exactly S is treating me to this intolerable intervention of hers.

'I wonder if I can have a quick word with you, please?' she repeats, already tugging on my arm.

'Excuse us, Alex,' I mumble as I am taken to a quiet corner. 'What is it, for God's sake?'

'I saw that Selim Mehmet lurking outside. He was talking to himself.'

'What? Selim? What the fuck is he doing here?'

'Apparently he tried to get in—'

'I didn't invite him – how the hell did he even know about it?'

'Well, it's been advertised on social media for weeks. Maybe he's cyber-stalking you?'

'Okay,' I say and think. 'Am I supposed to be worried?'

'I don't think so but I thought I should let you know.'

'Can you do it less cryptically next time?'

'I've had too much champagne – I was undecided about telling you, then I thought I better and then...' She goes mute as Mother sidles up.

'What's going on?'

'Nothing, Mother – do you remember that brat, Selim Mehmet?'

'The one who sent that malicious note to Maximillio?'

'Yes. Well – I suspect it was him, though I can't be sure. He's outside.'

'Do you want me to get rid of him?' S jumps in, sensing the alarm she is causing.

'Don't be silly – Mother, it's fine. He's harmless. I'll see you later.' I extricate myself from them and grab Alex on the way out.

Outside, Selim is pacing the sidewalk – as the Americans insist on calling it – with palpable resolve. I freeze as he barrels up to me – I must ask him straight out if that pathetic threat via my gallerist was from him, otherwise how could I feel safe in his presence? – and I can see that, unlike Alex, he has aged badly even though it has only been a matter of months since I last saw him. What has happened to him? He is slumped at the shoulders and his features are slack, reminding me of a shaggy dog banished from his home for eating the sofa cushions. Selim Mehmet, my wannabe protégé, looks wrecked. When he speaks to me he cannot hide the quavering anguish in his voice – something is clearly strangulating him from the inside. He tells me, in Turkish, that he was hoping to catch me as he was in town visiting friends and one of them told him about my private view and – he switches seamlessly to English when he finally clocks Alex's presence – he had to try and see me.

'What a coincidence,' he ends and decides to shake my hand at that point. His once respectably firm grip is trembling, his fingernails are dirty and his frowzy hair appears to be unwashed.

'How are you, Selim?' I say in a neutral tone and introduce him to Alex. I plan to enquire about the note he may or may

not have sent at a more opportune moment. 'Anatolian asshole'
it had said. I wonder if that sort of alliterative racism was in
Selim's blood. People can be quick to anger and blurt out the
most offensive things only to regret them seconds later – hoping
that the words fade to nothing in the ether. But the note had
been constructed with care and I imagined that the author had
spent several minutes finding, cutting out and pasting together
the letters required to spell out 'Anatolian asshole' – it seemed
ridiculous now that someone with a grudge would bother to
resort to such archaic methodologies when social media was
a perfectly easy way to insult somebody. Perhaps the medium
was the message?

'Hi,' Alex says.

'Hello, good to meet you.' Selim's brow twists together. He
shakes his head. 'Look – sorry – I was lying. I took a last-minute
flight from İstanbul when I saw you were going to be here!'

He crumples into himself as he lets out a hacking cough of
a mirthless laugh. God, he has let himself go; a sizeable paunch
is visible beneath his un-ironed shirt, popping out from behind
a cheap blazer.

'Have you been in? I didn't see you—' I begin with faux
merriness.

'Oh no, I couldn't bring myself to...' His face melts into a
confused frown and then he relaxes, remembering that he has
abandoned his mendacious backstory. 'They wouldn't let me
in,' he confesses with an exaggerated shrug caught somewhere
between humiliation and the release of telling the truth. 'And
I didn't want to make a scene. I suppose it sounds really stupid
to come all this way without an invitation. I thought I could
blag my way in – you know – I told them I knew you. I mean, I

know we didn't end things on a great note but...' he trails off, the embarrassment of his situation engulfing him suddenly. It is quite a sight to behold a young, once arrogant, man – who glared at you with contempt when you forced him to face his own delusions head on – so cowed and yet still battling some internal conflict that won't allow him to accept reality and move on. I register the *Schadenfreude* with little pleasure.

'Well, it's nice to see you, Selim. Take care of yourself,' I say and turn to go.

'Hey!' Selim reaches out a supplicatory hand towards us. 'Wait. Let's have a drink?'

'Now?' I ask, knowing in my bones that Selim caught his flight with only the clothes on his back and his passport in his pocket. He is riding on an adrenaline rush tempered by jetlag – of course he meant now. He doesn't have a hotel to go to, no friends to visit. He needs a drink all right. My instinct is to flee the scene but there is a magnetic mystery surrounding Selim's being here and for a few seconds I am rooted to the spot. Alex looks at me, waiting for a decision.

'Sorry, did you have plans?' Selim all but squeaks.

'Actually we were going to get a drink ourselves,' Alex says equably with an expression of searching concern directed at me. I let out a small sigh.

'Oh, right,' Selim says with the false jollity of the unloved and desperately lonely. Alex elbows me surreptitiously and I realise that I can hardly turn him away in the derisible state that he is in.

I want to know more.

At the Roxy Hotel bar, down the road from the gallery, some sort of jazzy ensemble is performing its tiresome versions of world music tropes. The three of us sit huddled together in a dark corner booth in an awkward triangle and drinking rather too much. Alex looks blathered already and I am definitely tipsy whilst Selim seems to be on the verge of an emotional breakdown – his mood vacillating between disaster and delirium. He is talking as if he has a score to settle with me but is being polite in front of the third party.

'You see, Alex, I was barking up the wrong tree. I was never meant to be an artist – I don't have what it takes and I didn't know it until this man told me to my face. He ignored my protests and proved his point by saying that if I was arguing about it then I'd already lost the argument—'

'Did I say that?' I ask, rifling through my memory banks for the exchange he is referring to. Clearly, we all have different memories cherry-picked from reality that are then edited by our brains into a pleasing narrative that fits our own version of the world we live in. His recollections are a collage of rage, disappointment and epiphany by the way he tells it now, as if renouncing his faith in art was a blessing that has allowed him to blossom as a human being. 'So what are you doing with yourself now?' I query, genuinely fascinated to know what has become of my erstwhile protégé's soul.

'Writing a screenplay,' says he and I feel a jolt. It comes from the very marrow of my pelvic bone as I reflect on Mother's words not so long ago on how I gave up on Hollywood too readily.

'Next stop Hollywood!' grins Alex. I'm almost insulted on Selim's behalf.

'That's so dismissive, Alex. Please.' I frown.

'Why are you being so negative?' implores Alex and for a moment I have to rein in my instincts in order to stop the expression of doom that is beginning to pervade Selim's face.

'Selim,' I say, 'I'm being provocative that's all. I'm sure it'll be a fine script. I'm just saying that there's more to film than bloody Los Angeles. I'm so glad that you've found something you are passionate about.'

'I'm obsessed by it,' he says, becoming animated.

'What's it about if you don't mind me asking?' That's Alex, leaning into Selim as if he's in the presence of the next Orson Welles.

'It's about how Turkish people are struggling to exist in an orientalist world, their work dictated to by the gatekeepers of the West.'

'That sounds amazing,' says Alex, teetering on his seat – and on the edge of alcohol poisoning judging by his foggy eyes and slurred speech.

'Sounds like a PhD thesis to me,' I smile, knowing that the implied accusation of academic intent will run counter to Selim's notion that he is still making art.

'So what do you do, Alex?' asks Selim, ignoring my jibe.

'Me, I'm sort of still hanging on to the art thing – it's a long story but in a nutshell, I deal with the notion of identity politics—'

'He's a photographer by trade,' I interject before Alex is allowed to bore us to tears with his fruitless exercises on the periphery of legitimate contemporary artistry. He is a bore when he's stone-cold sober so I shudder to think what he could do in his current state of inebriation.

'You say that as if photography can't be art,' Alex whines.

'Art depends on the dichotomy between the representation of something and the object representing it. That's why I never understood the sudden craze for hyperrealism. Sure, a ten-foot-high baby has some appeal in terms of scale but that's such a cheap trick. Where do you go from there? A giant baby. And so what?

'That's what academic writing is all about too,' bleats Selim. 'You always have to ask yourself, so what?'

'But photographs are made up from millions of tiny pixels of light and colour—'

'Like paintings?' I interrupt sarcastically.

'Well, yes,' Alex burbles in exasperation.

'What did I just say about hyperrealism Alex, for God's sake – I'm sorry to burst your bubble but photography is a pseudo-art that has had its faddish limelight, its fifteen minutes of fame. It's over for you.'

Alex's eyes well up then he cinches them shut and tries to focus. He excuses himself and staggers towards the toilets. With enough alcohol consumed thus far to render the past between Selim and me immaterial, the conversation is flowing more easily and I decide not to bring up the note, for now.

'He looks like a stunned seal, doesn't he?' I confide to Selim.

'I see your taste for humiliation hasn't waned.'

'That? Oh that was nothing. Wait until he gets back.'

'I'm not sure I want to see that.'

'Oh don't be a child, Selim.'

Alex returns presently, looking determined to avoid my gaze. I change the subject by evangelising about one of my favourite entertainments.

'Speed-bitching,' I repeat when Selim fails to take in my freshly coined compound word the first time round. 'You go to a bar on a busy night – such as this – and you find a target, any target will do. The point is not to be picky, the point is to make it as random as a speed-dating night—'

'Oh, I see what you're getting at now,' says Alex, bleary-eyed. Selim nods as if I'm explaining the intricacies of quantum mechanics to him.

'You go up to the target and initiate a conversation and all the while you're looking at them and judging them. It doesn't matter how long the verbal exchange lasts because this is all about speed. Then you start to bitch – about them, at them. If you don't like the way they dress, the colour of their hair or the distance between their eyes, you tell them straight – in one unbroken stream of bitching if you can and then... move on to the next one.'

'That sounds mental,' laughs Selim, somewhat mentally unhinged himself, I'd say.

'Sounds cruel and unusual to me.' Alex frowns with disapproval.

'I once speed-bitched two dozen people at a birthday party and – this is the crux of it – you're just being honest! Isn't that what everyone wants today? Honesty and truth? If they can't handle it then they know, if they have a half brain, that it's their own fucking fault anyway.'

'I don't know, it sounds kind of sadistic to me,' Alex pronounces with an agitated air. 'You didn't do it to me once, did you?'

'I think you'd have remembered, darling,' I tease and then, still staring at him, 'Perhaps we could have a go now?'

Özgür Uyanık

'Me?' he says, visibly anxious.

When I have finished with him, Alex has the fixed, quavering grin of the stunned and humiliated. He is soon gone – staggering away to the exit and, hopefully, out of my life for good. Regarding Selim, who seems rather unperturbed by my treatment of Alex, I swear that he has morphed into another man. This new Selim, who had given up on his unreachable dreams, had a look in his eyes that got me to thinking he might be open to the possibilities of a torrid one-night affair. I dimly recall an earlier limerence for him even though he had now become less attractive – but his gorgeous blue eyes still had a powerful pull on me.

'Perhaps I need a round of your patented speed-bitching too?' he says coyly and I wonder if this is his attempt at flirting.

'You don't have to be so hard on yourself,' I soothe. 'Alex and I are almost strangers – we had our time together but it didn't take me long to realise his limitations. You, however, have surprised me by rejecting failure and finding new avenues to pursue.'

'I used to blame you but then I realised that you did the only thing you could do in the circumstances. I don't have "it" – whatever that "it" is.'

The forthright acceptance of culpability in the collapse of out mentor-mentee relationship takes me aback and for a long, drawn-out moment I feel strangely unhappy. He has depressed me with his ejaculation of measured self-pity mixed with keen awareness of his own limitations. It is such an about-turn from the terse and obstinate personality he had displayed the last time I saw him in London, when I had laid out his weaknesses for him, that the duplicity of his personality angers me. I want to shake him by the shoulders and tell him that he should never cast blame on himself and be true to his nature as a failed artist. I almost wish that he had persevered and proved me wrong. He ought to take stock of that fact and give himself over to politics, business or other activities where his restricted creativity – too meagre to blossom into full artistic success – could be put towards a more productive purpose. A doctorate in creative writing was just another blind alley for him.

Selim had faltered by listening to his heart and not being ruthless. His undoing as an artist began there. I had the ice in my heart to thank for my ability to suppress my emotions so that I can produce good work. I have stamped out my empathy and that is what successful people do; they stifle the impulse to see through someone else's eyes and demand that others see everything from their point of view.

'Your trouble is that you're too nice,' I say and touch the small of his back. He does not recoil.

'Well, I guess you have to be a cunt to make it in your business.'

'Why should you be something you're not?' I tentatively make little circles as I lightly rub his spine and he does not flinch. His body relaxes and I can see from his sleepy eyes that he is close to passing out. I take away his half-drunk glass of vodka and scoot closer to him.

'It's difficult to admit that one is wrong and that one has to change direction in life,' I slur. By this time I too am very drunk and ready to make a complete fool of myself.

*

At my SoHo hotel on Watts Street, where apparently 'Elegance meets the Edgy', things move quickly. When Selim pops to the bathroom I shed my clothing and await him on the bed, stretched out horizontally in what I hope is an attitude of seductive nonchalance. My head feels as if it's on a spinning platter and I try to concentrate my willpower on my middle ear where the sense of balance resides. It is a losing battle and the room swoons endlessly down, fading into blackness; then it is miraculously resurrected from the inky stupor and hangs there for a moment or two – tantalisingly still – before resuming its stomach-churning slide to oblivion once again. I pray for a quick end to the night. Perhaps I will pass out and he'll discover my naked person snoring and leave me to sleep it off. Probably for the best. We could then either pretend it never happened or laugh about it over a pint in London some autumnal afternoon with Manhattan just a degenerate memory. Then again, I am at my most confidently lascivious and so my will to see this act through overcomes any attempt by the alcohol to put me to sleep. When he comes out, he sees me there and after a tiny pause of surprise, begins to laugh.

'That was not the effect I intended,' I say waggishly, camouflaging my shame with humour. He keeps laughing, guffawing and slowly collapsing to the ground. I snatch my clothes from the floor and scamper into the bathroom almost tripping over Selim, who is recovering from his attack of mirth, wiping the tears from his eyes and breathing gulps of air, reminiscent of a dying fish.

In the bathroom, incensed and humiliated, I think I must have blacked out because the last thing I remember is the blurred glint of metal on the glass shelf above the sink and then – as if a supernatural editor has cut out the intervening time from the film reel of my recall – I am straddling Selim on the bedroom carpet with a pair of stubby scissors in my fist and his pig-iron fingers squeezing my neck. I have somehow been provoked into this, I must assume; this is an act of pre-emptive self-defence. I bring the scissors down on to Selim's shoulder, meaning to cause him a short sharp shock so that he will desist from strangling me. One hand releases my throat and goes to my blade-wielding arm, his face screwed up horribly with the effort, but I am stronger and have gravity on my side. I use my whole weight to defeat his attempt to repel the weapon inching down towards his body but we appear to be too evenly matched for a decisive victory. The tips of the scissors approach his face as I direct my efforts towards a more definitive strike. At this point the balance of our bodies abruptly switches in some balletic wrestling move he executes, and I find myself sprawled on the floor having been divested of my instrument of protection, which is now in the grip of my determined opponent who, in a flash of movement, jaw clenched and arm slashing, begins to stab me repeatedly in the stomach and chest; tiny little hammer blows. I become engrossed in the shapes created by his snarling lips and teeth – a flashback to the ancient predation of our forebears that brought us to this moment in time. His eyes appear non-human and emotionless, reminding me of the glassy scowl of an unwavering wild dog caught in a frenzy of bloodlust. Flecks of hot spittle and spots of blood splash on to my eyes and burn them. The slim steel blades of the tiny scissors – I recognise them as the ones I use to snip my nose hairs – pop holes in my skin, slice flesh and fat. Alarmed that my remaining kidney will be harmed, I yell out a warning but there is not enough air in my lungs. My arms flail about in front of me as if belonging to an alien body and he does not stop his work and keeps stabbing and I keep swinging my fists at his face, both of us squirming about like a pair of oily fish locked in primordial combat. The silence in the room pounds my ears as tinnitus does and I can only feel his rhythmic coarse breath on my face as my other senses shut down – my own breathing, despairing and wispy, is distant and weakening with each passing second. We will not be laughing about this over a pint, I say to myself humourlessly. I feel the icky wetness of cooling blood pasting my bare back to the carpet when the thought occurs to me that I am dying. The cleaner will find my corpse glued by my own bodily fluids to the short-pile flooring and she, or he, will stifle a terrible scream and report that there is a body up in here. A body robbed of its humanity, its future, and cast back into the eternal nothingness from whence it came. A brief and clichéd time lapse of my life spools out, from birth to earth... then I start to discern a sickening moan. It is coming from him. He has paused to gather his energies. I ask Selim with an incongruously heartbreaking tone of friendliness to stop stabbing me but he surely can't hear my close-to-death whispering voice; his eyes are ferociously blank, the pupils pinpricks of concentration. This, I gather, is merely an interval. I doubt whether he even knows what he is doing any more. He looks down at me pitilessly and starts slashing again with my scissors, now slick with blood, his arm a cartoon loop of dedicated motion. His efforts are concentrated round the area of my heart and lungs, finding the gaps in my ribcage. Blood gurgles in my throat and my chest cavity takes in air from the scissor holes and one of my lungs begins to collapse.

After a while – time has ceased to exist in any meaningful way and Selim's actions may have been the work of seconds – he stops and flops to the ground beside me, exhausted. I can't move and, as the warm red blood empties out of me, I realise that I have never truly loved anyone except Samantha. It is my one and only regret that I did not allow myself to open up to her as my poor desolate heart squelches its last fistfuls of life force through my failing frame.

*

The celestial maestro has executed another abrupt splice in time and I find myself tumbling to the cold grey pavement off Watts Street. Somehow I am still alive, but barely. I stand weakly below the fire escape steps and I have the ludicrous idea that my last deed on earth ought to be that of the *flâneur* – wistfully floating along these city streets constructed for my amusement, to pass through unnoticed as though a fox (or should that be coyote?) in the night; all-knowing and yet flitting in and out of the liminal dark folds between being human and being animal. Bleeding profusely, I suspect I have little time to enjoy my anonymity. So, using the red brick or white stucco walls of the various buildings I pass in the main streets, bereft of humans at this ungodly hour, I make my way forwards to what I do not know when my nostrils are assailed by a solvent-based gaseous emission. I follow that stimulating smell, wobbling on my feet, and suddenly become aware that I am wearing nothing. I feel the hot blood goop along my thighs and calves as I enter an alleyway and approach a hooded denizen stencilling something on to a grimy wall using a spray can.

'Excuse me,' I burble placidly. The man turns ever so slowly and regards me from the void of his tracksuit's cowl.

'I must look an awful mess I know, but that's okay.' I smile and make a useless gesture that I imagine might infer how calm I am in the face of impending death. I see the half-finished product of this street artist's efforts – a splashy multi-hued protest of sorts whose meaning I cannot be bothered to decipher in this moment.

'Ah so... my nemesis. How strange and disappointing a coincidence,' I say, splattering blood from my lips. He makes no reply. 'May I see your hands?' I enquire. The man puts down his can of spray paint and holds out his hands palm up. I take them and turn them over so I can examine the backs.

'You have the long tapered fingers and broad flat hands of the man featured in the documentary that purports to show you at work,' I say. 'They resemble my father's hands actually.' With a throaty gasp I exclaim, 'Dad?'

The figure chuckles sadly.

'No,' I say. 'How silly. Of course not.' The man gently pulls his hands away from my blood-soaked grip and his head bows in thought. He appears to be considering the bloodstains on his fingers. Then his head looks up again and from the inkiness in the hood I feel that his eyes are piercing me.

'Well?' I say. 'Will you not let a dying man look upon you? Where I'm going I doubt anybody will care who you really are. Only the living are obsessed by the who, what, where, when and why, no? It's like an itch we have to scratch. I want to see your face and know your name so I can indulge that most satisfying of social tics and put a name to the face before I die.'

His head bobs in understanding and in the next moment he peels back his covering and stands before me bathed in yellow sodium light, a monk about to grant a dying man the last rites. To my surprise I am looking at someone all too familiar, so familiar that I burst out laughing but have to stop because of the acute agony in my chest as well as the fact that my lungs are both quickly filling with blood.

'Oh my God,' I say. 'What a joke.' And then I fall down dead.

XI

Well, I thought I was dead. When I see how much blood is soaked into the carpet round my body I think, not unreasonably, that I must be a ghost staring down at my own corpse. Then I feel my toes on the sodden floor and it dawns on me that I am standing up and gawking down at Selim. He and I seem interchangeable in the soft light of sunrise infusing this room with a heavy melancholy. We look very alike – similar height, hair and pallid skin colour, and even our weight is similar, despite Selim's flabbier midriff. We both have stick-thin legs, broadish shoulders and ludicrously slender, almost feminine, necks with only the suggestion of an Adam's apple. It is a striking resemblance made more so by the fact that his face is congealed with caked blood. I must stop this inappropriate rumination at once and do something. I have an indistinct notion of a dream image of me dressed as a monk staring back at me from the shadows of some rat-infested back street. It quickly fades away.

Selim wakes up and, seeing me there, panics and scrambles away. I fall on to the bed in an attempt to reach the bedside table where the hotel phone is. I press '0' for reception. However, it doesn't connect, so I crawl across the sheets to grab at my trousers that had been thrown over the back of an armchair in last night's abortive seduction. I pull out my mobile and speed-dial S and, through bone-dry lips, tell her to send an ambulance. Preferring not to die in this tiny room, I drag myself up and towards the door. In a fog of numbness all I can think about is how surprised I am by the turn of events. It occurs to me that Selim, as a failed artist, is on the brink of success in his new career as a killer. With some satisfaction, I note that my allusions to maniacs earlier have become prophetic. As I pad down the corridor, supported by the walls being imprinted by my blood-glossed hands like prehistoric cave art, I wonder briefly if he has run off to fetch medical assistance – which would mean that he has failed to become the cold-hearted murderer that he obviously wished to be – or, as is more likely, he has made his cowardly escape without finishing the job. Typical of his loser mentality. He would not get away with it so why would he be running? Knowing Selim, he probably wants to get caught and be incarcerated for the rest of his life so he can write a book about it. Possibly this was a convoluted cry for help and he had planned the whole thing out to end with him behind bars where he believes he belongs. Some people can't handle making their own decisions and so orchestrate elaborate ploys to get themselves infantilised – when they feel most secure and content, as does a pet dog – by being put in prison, or exile. Yes, sometimes people choose, albeit subconsciously, to renounce their freedoms.

I make it to the elevator and, with a supreme effort of will and rasping feverishly, I rise up high enough to stab at the call button. A nauseating sound – the emptying of a partially blocked kitchen sink accompanies my every breath as the lift arrives and the doors yawn open. Having wriggled inside on all fours, quite unable to walk any further, I have the hardest time trying to reach the button for the lobby, even though it is tantalisingly close to my fingertips. Then I collapse. Probably the blood has drained all but completely out of my body by this point. Luckily, someone calls down the lift and, after what seems an interminable age, I arrive at the lobby with a cheerful 'ding'. The lift doors slide apart as if in slow motion. I see the empty hall gazing back at me, reserved and tranquil. Losing all vestiges of hope, I rest my cheek on the musky carpet when I spy, in the corner of my eye, an elegantly attired old Manhattanite woman gliding towards me and I hold out a wet crimson hand. Where elegance and edginess meet indeed...

*

Paramedics had resuscitated me at the hotel before I was shuttled by ambulance to the NewYork-Presbyterian Hospital in lower Manhattan where personnel at their Emergency Medicine Center established that I had over fifty puncture wounds, a collapsed lung and had lost almost a gallon of blood. My physician was amazed that I had survived on the few pints remaining, it was later reported to me by Mother, who had flown over as soon as she could. With freshly donated blood in my veins and my lung patched up and re-inflated to their satisfaction, I was placed on a flight back to London where I am presently installed in a private room at St Mary's in Paddington. Well, the room is currently empty but for me, although there are two other beds available. Lacking private health insurance, my well-being is in the capable hands of the National Health Service.

I well up with spontaneous tears when Father arrives from İstanbul to visit me and Mother is also here. The barriers of contempt between them – already eroded by time – crushed out of existence by the plight of their second child returning from the jaws of death. Death, births, marriages and attempted murder are the fundaments of forced reunions, it seems. As they sit there by my bedside, I see them as the taciturn and ageing couple of my fantasies, two people who have battled through the hard times and stayed together no matter what, thinking not of themselves but their children.

We cry together and our tears carry away the poisonous past as a cleansing stream washes out to sea the debris of toxic garbage. Next day, I cry for my brother in pity, and the next and the next. I wring out of me the bottled-up grief that has for so long been the root cause of my dysphoria. I lived on and he ceased to exist – and why? A genetic frailty, a throw of the dice and his time was over. I feel a sudden hot envy for people who believe in gods and the afterlife, then, relying on my usual mind trick, I box up the complex tangle of emotions that I do not care to deal with right now and allow the container of mysteries to float merrily away down the cool fast-moving river where the box of the unknown – and unknowable – disappears out of view and out of my aching heart.

Speaking of the heart, all of my major organs remain intact apart from the perforated lung. Once my emotions have settled back to their baseline levels and cool-headed self-analysis kicks in, I am shocked to discover that I had been crying about my brother from relief, the relief that came from accepting that I had in fact hated him when he was alive. You really only have to work with four simple emotions, love, anger, envy and fear – or a combination thereof – to produce other seemingly very different yet actually compound emotions; fear (of death) and envy (of people who have not lost their loved ones) combine to produce grief, for example. Love mixes with envy to form jealousy. A fear of failure and being envious of those still young enough not to have experienced profound disappointments in their lives manifests as bitterness. My favourite might be the deliciously primeval combination of anger (at oneself) and fear (of being found out) that produce shame in most people.

As for myself, I had hated (anger plus fear equals hate) my brother for being sick because I was morbidly distressed by the sight and smell of decay and incensed at him for being a drain on the family's meagre resources of support and finite reserves of happiness. In short, he had been ruining my childhood and even then I knew it was a precious time of cossetted entitlement. My gut-intelligence range at the time did not allow my brain to mix and match certain of the basic emotions to turn my guilt (anger at myself for hating him) into the usable social currency of grief. The repressed grief formed within me a hidden ocean of untapped psychological material born of a grotesque sadness. Admitting, now, after my near-death experience, that I had hated the little bastard's temerity for dying too soon – how brilliantly childish! – brought with it a clarifying tide of truth that swells up the estuaries of my senses and washes away the emotional glitches from the creeks, streams and lakes of my subconscious. These glitches had hitherto thwarted my full development as an artist and removing them, the pesky obstacles to my ultimate self-actualisation, I am flooded by elation at this momentous discovery!

*

Samantha appears, wraithlike, one evening and settles next to my bedside with the plight of unrequited love in her eyes, clutching a thick paperback, here for the long haul. Upon seeing her I understand in my frosty core, similar to a lonesome proto-planet on the edge of the solar system forever trapped in the orbit of a star too far away to warm it, that I cannot in truth love her back. If I am to harness the sum total of what my life has hitherto given me as material to use in my art then I must slam that door to indulgence shut and dam up my feelings to refill the reservoir of creativity that had been leaking its contents, like the blood from my body on the night of the flailing scissors, ever since I started calling her by her full name.

'Isn't the word "love" terribly wanting?' I venture.

'How do you mean?' she says, nestling down, wedging her book between her thigh and the chair.

'Well, let's think about the synonyms for "love"... there just aren't any.'

Furrowing her brow she consults her internal thesaurus. 'What about "passion"? Does that come close?'

'Do you know how many different words there are in Turkish for "love"?'

She shakes her head, her sweet little shampoo-scented head.

'In English you can say "I love this book" or "I love my mother" or "I love sausages" and it's the same word modified by context. In Turkish you have words for love that don't require a context in order to have different meanings appropriate to the subject.' I look at her sitting there at chest-level on the armchair and she seems to be teetering on the precipice of an emotional spillage. She stifles a hiccup – perhaps it's an attempt to stifle a deluge of tears? I can't tell what she is thinking or feeling any more. I lose my train of thought.

'Are you all right?' I ask with a neutral smile, trying to lighten her mood, or at least attempting to ask her to modulate it.

'Yes, sorry,' she says, taking the hint expertly, and standing up to address the door. 'I'm upset by... what happened to you.'

'What's there to be upset about? I'm alive,' I respond and, since she is having trouble curbing herself, I add, 'but I'm tired.'

This gives her the cue she needs in order to make her exit, forgetting to take her book with her. Hospitals can have that effect on people and their... well, emotions. I humbly acknowledge the attachment that has formed between us on an interpersonal level as I reach down to pick up her book and it will take quite an effort of will to completely banish the lustful hankerings that plague my weaker moments, usually when I am inebriated or asleep. She has entered my dreams many times.

XII

Selim committed suicide a few days after he had tried to murder me. He jumped off a block of flats in İstanbul, apparently. He did not die outright but persists in a living death of sorts – a coma, plugged into a life-support machine. He did not leave an explanatory note, therefore it is simply guesswork on my part when I surmise that the guilt stemming from his ghastly attack on my person, a deep sense of associated failure from the debacle that was the mentor-mentee liaison and a psychosexual conflict, that rendered him spiritually enervated, primed his ego to choose oblivion over crushing reality. I now wish I had asked him about the sordid little note to Maximillio. I am home after my stint in hospital. Father has flown back to Turkey to be with his Celine. I forgot to ask him about what she thought of my performance piece but then again it wasn't the right time to ask him anything that might require honesty, seeing as how I was newly delivered from the jaws of death – anything he said would have been prejudiced.

Stretched out on my kilim in the gloaming evening of Rotherhithe, I reflect ponderously on life. Sometimes life is too much for weaker souls not gifted with a fully functioning self-preservation gene, I contend. It's as if they lack the plastic flip-cover guard over their suicide switch. Most of us have fumbled for that switch in our past at some point but the bright red carapace cuts short our impulsive gesture, brings us to our mammalian senses and our selfish gene goes on to fight another day. I imagine a tiny *hoca* or priest sitting astride the self-destruct button and staring with compassionate scorn each time I dispassionately consider an early exit.

Perhaps I can never prove it; however, I feel strongly that Selim harboured a latent sexual appetite for me that overflowed with abandon at the sight of my availability to him that night in the hotel room. His laugh, I now realise, was a profound release of tension that he had stored up over the time we had known each other. I was quite sure that had I not become sentimental and been prematurely stung by his guffaws, I would have found that, once the inappropriate but cleansing gaiety exasperated by alcohol and whatever else he was taking that night had subsided, Selim would have been receptive to my advances and an alacritous bedfellow. Alas, even with rigorous analysis and informed conjecture, the possibility of knowing his true motivations for taking his own life remain shrouded in mystery. Even so, I am considering reaching out to Selim's family to console them in these most dreadful circumstances and, as a corollary, perhaps investigating further Selim's mindset before he launched himself to his rendezvous with nothingness.

Aside from figuring out what made him tick, I am also trying to feel compassion for the man who was clearly a lost soul but, after what he had done to me, I have found it almost impossible to forgive him. I don't mean the murder attempt. That was a heinous crime committed by a desperate man. A crime like that can only be punishable by law and my own sense of justice or thirst for revenge has no place in the equation of justice. I wonder if he will be tried in *absentia* by a court if I press charges. I must make a note to speak to a lawyer. As long as he has a heartbeat then he is alive, I suppose, and so could face some punitive action or at least monetary fine since he cannot, presumably, be jailed in his condition, No, Selim has already paid a high price for his cowardly act of unspeakable violence. What irks me immeasurably more than his pathetic attempt to kill me is that he did it over something so inconsequential. His slighted little ego.

*

I try to contact Selim's family in an effort to convey my deepest sympathies and wish their son well. However, I am met with a wall of obdurate muteness. I am not sure if they know of my relationship with Selim before his attempt to murder me or whether they have been advised by lawyers not to communicate with their son's victim pending my compensation claim against him in civil court. Father, predictably, advised against pursuing this line of enquiry. More surprisingly, Mother too, was wary of my talking with the grief-stricken parents and, of all people, even asked me to withdraw my court case against them. She felt it wiser that I forget about what 'that insane young man' had done to me, and be thankful that I had survived. Examining my motivations for pursuing the matter with the Mehmet family I can appreciate how one might treat the experience as an act of nature, as if a typhoon or a tsunami had struck: rejoice in making it through alive and then move on. But this can only be effective if the incident carries with it the basic pillars of a natural disaster, a calamity visited upon one by a relentless force far greater than anything that is possible to humanly resist. If a psychopathic killer or some drugged-up lunatic had fallen upon me impulsively like a lethal locomotive of unstoppable violence then I could categorise the attempted murder as a *force majeure* event. However, critically, Selim Mehmet was a middle-class loser who had premeditated his scheme to kill me. He had tracked me down to the gallery showing, led me on, lured me to the killing ground and cold-bloodedly scissored my person then fled, guilty as hell. The fact that he was in a coma was not material to my seeking judicial retribution. I can easily separate in my mind the court case against Selim and my perfectly charitable approach to his family as one human being to another, able to console them over their brain-dead son whilst looking for redress in the courts. I feel put out by their lack of politeness. I have called them at their home on several occasions and they hung up on me each time.

XIII

Today I am feeling almost one hundred per cent and decide to give it another go and call Selim's family once again in order to say how sorry I am about what has happened to their son and to give them one final chance to behave in a civil manner towards me. The patriarch of the Mehmet clan picks up the telephone and as soon as he realises who it is on the other end of the line he lets loose a tirade of curses that leave me shaken and my ear sweating against the phone by the time he wraps up his diatribe. I have seen photographs of him on the news in a group picture with Selim. He is a big man and his upper lip is luxuriously furnished with an immaculate jet-black Anatolian moustache – he probably dyes it. During this telephone conversation, which is more accurately a monologue, it dawns on me that he has simply conflated the issue of my suing them for damages with the totally different issue of trying to connect with them emotionally, to seek closure if you will.

After his vituperative outburst he gives a massive guttural sigh – a walrus post ejaculation – and seems to have calmed down. I stay silent just long enough for him to unburden further and he tells me that I am a two-faced hypocrite and that Selim told them about me many times; how I tried to force drugs on him one time during the chaotic mentoring period (I recall only suggesting to Selim that he pop one of my beta-blockers and I hardly count that as an aggressive or irresponsible action) and how I had allegedly flirted with him and g the impression that I was interested in having sex with him in return for helping him meet influential gallerists in London and New York, so on. Clearly Selim was sicker than I was able to glean at the time and had somehow misconstrued his own sexual urges and projected them on to me. His sexuality was repressed by his conservative superego, modelled of course by his father's staunchly heterosexual belief system, and would have blocked any hint of transgressive feeling and, whilst his conscious mind was looking politely elsewhere, he'd have dumped his toxic denial on to yours truly and been convinced that I was flirting with him when in fact, subconsciously, he was flirting with me!

Drained by being forced to think about the horrific intricacies of delusion and prevarication that entombed and warped Selim's mind and heart, I hang up the phone whilst the old man is gently crying about his son's ignominious fate and how much he wants to 'finish the job Selim started' by shooting me, on in a strangely fond tone 'like a rabid dog in the street'.

A few moments later, I collapse from the fatigue of being unjustly harangued, threatened and insulted by the progenitor of my would-be assassin. they all liars and murderers in that family? I ponder in amazement as I awake from an unexpected nap that had drawn me down into its sweet, coddling embrace. I crawl out from under my maple dinner table – a place of cool shaded sanctuary – and push myself off the floor, mindful of the stitches holding my puncture wounds shut, and slowly down a glass of ice-cold water in the kitchen, enjoying the buzz and freshness of the gaping refrigerator – currently full of the produce that Mother bought and sent over with S. The cold liquid glides into my stomach like a glacier. I must eat. It was my own fault for asking that everyone leave me be for a spell each day so that I can be alone with my thoughts. Eschewing ready-meals and takeaways, I was also intent on cooking again to revitalise myself yet I have not been able to so much as look at the stove. My horrendously outdated Gino Bombo stools taunt me as I realise I never got round to replacing them. Then I lie down on my bed and mechanically fill out a donor card as a gesture of goodwill to humankind so that at my demise my perishable organs can be re-used as needed to help someone live, or see again. Even though I am squeamish about my eyeballs being requisitioned, I include it in the list of organs I wish to donate. I wonder if Selim ever had one of these donor card things? If he never regains his faculties then it would be a terrible waste of body parts.

At least, according to Muslim custom, he will be buried in a shroud in direct contact with the soil so that he eventually releases his minerals and benefits the ecosystem. A far better burial ritual than the insanely individualistic embalming process followed by encasement in thick hardwood and, some-times, concrete. What are you preserving after all – just a useless corpse injected with polluting chemicals? Then I remember that Christians look forward to a potential day of resurrection when the dead – righteous in life – will rise from the ground and all their horror stories of revenants, zombies and the ghastly superstitions of their Jesus cult come into sharp relief.

*

A few days after my telephone call to the Mehmets, a helpful-sounding police officer calls on me to explain that my actions amount to harassment and that I should desist from contacting Selim's family otherwise they will, apparently, escalate the situation and I could be arrested under the Protection from Harassment Act 1997. I do not want to get involved with the police in any way whatsoever. Authority in the hands of ordinary, average people trained to believe that they are superior to everyone else is my nightmare fuel. The police are a necessary evil of modern societies, perhaps – they are the sheepdogs of humanity, vested with the power to detain and hold you against your will. Their power reduces you to the status of a helpless child and the very thought of it makes me queasy. To combat an unnerving welling of panic, I call S and fire her. Somehow, being more isolated is what I need right now; a free solo climber contemplating a vast granite edifice that could be his making or his end. I must face my mortal enemy without the pressure of witnesses. I have cast aside my ropes and carabiner to tackle this immovable mass of terror – my objective demands nothing less.

*

The slap on the wrist from the authorities has given me pause. I know I am lucky to be alive. We all get depressed and wish for nothingness – that sought-after absence of suffering that some say is synonymous with happiness – but apparently any such happiness is only available to us humans in small restricted doses, dished out in bite-size chunks by some benevolent godlike thing comparable to a person dispensing joy-bringing meaty snacks to their pet animal. I have my own godlike being somewhere inside me and its name shall not be spoken.

As I meditate on these musings, it is as if I am packed in jelly, able to perceive my environs only through a translucent yellowy haze, able to reach out in slow motion and speak dully, my hearing insulated by layers of stuffy misery, but unable to make a connection with the outside and its population of other humans, unable to breathe in the air and feel it nourishing my blood or breathe out and feel the waste being aspirated. I am trying to shake these feelings. It is in the midst of this abjection that I must somehow enjoy the moment as if there is no past, present or future but only one gigantic dollop of time, a huge miraculous slice of 'nowness' to gulp down and feast upon – when this state of mind is achieved, usually fleetingly, one feels a sense of life-affirming vertigo. I feel a similar vertiginous melancholy when I look at Mother and, involuntarily, imagine an existence where I won't be able to hear her life-affirming tones or speak with her, my mother, over a spread of tea and ridiculous finger sandwiches whose unconditional affection resembles nothing else and cannot be substituted, replicated or reproduced. This moment results abruptly in a chasm – without pity or warning – yawning apart inside me, a rushing panic that sends me reeling. I am not afraid of death per se, for the fear of death is paralysing and fires the furnace of organised religions that – despite the initial good intentions of the many prophets – have been disfigured by man's ambition to rule over others, but I don't want to be the one left in the corner of the party either. I need to bounce my psyche off someone else, an ally; someone

to fill the gap that will be opened by the grief of bereavement –
not a substitute for that pure motherly love gone forever but a
balm to soothe the aching suffering that ensues. It is time for me
to join the party once again with a positive attitude and a stoic
understanding that humanity is imperfect but I am a part of it
nevertheless, a biological being with certain needs. So I invite
S over for dinner, hoping to erase the unpleasantness of our
previous dining experience. Since she is no longer an employee,
I am discharged of my rule about not sleeping with the help. I
don't mean that I am planning on sleeping with her, mind. It is
simply an option that has presented itself.

*

I am taken aback when she arrives dressed in an immaculate
dark grey woollen suit. She works in a back-office job at some
bank, she tells me in answer to my look of surprise. She is as
warm and charming as ever and conducts herself with poise
even after we move on to the second bottle of red wine of
which I imbibe more than my fair share. As we sit together
in the living area, I note that her footwear denotes her new
mundane occupation – a pair of commonplace medium-height
heeled shoes. Her feet are crossed at the ankles as demurely
as ever during our horribly restrained conversation about her
training in annuities and the intricacies of compliance at the
bank. Then the alcohol finally kicks in.

'Life is short,' I say and wince. 'What I mean to say is that,
well, any one of us could go at any second right?'

'It's scary.'

'Yes, it is. Who will stand by you in the end and mop

up your shit when you wind up having to wear a nappy or something? Lingering on and on, not knowing how or when to die – no exit plan. We are living longer but not better. We are doing something very wrong with our lives – we haven't cracked it because we don't know how to die. The first half of life you're moving away from birth and in the latter, you're moving towards death. It's that tricky second half when we are left adrift.'

'I suppose that's what religion is for,' she mutters.

'Yes! Exactly. It's a cack-handed attempt to prepare us for death – a noble enough effort but it's no good to us any more. How can we sign up to religion when faith is something that science has given such a battering?'

'I try not to think about,' she says and sips her wine.

'Animals. They know how to die. They're masters at it. The cat takes itself somewhere quiet and waits for it calmly. The elephant makes its way to its graveyard alone and without fuss. Dying is a normal part of their life and they're not worried about their – their fucking legacy, are they?'

'Is that what keeps you going, legacy?' she enquires and I reflect on the notion that all I have ever done is for something that I will never enjoy in person.

'Since I can't believe in an afterlife where I'm looking down at the living enjoying my legacy – it seems like...' I trail off and my father comes to mind. 'It's a waste?'

'I guess nothing was ever achieved by a happy person,' she says and I nod along then return to my earlier thought:

'They don't have the consciousness of consciousness, do they?' She frowns, lost. 'Animals, I mean.'

'Oh, I guess...'

Without waiting for her to catch up with me, I continue:

'The curse of the human animal is that it is aware of its own inevitable death and unable to deal with it. So the dying is messy, do you see what I mean? It's all medication, tears, beating of breasts, agony, final words, documents, wills, inheritance, bequests, more tears, death-rattles heard by all and sundry crowded about a death bed. Why can't we just take ourselves off somewhere and disappear without ceremony like the cat or the elephant? Why do we have to put our loved ones through the horror of seeing how they too will have to go one day? Washing of bodies, funerals and wakes – all fake remembrances and pathetic attempts to deny that death has the upper hand irrespective of your rituals. You die when you die and this obsession with immortality is bollocks. Is Alexander the Great still alive because we read about him in history books? Is Einstein still alive? Marilyn Monroe? Amy Winehouse? No, all dead. Dead, dead, dead. Just as you and I will die at some point and only the living will care about what we left behind because only the living have the privilege of worrying about dying.'

She needs a moment to gather her thoughts after my admittedly ghoulish soliloquy but it feels good to let it all out, even though I see her eyes wavering and her back curving over with fatigue.

'So wait, you don't care if people remember you?'

I think this over for a few moments and reply, 'I do care. No matter how much I tell myself it doesn't matter, it matters.'

With that shallow admission, I take refuge in the kitchen where I add pomegranate molasses and olive oil to the salad before checking on the stuffed peppers in the oven. S asks how

Mother is and whether I have plans for a holiday or will I be getting stuck back into work as soon as possible? I answer her questions on autopilot as she floats about watching me work. Then, in the middle of dessert, 'There isn't a day that goes by when I am not thinking about you,' I blurt out over poached quince with clotted cream, a favourite Turkish recipe of mine. She stares at me blankly for a while and then gives a deep plaintive sigh.

'What do you want from me?'

'Nothing. I thought we could catch up, that's all – after all there is no reason why we cannot remain friends.'

'That's really difficult for me.'

'Why? You're here – we're having a good time, no?' I grin, my gut clenching.

'I find it impossible to be friends with you.' She smiles in bewilderment as if this is an obvious fact that I have clearly not yet appreciated.

'Why?'

'I can't be the one to try and explain it to you,' she says and seems genuinely exasperated. I note that her hands are trembling delicately, conjuring up an image of vine leaves on a hot Aegean afternoon.

'I suppose I am asking too much of you,' I say finally.

'I'm seeing someone.'

'Oh, great,' I say as I skulk to the sink with our empty plates. The quince was delicious and a fitting end to a light but extremely filling meal.

'Who is it?' I say, dizzy.

'It's early days yet...'

'You're being evasive.'

'I didn't want to tell you yet but since—'

'Since you brought it up?'

'It's Joseph.'

'Joseph,' I repeat, the name oozing out of me.

'We met at—'

'I'm not sure I care much where or how you met.' I smile and try to figure out what to do next as I stand there foolishly in the kitchen.

'So you see, apart from anything else, it's going to be difficult being friends,' she says and I sense a triumphant tone almost as if she came over here just to see the look on my face at her revelation, which was also the solution to her never having to see me again.

'What do you mean, "apart from anything else"?' I turn to a cupboard and open the door like an automaton to see a *cezve*, a small copper pot the size of a woman's fist with a wooden handle. I reach for it, somewhat breathlessly. 'We'll have some coffee and I'll teach you how to read my fortune in the grinds.'

'As usual, you're not really listening to me.'

'Why did you come?' I enquire, opening a jar of ultra-finely ground Turkish coffee.

'What you are doing to that poor man's family is... it's not right.'

'Who, Selim? What are you talking about?'

'After you fired me I called your mother—'

'You did what?'

'I was worried about you...'

'Okay, sure,' I say, sarcasm my only defence at this point. I'll have to bring this up with Mother later on and find out what was said. The shadow of betrayal falls across my heart but I dismiss the automatic reaction before it gets hold of me.

'How… is he?'

'You mean, is he dead?' I ask, spooning the coffee into the *cezve*. 'Now, how do you take your Turkish coffee? Plain, medium sweet or very sweet?'

'I know he's not dead,' she says, ignoring my question. I go for medium sweet, guessing that she would want a mildly sweetened cup. I normally don't use sugar to sweeten my beverages but a Turkish coffee – similar to the espresso – demands it. I then pour room-temperature mineral water into the mixture.

'I'm talking about how you're contacting his family and I don't understand why you would do that,' she goes on, her voice pitching into desperation. I fire up the gas and turn round to regard her with dispassion.

Frankly, I cannot decipher her expression. Normally I'm quite good at reading a person's countenance and garnering meaning. Right now there is too much happening on her face, in her tight little shoulders – the way her eyebrows are gathering together. Anger? Hysteria? I conclude that she is struggling to steady her features to form a look of earnest confusion.

'He tried to kill me. It was attempted murder. Are you saying that I should just let it go?' I place the *cezve* on to the flames.

'Is that why you're suing them for damages?' She asks casually, averting her eyes.

'Well, I took a view on it and decided not to, if you must know.'

'You did the right thing,' she says and adds, rather redundantly, 'in the end.'

'Obviously you didn't manage to wring out all the information you were after from Mother,' I mumble defensively, then focus again to say, 'I did it for justice.' The word hangs there limply.

'I don't believe you care about anyone else but yourself,' she retorts. I decide that she is definitely exhibiting the body language of an angry person. Her legs are crossed, her arms are crossed – one foot is waggling in mid-air and her heel is almost about to pop out of her shoe. I stand there quite still as the brew begins to bubble.

'You put them through a living hell.' She is bristling now. 'Letters from lawyers, court summonses – when their son is dying... What kind of a monster are you?'

I peer down at the stove. The trick with Turkish coffee is to kill the flame at the precise moment when the *cezve* is about to overflow and not a millisecond before. It is heating up nicely, the rich chestnut-brown liquid frothing round the inside of the copper pot – creeping up to the rim.

'Hold on – he's the one who tried to kill me...' I say calmly, although the muscles round my mouth are hardening. Her hands are bunched into cute little fists as she stands up and appears to be holding in her breath behind tightly compressed lips that have lost their colour. During all of this I am distracted and miss the crucial moment to whip the *cezve* away from the heat and the coffee spills over and hisses on the gas flame like a basket of cats.

'Shit,' I exclaim as the boiling liquid splatters on my forearm. I take no heed of the burning pain. 'You've had too much to drink – the coffee will be ready in a minute,' I say evenly, washing out the ruined batch for another go, as she steps towards me, quivering.

'You should've died because Selim is the one who deserves to have a life. Not you. You're evil.'

'Evil,' I say in order to hear if the word has any meaning to me. It does not. I smile and turn my back to her to grab more coffee. I won't bother with the sugar this time.

'You're a psychopath or a sociopath or whatever the hell it is.' She seethes, the wine taking her over. 'I saw what you did to him when you were supposed to be his mentor – you drove him mad. And you've driven me mad – look at me, this isn't who I am!' she warbles, her heels clopping on the hardwood flooring as she approaches me. I don't look at her.

Undoubtedly, she has lost control of her pent-up frustrations that have been coiling round her like a python for some time. She was always so reserved (that damned British reserve does more harm than good!) that I never imagined she could get so passionate that it would skew her reality enough that she would concoct such a variation on the truth about Selim. I'm sure that blathering fool Joseph did nothing to rein her in. I must take this up with him as soon as practicable. I turn to her.

'I can see that you're upset but Selim is no angel, I can assure you of that,' I say with as much sympathy on my face as I can muster. There is a drawn-out silence with me standing there, pot in hand, about to approach the stove again.

'Fuck you,' she exclaims and turns to leave. If there's one thing guaranteed to trigger a response in me, it is the vile act of someone walking away from me in a self-righteous pique. She is at the door, actually about to exit when, despite my best efforts to control my temper, I explode like the pot of coffee. I lunge at her. She tries to dodge my thrusting arms as I capture her in a bear hug. This is the one person I trusted implicitly and the one person who – it unexpectedly becomes clear as I haul her to the dinner table – I had planned to continue trusting well into my old age and she is betraying me. We hadn't even had the chance to discuss the possibility of us marrying someday in order to take advantage of married couples' healthcare plans, never mind the tax savings. There is a lot to talk about – inheritance of my estate, the future custody of my art – and she is trying to walk away! She writhes and even claws at my face as I tightly clasp her in my loving arms and entreat her to relax and face the fact that she is still wildly attracted to me. She denies it over and over again but by the time we have finished she is totally spent and can barely crawl on her hands and knees across the floor, where – quite to my surprise – we have tangled together in an act of animalistic congress. When words fail to express certain urgent and formidable notions, when the timing is all wrong or, as in this case, there has been a monumental misunderstanding – then only actions will do.

I notice that she has an ugly bruise forming on her temple. No pretence of shopworn civilised conduct has marred the occasion. We are biological beings evolved from mud and we'd do well to remember that. The act of physical love cannot be condemned by a duplicitous society of two-faced morons, terrified of their own potential for animalism born of human prerequisite. Yes, I made a candid primal connection with her and it is up to her to rise to the challenge of interpreting my deed correctly, ignoring learned modes of thinking that are as false as a politician's smile or the applause of a claque. Grappling with these profound thoughts, I sit down heavily on a chair. I watch as she ever so slowly gathers her things, the shoes that had become dislodged, the handbag with its spilled contents. I say nothing as I rise to my feet and plod over to the kitchen and contemplate the mess of caked coffee residue on my cooker. I'll have to take care of that later, I simply don't have the energy for it right now.

She is making soft whimpering noises as she scoops up the contents of her bag and, with shoes in hand, shuffles towards the door for the second time. I don't want it to end this way, in ambiguity. I need to know where I stand so I call after her and rush over. She doesn't turn at first, her white fingers clinging loosely to the door handle, but by a tender gesture of affection I hold her chin and pivot her head to face me. I adopt a rigorous expression of stoic empathy and brush aside the hair that has formed a damp veil across her still features, a childish veneer of placidity convulsed with torrid tides below its surface. She reminds me of a girl, lost in the woods, who has stumbled upon a familiar clearing and is filled with the hope of finding her way home again. Her glistening, red-rimmed eyes tell a story of bitter regret. I know that she has not been honest with me about her feelings and that the piquant things she said have come from elsewhere, pushed upon her by a judgemental and entirely wrong-headed appreciation of my personality deformed through the envious lens of others. She is, in short, confused. I hold her to me, binding our warm bodies together as she snivels. She is trembling. Her breathing is smoothing out as it becomes shallower and trancelike in its rhythm. I'm not aware how long I hold her but her hot breath is marking its territory across my collarbone when she wriggles free. She coyly avoids my eyes as I open the door for her and, with silent understanding, we, as adults and people of the world, part ways.

As I reflect on the unexpected events of the night, it occurs to me that she and I have a very plausible future life of togetherness to look forward to. She tacitly knows who I am at my core and her conflicting feelings of loyalty pushed her into that charlatan Joseph's soft arms. Her angry words tonight were as hot pus discharged from an overburdened boil or cyst – she was sinking under the weight of expectation that had turned her initial crush into a dangerous obsession. Now, having evened out the keel and taken our relationship to the next level, ejecting the toxins of accumulated angst, we can move on with our lives, I am sure.

XIV

In Turkish the word for wolf is *kurt*, which means maggot. That's because in Turkic culture, saying the name of the thing you are afraid of will make it appear. That's the reason why people don't often use the Turkish word for 'no' any more but prefer *hayır*, which is an Arabic word that means 'auspicious' since saying 'no' all the time just feels like a great way to invite negativity into one's life. Even when we curse we'll yell to the object of our rage, 'I hope God does not damn you!' What goes around comes around after all. No particular belief system has a monopoly on superstitions but the shamanic Turkish rituals are far more soothing, I'd say, than what the Christians have at their disposal for example. They are simple and emphasise the restorative power of ritual. Like pouring water after someone who is going on a long journey so that they may go like water and return like water – how many other helpful rituals that may soothe our daily lives, I wonder, have slipped away from our collective memories since we abandoned the steppes and sought out new lands where the sun god Tengri disappeared beyond the horizon to rest? I am just the same as those ancient folk who would not call a wolf by its given name. Perhaps it is why I refuse to name my own personal God. In case he comes for me. These reflections have come about all because of a dream – one of those that you end up remembering in every detail after an afternoon nap:

I'm riding, sedately and with great composure, an ox-type creature across a muddied medieval landscape on the edges of some distant empire and then for reasons unknown my beast of burden takes offence at my hauteur, of my ordering it about wordlessly with a pull on the reins or the squeeze of my spurs against its hard flanks and it rises with acute irritation to reveal its true nature – a sentient being on two feet, towering above me, its grey muscular neck and shoulders wide as a plough now proudly holding aloft its enormous skull and black shiny horns. I slip to the ground from its sloping granite back as my legs weaken in its awesome presence. Whereas a moment ago I was its master, I am now agog with wonder at its imposing stature, fearful of the look on its half-turned face, looking down at my puny form with scorn. I have clearly done something terrible – its eyes tell me from deep sockets compressed by an angry brow – and its hot breath comes in measured rasps from a vast cauldron of a chest. I run.

But no matter where I go – up a tree, into a ditch, a hole in the ground or the roof of a dilapidated barn – it is there snorting with fury, horns piercing wood and smashing asunder any obstacle in its way to try and crush me. Stoically, I continue to dodge each attack and nimbly seek out any haven of safety I can find in this strange land where only I and this crazed, affronted brute seem to dwell. Finally, I am exhausted and vaguely aware that I am trapped in a lucid dream. Suddenly, I am in a room lit by a lantern – there is a bed and the ox-man is preparing to settle down for the night clothed in hessian pyjamas and a huge nightcap that obscures its fearsome features. I am relieved that the chase is over but then it sees me...

*

I have to consult with Joseph – the man I have disparaged so often and cast aside is the only person left that I can turn to now. Vague misgivings aside, I feel that I can rely on his mild-mannered good nature to act as a tonic to my recent woes so I arrange a meeting.

The very next day, I am heavily disguised in a petrol-green felt fedora, aviator sunglasses and a pink and purple Moroccan scarf, looking elegantly ungendered, non-binary, queer or whatever they call it nowadays – when I meet Joseph over breakfast in Saint Christopher's Place off Oxford Street. The place is brimming with tourists and the life force of the human herd is agreeable to me today whereas normally this kind of place would be quite abhorrent. I'm having poached eggs. Joseph is not eating. My egg's yolk splits under the knife, spilling its beautiful orange liquid contents on to the sourdough toast beneath.

'You're sure you don't want anything to eat?' I ask and he shakes his head, still avoiding my eyes. He seems terribly pained as I recount the recent episode with S.

'She's turning into quite a woman,' I conclude and sip my iced orange juice, feeling much better about myself after unloading the unpleasant details of the passionate night with my erstwhile assistant. Joseph thinks for a while – a curious smirk fixed on his pallid face – before saying:

'Samantha wouldn't tell me what happened. I could only guess it wasn't good by the way she turned up at my place in the middle of the night crying.' His hands sit in rigid repose on either side of his coffee cup.

'Oh?'

'She told me you'd been abusive but—'

'Well I've told you what happened. I'm sorry but there was a tension in the air that had to be defused and we couldn't help ourselves. Don't blame her,' I offer with a sympathetic tilt of my head.

'I was hoping I was wrong,' he says.

'It may be difficult to hear the truth, Joseph. However, it is surely better to lance the boil sooner rather than later – I'm sure you will both do just fine. Now, what I need is to get back in the saddle—'

'What you need is a lawyer,' he says apropos nothing and adds redundantly, 'a fucking lawyer is what you need.'

'I already have a lawyer, Joseph. Well, house counsel – and what are you talking about, anyway?'

'What am I talking about?' He looks away, jaw clenched tight. '—'

'Just shut the fuck up.'

I wasn't expecting that. Where is all this animosity coming from? Has Joseph grown a set of adult male genitalia all of a sudden and is overridden with testosterone and aggression thanks to the jealousy awakened in him by my dalliance with his partner or is this hubris a sign that he cannot be successfully re-employed as my agent?

'I sense a lot of hostility in you, Joseph,' I say and I might have stammered a little bit. I am angry and offended by his truculence.

'You bring me here to ask my advice? Why? How stupid do you think I am?'

'Not at all stupid,' I say and munch my crispy toast before it gets any colder.

'How can you be so fucking casual about it?'

'About what?'

'Rape,' he says. The word hangs between us as if it has pulled up a chair like an eager, uninvited guest.

'How rude,' I retort pertly and hold his annoyingly perturbed gaze. 'It was nothing of the sort. Who said the r-word, anyway?'

'I said it. And she is going to say it, too. You prick.'

'Can we dial down the expletives, Joseph? It's too early in the morning for me. You're very, very hot-headed today. She's lying, by the way.'

'I ought to punch you in the face right now for what you've done,' he says with a disastrous attempt at authority.

'Really?' I smile, fold my arms casually and sit back in my chair just in case he attempts to take a swing at me.

'That poor girl. She had a crush on you. God knows why. You used her, took complete advantage of her, and then decided to throw her aside. She's a lovely, kind person and now...' He struggles to maintain his composure. 'Because of your vile actions, she... by God, you will pay,' he seethes at me.

'Joseph, I have no fucking clue what you are talking about. A crush? On me?' I say. 'And how dare you use that word with me?' My voice falls to a whisper. 'If you get that word into her head then she might get to the point where she starts believing it, Joseph. Don't be so irresponsible.' I realise that I am squeezing the glass of orange juice tight enough to break it. If this line of fabrication escalates then – then there'll be a bloody court case with... with the likes of Joseph standing there piously passing judgement on my character, my soul. I am not having that.

'You! Judging... me!' I cry out at him, spittle flying. 'You dress like a tramp! Look at you, you self-important stupid twat.'

I have, I know, lost my temper somewhere in the middle of that last train of thought and I know that my hands are juddering with the adrenal fluid coursing through my dilated arteries because the cutlery next to my plate is clinking together. It is a distracting noise. I barely have the self-control to keep from accelerating the situation and keep staring down Joseph who is wearing on his soft doughy face the puckered indignation of a schoolboy unfairly reprimanded in front of his classmates – brimming with indignation and that British air of self-righteous astonishment – the coloniser stepping foot on foreign soil to find the natives naked and content, the look that says, 'how very dare you!'

'You'll go to prison for this,' he says between rigid lips before he swans away. Needless to say, I am left fuming and, frankly, totally alone. You don't realise how alone you are when someone who you thought was beneath you turns round and tells you to go fuck yourself; a real wake up call. I finish my breakfast in a sullen mood and take it out on the waitress by leaving a tiny tip despite her smiles and readiness to serve.

On a double-decker bus bound for Knightsbridge, I call Mother in a state of bottomless depression but she does not pick up her telephone even after several tries. I am on the top deck of a red London bus resembling a clueless tourist, for God's sake, and it dawns on me that this is a cry for help but no one is within earshot. No one on this bus can detect my suffering. They are thinking about what to have for lunch and whether they have enough time to pop into Harrods to ogle the charmless statue of Dodi and the Princess. Mother is either in the bath or having her hair done, I decide. Either way, my solitude is complete. Could it be that the only person I can speak to right now is Father?

Then, fortuitously, Maximillio calls to tell me that we have a buyer. A shadowy American collector is offering the asking price of $550,000 and has jumped to the head of Maximillio's waiting list (if a list actually existed) by virtue of said collector's solemn promise, no doubt enshrined in a water-tight contract, to bequeath the piece to a museum so that it will never enter the secondary marketplace where its value would be left to the vagaries of art-lust between competing oligarchs and the guile of an auctioneer one evening at Sotheby's or Christie's. This rather ludicrous figure for a small artwork by a mid-career artist who has never been offered a retrospective, museum group show or placement in an important collection is a ballsy manoeuvre. Maximillio helped sell the work by producing a lavish catalogue of new works from his gallery, showcasing mine on the cover, that he had sent to several hundred collectors by courier. This self-assured gesture (well done, Max) apparently got many of the collectors thinking they might be missing out on something big and, motivated by the morbid fear of 'non-buyer's remorse', a lot of them had rushed to his stand at Art Basel to view the piece before anyone else. I thank him for his hard work and hang up.

There is no rushing in of joy. I feel carved out like an avocado, flabby and melting like butter under my now inappropriately merry green hat. Joseph had destroyed my mood so that even this momentous news is wasted on me. Still feeling the urge to unload, I dial and wait for the international call to be connected. I hope that he will not pick up the phone so that I can scrape through this embarrassing morass of pessimism until Mother is available but I need the comforting sound of a long-familiar voice to reassure me that there is a reality I know still ongoing beyond my immediate and claustrophobic circumference.

'Hello... Dad.'

'Oh, hello son.'

Son.

Pathetically, I feel human again thanks to that one single word.

'Where are you?'

'London,' I say.

'You sound funny.' A rueful hush descends on the already halting conversation. There is so much need for me to spew out that I begin to gag, throat constricting.

'How did that thing of yours go?'

'The thing, yes. It went well,' I say.

'I don't understand it, I really don't,' he says and, like son like father; he wants to spew his accumulated poison at me as well. I let him take the opportunity to unburden himself by pausing and then sighing hopelessly through my nose.

'I can't see how you manage to live. I mean, you don't have a job, where's the money coming from? I'm afraid to ask,' he continues along his favourite trajectory. 'My biggest mistake was letting you go to art college. I've never forgiven myself for that. Now look at you, you don't have a home, you don't have any prospects for starting a family. How do you survive, I just don't get it.' I can hear him grimacing in despair.

I think about telling him that my work has been sold, that my career is finally taking off and that he can stop worrying. Then I realise that I want him to suffer so I tell him nothing. He worries incessantly as parents do and children cannot comprehend it and feel put upon until they too have their own children. It's biological, chemical. You can't stop evolution from trying to interfere in your business. Those genes you're carrying? They own it all and they want to keep on trucking long after your cells are mulch.

'I have to go, Father,' I say. He mutters a platitude and, annoyingly, manages to hang up before I do.

I alight from the bus at Trafalgar Square and trot with my heavy head lolling down – a despondent street dog who doesn't know if the sun will shine on his backside today or if the day will kick him in the balls. Then along The Mall I go as I have done many a time before, with the Palace rising above the burgundy tarmac, framed by the overhanging trees lining this ceremonial tract and I am rewarded by the sight of cantering horses of the royal stables with the splendidly uniformed cavalry perched atop them with their polished helmets and swords. I crunch the gravel underfoot along the edge of the pavement slabs and stare down and feel myself scaling up as if the tiny stones and puffs of dust below as I walk are the rocks and alien winds of a faraway moon. It's as if my genes are whispering to me – easily mistaken as a message from God – but I am too focused to be fooled by these voices; there is no God but the god I create and name.

XV

The next day, I walk briskly across the human traffic of Oxford Street as if I am traversing a river of sewage and dive fitfully into Mayfair. The night before, I finally got through to Mother and told her everything. She only said, 'What have you done?' but I cannot – I must not – dwell on that for now. I'm sure that when we meet face to face she will unleash her considerable acumen on the problem and we will have it sewn up in no time. For right now, I seek solace in a small branch of my private member's club, Home. It feels far from homely, however, and I encounter instead a gelid efficiency from the staff and too many prying eyes peeking over newspapers and a variety of screens for me to enjoy the pot of Earl Grey brought to my table by the usual faux-Parisian waiter. I almost ask him why everyone is staring at me. He wouldn't know, of course. But I have my suspicions. Having been through my ordeal of the fifty-six stab wounds, people probably pity me. They can't have heard about the allegations this fast, surely? I leaf through the art section of the first newspaper I find lying on the table, confidently paranoid. When my phone vibrates I take the call in the stairway, as per the house rules. It is her.

'I felt sorry for you at first,' she says by way of a preamble. 'Then I remembered something about what you said in Cyprus, about the soldiers.'

'Can we be adult about this—'

'Shut up. And listen,' she says with such feeling and purpose that I comply, somewhat aroused. 'There was an assault and a rape. But it wasn't you, was it?'

'I asked you never to bring that up,' I retort. How could she…

'You lied and I felt sorry for you – God, I'm so stupid – I even thought about forgiving you, you… you evil, evil man.' She is on some sort of a roll now and I let her ramble on. 'Did you even have a twin brother? Was that lies as well? Or did you tell the truth for once but lie about your blood types not matching? Did you refuse to give him your kidney? Did you let him die—'

'If you think I'm going to take lessons in veracity from you then you're very much mistaken,' I fume with dignity and hang up.

Truth. What is truth, anyway? I crumple up a piece of material and declare it to be art. That is *my* truth. The only truth there is.

*

My *Gesamtkunstwerk* – what an unlovely yet pleasing compound word don't you think? – cannot be an anaemic imitation of what has come before. Rather than appeal to the five senses and harangue the viewer in the Wagnerian sense, I feel strongly that the work has to *be* the five senses; sight, sound, smell, taste and touch. Of course! The era of ephemeral concepts is over – we need something concrete, graspable and as the pyramids stand as monuments to a dead but unforgotten creed, so art must stand for as long as stone and mortar, solidly for eons to come!

I've done it before and I can do it again, but this time expanding the theatre of operations and the depth of the piece by harvesting the very biological artefacts that together constitute our earthly, non-transcendent, rather insufficient existences. It will be Selim's apotheosis, a solemn and sacred olive branch between us that will resonate through the ages long after we are ash.

I'll need some considerable help to harvest Selim's eyes, eardrums, olfactory bulb, tongue and fingertips. I can't imagine why he would not survive the operation and, as he is not using any of his bodily attributes, it seems churlish to have these vitals hanging on some sort of human vine unused and fated to wither, having achieved nothing. With this fresh objective ahead of me, I relax – contentment and serenity warmly radiate from where it always begins, in the belly button. Is it any accident that this most harmonious of feelings is at the site of the unplugged umbilical cord that once kept us nourished during that finite eternity of bliss before birth? A kind of phantom connection that comes alive when we are at peace and mindful of the supreme luck of our own existence, without doubt, without thoughts and simply and only *being*.

Excited by my new idea I return to my flat and imprison myself there in order to enter the state of mind that will best yield the working outlines of my next work of art. I pull out a bottle of vodka from the freezer and prepare to slide into blessed oblivion.

Then there is a knock on the door. It is the police.

Conception

A PERMANENT STATE OF EXTREME SUFFERING
by

████████████████████████

2010

signed, titled *Untitled* (or, *A Permanent State of Extreme Suffering*) and dated *2010* under the base. 24-carat gold leaf, human excreta (artist's own kidney, ingested), wood, crushed velvet and glass.
8¾ x 7½ in. 22.22 x 19.05 cm

Provenance

Private collection
The Zvwark Gallery, New York

Recent Exhibitions

Make/Shift, Thomas Dane Gallery, 3 Duke Street, London SW1, UK, February 27-April 1, 2010

Othering the Turk, Sperone Westwater, 257 Bowery, New York, USA, November 3-December 25, 2009

Tantalus, Galata Greek Primary School, Galata, İstanbul, Turkey, İstanbul Theatre Festival Special Project, May 11-29, 2009

Behind + Ahead, ARTER, İstanbul, Turkey, September 11-December 15, 2008

Times of İstantinople, İstanbul Modern, Turkey. November 17, 2005-March 9, 2006

Heimweh, Museum Ludwig, Cologne, Germany, September 1, 2003-January 31, 2004

(++/+++), Thomas Dane Gallery, London, UK, March 13-April 17, 2001

Catalogue Notes

'The work is a forthright contemplation that eschews easy definitions yet courts them feverishly, constantly agitating the viewer. The artist[1] addresses, by an act of anthropophagy, the deepest fears of (hu)mankind; the fear of being judged by history, the fear of injustice and the fear of desolation in the face of mortality. Cannibalism as taboo and as outright affront, a sure course to purgatorial shame, is subverted to confront such primeval horrors. As Abraham sacrificed Isaac and Prometheus was bound to a stake on Mount Caucasus to have an eagle feed perpetually on his liver before God released the former from the burden of unthinking obeisance and, in the latter case, Heracles set free the Titan, so too *A Permanent State of*

---

[1] At the time of writing, the artist is facing serious allegations of sexual assault from his former personal assistant. Although he denies the allegations, the court of public opinion has seemingly already made its judgment and the artist has been vilified. However, the impact on the value of his work has thus far remained stable, a fact that has not gone unnoticed by commentators.

Conception

Extreme Suffering inveigles the outsider back into the inner sanctum of acceptance through his art. Although never overtly religious, the work attains the attribution through an oblique reference to denial by virtue of its own insubstantiality, *in absentia* - a Sartrean negation. Thus, denial, being the pivot-point of the conceptual arc itself, brings full circle the implicated subtext, laid bare yet confounded by the luster of surface language that would have enchanted Wittgenstein, within the fabric of the irrefutable collapsing in on itself, always shifting and forever shrouded in Byzantine layers of amoral intrigue with an insolent rictus-grin nod towards Said, Kristeva, Duchamp, Manzoni, and, naturally, Freud.

Spectacle as Mass Delusion may have been a more fitting, albeit didactic, title for this piece, which throws its maker and the Debordian spectator-mass into an eschatological continuum of tribal primitivism and existential, nay, nihilistic morass that has defined the milieu of the postwar Middle East typified (and transfigured) by that oft-proclaimed 'bridge between East and West,' Turkey-looking less like a two-way connection between the Occident and the Orient (unfashionable words these days) and more a one-way mirror, reflecting us watching ourselves with post-imperialistic scrutiny, poker-faced and deathly serious, as the Other - once again made invisible as compatible yet twisted dichotomies by a unilateral effacement, by force of Nietzschean will - and cloaked in mystery, observes knowingly from beyond the reaches of our imagination, customs and beliefs... and laughs.'

Celeste Arzoomanian, art critic

ACKNOWLEDGEMENTS

Writing can be a lonely business yet nobody writes a book alone – there were many people who lent their support along the way so apologies to anyone I have left out.

My heartfelt thanks to publisher Louise Boland and editor Urška Vidoni for recognising the potential and their thoughtful input throughout the rewriting process as well as everyone at Fairlight for turning my writing into a book. Oscar van Gelderen and Vicki Satlow have my gratitude for their championing of my work early on thus giving me the impetus to keep going despite the setbacks.

Thanks also to Dr Kate North and Dr Dan Anthony at Cardiff Metropolitan University who provided keen insights and guidance during my MA when the book began to finally take its eventual shape.

Last but not least, I give thanks to my family to whom this book is dedicated because without their unconditional encouragement and love I wouldn't have managed it.

ABOUT THE AUTHOR

Özgür Uyanık is a writer and filmmaker whose family emigrated from Turkey to the UK in 1980.

After graduating from the University of Kent at Canterbury, where he studied Communications and Image Studies, Özgür started a career in the film industry working as a runner and making short films in London until his debut feature film premiered at the 17th Raindance Film Festival in 2009. He recently gained an MA in Creative Writing and English Literature from Cardiff Metropolitan University and is currently a PhD candidate in Creative Writing at Cardiff University.

Conception is Özgür's debut novel.

Bookclub and writers' circle notes for
Conception can be found at
www.fairlightbooks.com

FAIRLIGHT BOOKS

LOU GILMOND

The Tale of Senyor Rodriguez

A dead man's house. A dead man's clothes.
And a dead man's wine cellar...

It's 1960s Mallorca. Thomas Sebastian, an English conman, is hiding out in the house of the late Senyor Rodriguez – carousing, partying, and falling in love with his beautiful but impossibly young neighbour, Isabella Ferretti.

As the boundary between lies and reality blurs, Thomas' fiction spirals out of control in ways that are quite unexpected.

'A gripping, atmospheric novel, with a brilliant twist.'
—G.D.Sanders, author of *The Taken Girls*

NIAL GIACOMELLI

The Therapist

*'I am levitating above the curvature of the earth.
Weightless, unencumbered. Flung like a comet out of
the atmosphere and into some great beyond.'*

In this bittersweet and hauntingly surreal tale, a couple finds
the distance between them mirrored in a strange epidemic
sweeping the globe. Little by little, each victim becomes
transparent, their heart beating behind a visible rib cage, an
intricate network of nerves left hanging in mid-air. Finally, the
victims disappear entirely, never to be seen again.

'I dreamt we were at sea,' she says.

*'If the population of the world had vanished while I was
reading Nial Giacomelli's beautifully observed novella, I'm
not sure I would have noticed. It's that good.'*
—Christopher Stanley, author of *The Forest is Hungry*

SOPHIE VAN LLEWYN

Bottled Goods

*Longlisted for **The Women's Prize for Fiction** 2019,*
***The Republic of Consciousness Prize** 2019 and*
***The People's Book Prize** 2018*

When Alina's brother-in-law defects to the West, she and her husband become persons of interest to the secret services and both of their careers come grinding to a halt.

As the strain takes its toll on their marriage, Alina turns to her aunt for help – the wife of a communist leader and a secret practitioner of the old folk ways.

Set in 1970s communist Romania, this novella-in-flash draws upon magic realism to weave a captivating tale of everyday troubles.

'Sophie van Llewyn's stunning debut novella
shows us there is no dystopian fiction as
frightening as that which draws on history.'
—Christina Dalcher, author of *VOX*

'Sophie van Llewyn has brought light into an
era which cast a long shadow.'

—Joanna Campbell, author of
Tying Down the Lion